THE
CARDINAL'S
COURT

The
CARDINAL'S
COURT

A HUGH MAC EGAN MYSTERY

CORA HARRISON

The
History
Press

This book is dedicated to my daughter, Ruth Mason, who, since the age of five, has been a huge fan of the Tudors. She has been of great assistance to me while writing this book and we've had many interesting discussions during its progress.

Cover illustration © Shutterstock/Rachelle Burnside

First published 2017

The History Press
The Mill, Brimscombe Port
Stroud, Gloucestershire, GL5 2QG
www.thehistorypress.co.uk

© Cora Harrison, 2017

British Library Cataloguing in Publication Data.
A catalogue record for this book is available from the British Library.

HARDBACK ISBN 978 0 7509 6839 3
PAPERBACK ISBN 978 0 7509 8359 4

Typesetting and origination by The History Press
Printed and bound in Great Britain by TJ International Ltd

1

At the time when the murder of Cardinal Wolsey's instructor of the wards occurred in the hall of Hampton Court, I had been in the adjoining chamber penning the first draft of the marriage contract between James Butler the son of my employer, and Anne Boleyn, the younger daughter of Thomas Boleyn. It would, of course, be a preliminary, tentative outline. I knew that. The girl's father would have something to say about it, Cardinal Wolsey would have something to say about it, even the king himself might be involved.

'What happened?' I tried to keep the note of angry impatience out of my voice and lengthened my stride to keep pace with the serjeant-at-arms who had come to fetch me. He eyed me sidelong, keeping, as was his wont, a few feet away from me. He never liked to be reminded that I was taller than he. Impatiently I moved a little closer.

'You weren't there, were you, last night, during the pageant?'

'No,' I said shortly. The serjeant, a cautious, secretive man, reputed to be hoping for the next vacancy in the judiciary, was famous for always answering one question by putting another. An annoying habit, especially in a time of stress. I liked him – he was an honest man who

served Cardinal Wolsey faithfully and did his best with
a difficult job – but I had no great esteem for him and
considered that his sister Alice was very much the more
intelligent of the two.

'But why is James involved?' There was something
ominous in the fact that he had come straightaway to
fetch me from my lodgings. Why did young James need a
lawyer present?

He shrugged, but there was an uneasy look on his face
and so I substituted: 'When did it happen?'

That was an easier question.

'Last night. It must have been early last night. The body
is as stiff as a board, now.'

I glanced up at the clock tower. Eleven o'clock of the
morning.

'Last night,' I repeated. 'Before the pageant? I heard
nothing of this.'

He shrugged again. 'We don't know exactly when it
happened,' he said. And then, rather evasively, 'No, not
before the pageant. We don't think so. No, we think that
it was during the pageant, during the storming of the
château vert …'

I turned back to stare incredulously at him. If a man
had been killed in the presence of the king himself,
during the time when King Henry and his courtiers were
busy throwing comfits, oranges and dates at the ladies-in-
waiting, supposedly imprisoned within the mock castle,
well, this was a terribly grave matter. Why was the serjeant leaving the great hall and coming to fetch me. My
first instinct was correct. James was in serious trouble, was
in some way involved in this death. I kept close on his
heels as we both went through the Base Court.

'The king's serjeant, Master Gibson, is very worried about it all,' he said, answering my unspoken question. And then I understood. John's face, always an easy one to read, wore a sullen, slightly angry expression. The king had departed at dawn with a riding party but he had left most of his household behind. Serjeant Gibson was the man in charge: the cardinal's serjeant, John Rushe, would be well below the king's serjeant in status.

'And James is supposed to have something to do with it, is that right?' I asked. My own face, I knew from experience, would show little other than that firmly closed mouth and pair of enigmatic grey eyes beneath level dark eyebrows that I saw every morning in my steel shaving mirror. As always I kept my voice low, though it was bitterly cold and there was no one except ourselves in the courtyard.

'It was Harry Percy,' he said. He stopped in the middle of the Base Court, though I wished that he would not. I wanted to see James, to find out what he had to say, and, perhaps more importantly, to find out what people were saying about him.

'Why? What's it to do with young Percy?' I asked. In the cardinal's court I had the reputation of an imperturbable man and I tried to live up to it.

'The man, the dead man, was shot with an arrow, a real arrow, bodkin-tipped. Harry Percy says that he saw your James take a real arrow from his arrow bag, not one of those mock ones, not those lightweight arrows made for the pageant from leather mâché, from finely chopped leather, the ones that the pages were supposed to be using.'

I drew in a breath. I could see where this was leading. Bodkin-tipped. My pace through the clock tower courtyard did not slacken but I felt my eyes narrow as I took in the implications.

Cardinal Wolsey had eight pages, all of them wards of court. Seven of them used the traditional broad arrows whereas James, my James, a fanatical bowman, favoured the bodkin arrow. And, of course, the arrows they were supposed to be using in the pageant were wafer thick, designed to break into crumbs on impact – wouldn't hurt a kitten. No real arrow, bodkin-tipped or not, should have been used within the great hall.

'What happened exactly? Come on, man, tell me what happened.' All of this had a very odd sound to me. Why shoot someone in the midst of a crowd of merrymakers? I tried to keep a hold on my temper. It was pointless to get exasperated with John Rushe.

'It seems as though the instructor of the wards was standing by the tapestry, just to the side of it, probably half-concealed, keeping an eye on his pupils, perhaps, making sure that their behaviour and bearing was such as would please the cardinal.' John looked at me meaningfully. It was, of course, typical of Edmund Pace to be spying on the boys – and on everyone else. The man was feared and hated throughout the entire staff at Hampton Court, and at York Place, as well. A gatherer of information, a born intriguer and troublemaker. 'He was shot through the edge of the tapestry cloth,' he continued, 'then he fell behind it. You can see for yourself. There's a hole in the tapestry cloth just by the hub of the cart. You know the picture of the cart at the edge of one of the tapestries, the one that is nearest to the door.'

'And the body has only just been discovered?'

'It was noticed by the cook, Master Beasley. The cardinal sent for him to congratulate him on the magnificence of last night's supper and when Master Beasley had bowed and was moving away he saw the man's shoe. He bent down and found the body.'

'You were sent for me?' It would have been the cardinal who dispatched him. The question gave me time to weigh up some possibilities, though.

'I was there. I got up from my seat immediately. I was the first to view the body. And then the king's sergeant-at-arms, Master Gibson, came. His Grace stayed where he was, but after a minute he sent one of the gentlemen ushers, young George Cavendish, across to me to find what was wrong. He, the cardinal, came over then when he heard about the body. But there was nothing to be done. We saw immediately that he had been murdered.' That didn't really answer the question, but I supposed that I would have to allow him to tell it in his own way. Alice often raised a delicate eyebrow and sighed when her brother John began on a long-winded explanation. I waited for more, but he said nothing, just tightened his lips.

'What happened? What killed him? How did you know that he had been murdered?' I was beginning to lose patience though my voice stayed low and calm.

'One of the gentlemen ushers pulled back the curtain. He might have done it roughly in his alarm. There was an arrow. It fell from the wound, fell onto the floor. He picked it up.'

'Bloodstained?'

I wanted to ask when and why Harry Percy made his disastrous accusation, but John Rushe was not a man to be rushed, as he often said himself.

'Dark on the tip of it,' he confirmed.

'And everyone gathered around.' I could picture the scene. The tables abandoned, benches, chairs and stools pushed aside.

'Thank God that King Henry had gone back to Westminster,' said the serjeant reverently.

'Indeed,' I said politely and waited. We had traversed the length of the Base Court, gone through under the clock tower, crossed the clock court and were now standing in front of the doorway that led to the great hall. It was time for Master Rushe to live up to his name and to come to the point.

'And Harry Percy …' I prompted.

'Says that he saw James Butler, your James, take an arrow from his bag and that it was a real arrow, not one of those painted leather ones. And that's not all; that young lady, Mistress Anne Boleyn, the lady James Butler is supposed to marry, she backs up Harry Percy, says that she wondered what James was doing, wondered why he was not using one of those pretend arrows that the boys were firing. She was peeping over the battlements, waiting to be rescued.'

I drew in a breath. This was getting serious. One accusation – well, it's one man's word against another's, but two accusations, and one of them from the young lady whose betrothal contract I had been drawing up with such care. If I could not unravel this matter fast, young James could be thrown into the Fleet prison, or even Newgate.

'The cardinal ordered me to fetch you immediately.'

That made sense. Cardinal Wolsey was very fond of James, more so than of Harry Percy. However, it showed that he was taking the accusation seriously if he immediately sent for the boy's legal advisor. And then I thought of something else.

'You said Mistress Boleyn, Mistress Anne Boleyn, joined in the accusation. Is Queen Katherine still here, then?'

'Yes, she has stayed on. She wanted to discuss with my lord the betrothal between young Arundel and one of her ladies-in-waiting.'

It was all marriage contracts these days for the cardinal's four older pages. Each had been paired with an appropriate lady. Thomas Arundel was only the latest; there had been Harry Percy with the daughter of the Earl of Shrewsbury, Gilbert Tailboys with Bessie Blount.

And, of course, Mistress Anne Boleyn had been taken back from the French court to marry James Butler. It had been a brilliant solution to the disputed Ormond inheritance, dreamed up by the cardinal. James's father, the male heir and the choice of the Ormond family in Ireland, had the right to it according to Irish law. Sir Thomas Boleyn, father of this Anne, the king's ambassador, and grandson of the former earl, had under English law, through his mother, a rather shaky claim, in my view. In fact, I considered that his cousin, Sir George St Leger, whose mother was the older daughter, had a better claim, but King Henry favoured his ambassador.

So, the younger of Boleyn's two daughters had been summoned home to marry James Butler, the son of the man in possession of the Irish part of the Ormond estates.

It only occurred to me now that she might not have liked the idea, that Anne might have preferred another match.

Hers was the first face that I saw when I came into the great hall. Beneath the oriel window that was the pride and joy of Cardinal Wolsey, she faced the great man himself, black eyes snapping, long dark hair swinging with each toss of a head. Her face, lit by a stray shaft of sunshine coming though the stained glass, was a pale rose-coloured oval, delicately framing those dark eyes.

I saw James instantly. Standing by himself, gripping the rail of a heavy chair, upholstered with padded leather, fastened with round copper nails. His fair-skinned face was so white that his red hair, beneath the black velvet cap, blazed in vivid contrast. No one was with him, but I didn't join him. Murder was a serious accusation. Here in England, it meant a hanging or the axe and a block. I made immediately for the man of power.

'Give you good time of day, my Lord Cardinal!' I said the words formally and saw a gleam in his eyes in response as I replaced my cap. He had often accused my English of sounding like Latin and now he appreciated that I was trying to please.

'Go now, Mistress. I'll speak with you later,' he said to the girl and Anne Boleyn dropped a very pretty courtesy and went off as gracefully as though she were taking part in an elaborate dance, tripping lightly down the three steps that led to the main hall.

'Teach them well in the French courts, don't they?' I made the remark in a light-hearted way and he responded in the same fashion.

'All of the graces, *n'est-ce pas*, Hugh?'

'And all of the virtues, we hope, Your Grace. Especially that of Truth.'

'You Irish are so ignorant of religious matters,' he complained. 'Truth, you know, is not amongst the seven virtues. I should know. I've long coveted a set of arras hangings that show the seven virtues: Faith, Hope, Charity, Justice, Prudence, Fortitude and Temperance. So much more suitable for a man of the church than these *Triumphs of Petrarch* hangings, don't you think, Hugh?' Gently and almost casually he moved one of the two-tiered, six-branched candelabra so that the light would illuminate my face. A waterfall of solidified wax spilled down one side of each of the candles. Not the first time that it had been moved, or lifted, this morning. I took heart from that. The cardinal had probably eyed Mistress Anne Boleyn as closely as he was now scrutinising me. I nodded at the tapestries below us.

'I hear that the *Triumphs of Petrarch* have borne an unusual fruit this morning.'

He was a hard man to assess, Cardinal Wolsey. He had a gentle smile on his face and his brown eyes were twinkling. A sign of the seriousness of the matter, I guessed immediately.

'You are correctly informed. I hope that the damage to the arras is not irreparable. The loss of such a man, of course ...' and the cardinal raised his eyes to heaven and sighed.

'Irreplaceable!' I made the word sound as neutral as I could. And Edmund Pace for sheer malice and ability to make trouble would indeed be irreplaceable.

'And he was shot last night.' My voice inserted a question mark into my second remark.

'So they tell me.' His eyes slid past me and went not to Master Rushe, but to the king's serjeant, standing on the edge of the dais at a respectful distance from the cardinal. There was another man with him, a squat, thick-set man with bushy mop of iron-grey hair, standing above an oddly young, smooth and clean-shaven face. They were whispering together. For a moment I thought that I glimpsed a strange expression on Master Gibson's face, an eager, almost a greedy look. And then the winter sun was suddenly extinguished by a heavy cloud. The coloured glass in the great oriel window and in the side windows became dark and almost opaque. The rich garments of the courtiers, the servers and maids of honour were lost in the shadows; only the faces lit by the numerous candelabra, showed palely white in the gloom and every one of them turned up towards us. The face of the king's serjeant now seemed as impassive as the faces on the tapestries. Perhaps I had imagined that eager look.

'The arrow?' My voice must have been louder than I intended, as John Rushe came forward instantly, taking a box from the hands of his assistant and hurrying across to us. There was a movement in the hall and then a stillness. I took the arrow from the box, though I hardly needed to do this. A glance would have been enough. It was unmistakable. Made from well-seasoned ash, bodkin-tipped, and the initials JB scratched into its haft. And there was an ominous dark stain on its tip. I looked down at the hall. All pairs of eyes seemed to be on me. All but one. James Butler gazed steadily and fixedly at the leather seat of the chair whose back he still gripped.

'How long is Queen Katherine staying?' I kept my voice neutral, but ignored the outstretched hand of John Rushe. I would keep this arrow for the moment.

'She hasn't said.' Cardinal Wolsey's voice, also, was quite neutral. 'She received the holy ashes at dawn this morning. She is now praying in her closet with some of her ladies.'

'I see.' Queen Katherine, of course, was very pious and reputed to love the Chapel at Hampton Court. It was not surprising that she did not wish to travel with the ash still smeared on her forehead. Nevertheless, she was unlikely to want to spend the whole forty days of Lent at Hampton Court. But a couple of days perhaps; at least I hoped so. A lady with a calm, penetrating look. I had a feeling that I would like to get her opinion about the worth of the evidence given by Anne Boleyn. Harry Percy I could deal with myself. Even now he avoided my eye.

'Perhaps we should talk about this matter in private,' said the cardinal. 'My rooms, do you think, Hugh? Master Serjeant? And you, Master Rushe, please.' A man with a fine appreciation of rank, the cardinal had spoken first to the king's serjeant. Gibson would be the man in charge of this investigation.

'In a moment,' I said. 'I'll join you there. I must speak with James first.'

I didn't wait for an answer, but descended the three steps down from the dais into the hall and walked across to where James still stood, his head bent, his eyes averted from the curious gazes.

'Let's walk outside for a few minutes,' I said and I took his arm.

He shrugged it off instantly. I should have remembered how self-conscious he was about his lameness.

'It's snowing,' he said.

'You won't melt. Come on.' I waited, made sure that he was in front of me, but said nothing more. He walked stiffly, trying in vain to disguise his limp. A servant carrying a tray of wooden platters was ahead of us. We stood for a moment in the doorway watching him go. There were indeed blobs of snow on the man's shoulders. The clock tower courtyard was bitterly chilly, the grass bleached a desolate shade of yellow; even the crimson bricks lacked warmth under the leaden sky. The gravel beneath our feet was frozen into clumps and I saw James stumble. I took his arm and held it firmly, making him stop and turn towards me.

'Did you do it?' I had waited until we were alone in the square space before I asked the question. It wasn't a day for people to linger and here in the centre of the clock court, there was no danger of being overheard.

'Of course I didn't.'

I eyed him. Like other boys he would tell a lie sometimes if it served his purpose. He wasn't stupid, though. I was his father's lawyer, or Brehon, as we said in Ireland. He knew that I would look after his interests in this English court.

'I know that there was some fuss, some affair that Master Pace uncovered,' I warned him. 'There were rumours about it.' I eyed him keenly. 'Did you pay his blackmail?'

He was taken aback for a moment and then he shrugged. 'Well, you know what it's like. Gave him a crown to shut him up. He threatened to go to the cardinal. It wasn't anything serious. He had something on Gilbert, too. And Thomas. Probably Harry, too. We all had good matches, rich brides in the offing. He threatened that he could put a stop to the marriages if he told what he knew. He had us all paying him to keep his mouth shut, otherwise we'd have to behave like young priests.'

He's lying, I thought. There was something more than that. Even Cardinal Wolsey with the affairs of Europe on his shoulders had spotted something, knew that there was something amiss, had dropped a hint to me that was impossible to ignore. I wouldn't pursue it at the moment. The man was dead and I had to make sure that my employer's son was speedily freed of all suspicion. If we had been back in Ireland, I could have afforded to take my time. Under the Brehon law, in which I had been trained, the punishment would have been a fine. Here it would be death. And death was very final, held no room for mistakes, no possibility of redressing a wrong. I needed to work fast, needed to absorb all the available information.

'And this arrow, your arrow in the man's chest. I saw it. It was definitely yours. Bodkin-tipped, your initials …'

'I lost that arrow a few days ago; I told the serjeant that. I was aiming at a duck flying over the moat, just near to the west entrance, just by the stables. It was getting dark. I thought that I would search for it next morning but I forgot about it.'

I suppressed a groan. It was a possible story, but taken with the evidence put forward by the lady, Mistress Anne Boleyn, and by Harry Percy, it was not good enough. Admittedly it was likely, if the man was a blackmailer, that one of the other boys, all eight of the cardinal's pages, all of them armed with these toy arrows, might have had reason to shoot the instructor of the wards, but two people were prepared to swear that they saw James with a real arrow, bodkin-tipped, and that was the arrow which had killed Master Pace.

And the arrow itself was undoubtedly his.

'Anyone with you when you lost the arrow?' I asked the question without much hope and wasn't surprised when he shook his head. Not too many people would have gone out duck shooting on a freezing day in the month of February. The others were probably cosily tucked up by a fire, playing cards and discussing their marriage prospects. James was always driven, always setting himself goals. Perhaps it was the lame leg, or perhaps he had just been born like that.

'Did you notice anything, anything last night during that …?' I stopped myself using the word 'ridiculous affair' and substituted the word 'pageant'. No matter how puerile the amusements of the king, a man past his thirtieth birthday, it was unwise to voice such opinions.

James shook his head. 'No, but it was very noisy. Everyone was shouting and flinging things and the girls were all shrieking. Mistress Anne was crying '*au secours*' at the top of her voice and her sister Mistress Carey, she was '*Kindness*' and she was screaming – pretending to be frightened, and holding her arms out to the king – everyone knew it was the king, of course. He's the biggest of the lot of them. So we were all laughing at that and cheering her on. And then, of course, there were the sweetmeats thrown in my face and Her Grace the king's sister, the French queen, she emptied a pitcher of rosewater over young Tom Seymour's head and …'

'Were you near to Harry Percy?' I interrupted him. The cardinal was not patient man. In another moment a servant would appear with a polite message requesting our presence.

'I'm not sure. I can't remember.'

A question for one of the ladies-in-waiting. They were up high. The pretend castle had been erected by the carpenters on the dais. The girls would have been looking down at the melee. Not Anne Boleyn, nor her married sister, Mary, but perhaps I would question Bessie Blount, Gilbert Tailboys' designated wife.

'Let's see what the cardinal has managed to uncover,' I said. I went ahead of him, hearing him limp behind me. If things looked too bad I would smuggle him out of the country, and let the marriage to Anne Boleyn hang in abeyance. I did not think that I could face Margaret, Countess of Ormond, if anything happened to her beloved eldest son.

2

The cardinal's room above the entrance archway of the clock tower had a window overlooking the court so I was not surprised to see young Francis Bigod already posted at the doorway ready to bow us into the room. Francis was the descendent of earls, but the younger boys, even fourteen-year-old George Stanley, Earl of Derby, acted as pages in the cardinal's household.

'Thank you, Francis,' I said, but James, I noticed, could not even manage a smile. His face was whiter than ever and I swore under my breath. Francis looked embarrassed, his eyes avoiding James's. Perhaps by this stage I should have been down at the stables choosing two good horses to take us to Bristol. However, it was probably too late for that now. As soon as we came in the king's serjeant-at-arms stepped forward from the shadows. The cardinal, a man who felt the cold, had the stone walls of his room darkly panelled in wood. Not even the brightly burning fire and the many-branched candelabra could illuminate the gloom on this grey morning and it took a few minutes before the other shadows resolved themselves into shapes.

Six ladies-in-waiting, I noticed. Even the king's sister, known as the French queen since her brief marriage to the now-deceased Louis XII, although she was now Duchess of Suffolk, even she and the Countess of Devon were there. And so was John Rushe's sister, Alice.

Alice would be, I reckoned, about my own age, about thirty. She had been married, John told me once, at barely fourteen. An Italianate beauty, she had dark green eyes, almond in shape, olive skin, but her hair was a rich gold, the colour of ripe corn, an unusual colour where a subtle shade of red tinged the blondness of the smooth locks. It had been a brilliant marriage to a very wealthy knight, three times older than she. On the death of her husband a few years ago, her wardship had been given by the king to Cardinal Wolsey. He had made various attempts to find her a new husband, she had wealth and beauty, but she had always objected. In the meantime the cardinal benefited from her estates and from her presence. It was rumoured that Serjeant Rushe owed his promotion to his sister's elegance and charm. She was looking very serious this morning. The almond-shaped eyes that met mine held a warning, before they moved to focus on the king's serjeant-at-arms.

Deliberately I picked up a wooden candlestick and held the light in my hand, moving it slowly from face to face and watching the features spring to life. Harry Percy looking, not guilty, rather more excited, though his hands, pale in the candlelight, were twisted together, one entwined in the other in a nervous fashion. Thomas Arundel appeared embarrassed, confused, but looking away from James. Thomas and Harry were very close and now I could see how they seemed to range themselves together, as though to face an emergency. And Gilbert Tailboys, James's best friend, was looking frightened.

I glanced quickly at the king's sergeant and was not surprised to see that his eyes were fixed on Gilbert. The boy did look as though he knew something.

'James, Hugh, come in, come in. Come and get warm by the fire. Today is no time for the outdoors! You Irish. You're a hardy race.' Scolding lightly, the cardinal got us both sitting by the fireside while he himself took a chair behind a small table, resting his clasped hands on its carpeted surface and smiling gently.

'Now, Hugh, we know that you were busy last night so were not able to watch the pageant.' The cardinal, a consummate actor, bore a note of commiseration in his voice. He knew well that I loathed loud music and took any excuse to get away from it.

'That's right, Your Grace,' I said briskly. 'And now I very much regret that fact.' I looked grimly across at Richard Gibson. The king's sergeant would not find me an easy opponent. I had often beaten him at tennis and he knew I was ruthless under pressure. I kept an eye on him while I smiled politely at the cardinal and waited for the next move.

'And so, I've asked George here to describe the scene as he remembers it. George has a way with words and if he makes a mistake, then the others here can assist him. Come on, George, we are agog.'

It was George Cavendish, of course, one of the gentlemen ushers, the newest of them, not long in the post. He looked nervous as he came forward from the shadows, but when he began to speak, everyone perched on chairs or stools, or leaning against the panelled walls, stayed very still and listened intently.

How like the cardinal to have discovered a talent in this latest recruit. He was the one who had encouraged

James to become a master bowman, a skill where his lame foot did not impede him; the one who had continually lauded Gilbert Tailboys as the most sensible and the most level-headed of his pages and caused him to put his father's sad history to the back of his mind. And now this George Cavendish, nervous, tentative, probably quite unsure of himself while performing his duties in supervising the servants, scolding people for bad service, was being praised as a gifted teller of tales.

And George did it very well. He fixed his large blue eyes on me and spoke in a musical, almost rhythmic fashion.

'You must know, Hugh,' he said, 'that my lord would do anything to please the king, to relieve him, if only for a few hours, of the cares of state. And so, on this Shrove Tuesday, all was appointed for his entertainment. The castle looked for all the world as though made from stone, the ladies, the queen's gentlewomen, all sheltered behind its castellated walls, imprisoned by these young men, dressed as women from Inde ...' George waved his hand towards the cluster of the cardinal's wards. And, he, the kindest of men, flinched at the sight of James's white face and went hastily on with his story. I half-listened to the flow of words in the antique storytelling accent:

and on every braunche were thirty-two torchettes of waxe, and in the nether ende of the same chamber was a castle, in which was a principal tower, where there was a cresset burning: and two other lesse towers stode on every side, warded and embattled, and on every tower was a banner, one banner was of three rent hartes, the other was a ladies hand gripyng a man's harte, the third banner was a ladies hand turnyng a mannes hart: this castle was kept with ladies

of straunge names, the first *Beautie*, the second *Honor*, the
third *Perseueraunce*, the fourth *Kyndnes*, the fifth *Constance*,
the sixte *Bountie*, the seuenthe *Mercie*, and the eighth *Pitie*:
these eight ladies had Milan gounes of white sattin, euery
Lady had her name embraudered with golde, on their
heddes cauls, and Milan bonettes of gold, with jewelles.
Under nethe the basse fortresse of the castle were other
eight ladies, whose names were, *Dangier*, *Disdain*, *Gelousie*,
Vnkyndenes, *Scorne*, *Malebouche*, *Straungenes*, these ladies were
tired like to women of Inde.

George gesticulated towards the eight wards, who had
played the part of the unpleasant ladies with such gusto.
Something about James's white face must have struck
him, because he stopped there and he looked anxiously
at the cardinal.

'And you saw them aim their arrows at the attackers,
that's right, isn't it, George?'

George nodded mutely.

'And you would have been observing them carefully,
would you not, as I had given you the responsibility
for that part of the evening's entertainment?' queried
his master.

Never ask an important question if you don't already
know the answer to it was one of the many pieces of
good advice that Cardinal Wolsey had given to me and
now I awaited George's answer with confidence.

'Yes, I did,' said George stoutly. He cast a quick look of
defiance at the two serjeants, standing side by side, and
then turned back to the cardinal. 'I was watching with
great care the arrows that your wards were firing, Your
Grace, as I was the one that thought of using a mixture of

finely ground-up leather and glue to fashion them in the likeness of real arrows. I took the idea from some of the medallions in the great hall which, when painted, looked just like wood.'

'And it was a great success, George, wasn't it?' The cardinal's voice was smooth and he did not even glance towards the king's serjeant. I noticed John Rushe look at the man by his side uneasily, though. John was a decent fellow but he was keen for promotion. Master Richard Gibson had the ear of the king and John's future could depend on him. 'I saw one of them glide off the king's sleeve,' continued the cardinal, 'and I saw it fall to the floor. I picked it up. It snapped more easily than a cornstalk. You did very well, George. His Grace was pleased to say that he had seldom enjoyed an evening as much.'

George flushed a rosy red. He gulped, his large Adam's apple moving up and down his neck. In a flustered way he stepped back from the candlelight and remained silent as though the compliment had robbed him of words.

'No one thinks that those arrows did any harm, Your Grace,' said king's serjeant impatiently. 'But Master Harry says …'

'Ah, yes, Master Harry.' The cardinal's voice, used to the negotiating tables of kings and emperors, overrode the serjeant's voice very effectively. 'Yes, indeed, Master Gibson, you remind me of the tale that you told me. Stand forth, Harry. Don't look so worried, boy. Anyone can make a mistake. The wine flowed freely last night, didn't it?' And the cardinal gave a fat, comfortable chuckle ready to reassure that all sins could be forgiven.

Harry Percy was the heir to the Earl of Northumberland, not the most important of the cardinal's pages – that would have been young Stanley, already the third Earl of Derby – but he was probably the one that His Grace worried the most about. A dark-haired boy with a high complexion and a difficult nature. One who turned to wine not just for the fun of the moment but as a release from inner demons. It was rumoured that his father favoured his younger brother and openly regretted that Harry had not died of a bout of sweating sickness five years ago.

'I saw James with a real arrow in his hand.' The words spurted out and young Percy gave a defiant glance around the room and then a hasty, furtive look at Mistress Anne Boleyn.

'And you could see it plainly. God bless your young eyes. I couldn't make out much in the confusion. All that rosewater! And the fruit flying through the air. The candles flickering!' The cardinal threw his hands in the air, the gesture causing a stretching of the flames in the top tier of the candelabra in front of him. A drop of hot wax fell onto the crimson carpet of the table. George rushed forward and scratched it off with a well-trimmed nail, but the cardinal's eyes never wavered from the face of Harry Percy. I remained silent. The cardinal would do a good job of interrogation.

'I could see it plainly.' Once again there was that glance at the girl. A self-possessed young lady. She was standing very still and looking politely at the cardinal. She stood as gracefully as she moved, slight, small-boned, very slim, but quite upright, silhouetted against the dark brown squares of panelling, her bejewelled French hood, like a crescent moon, catching the light from a nearby candle. She wore a dark veil attached to the slender hood, floating down her back and it enhanced the rich colour of her very black hair.

Harry Percy could not take his eyes from her. 'Ask Mistress Boleyn.' He blurted out the name as though he could no longer restrain himself from attracting her attention. She looked at him then. For a second a half-smile flickered over her lips and then she looked back at the cardinal.

'And you, Mistress, what did you see?' The cardinal turned from Harry and she met his gaze with one of her graceful curtseys.

I saw the same as Master Percy, Your Grace.' Her voice was musical, well modulated, reached across the room with ease.

'And that was?' The cardinal raised his eyebrows at her.

'A wooden arrow, ten times the girth of the other arrows that the young gentlemen were firing.'

'And you could see that clearly, from where you stood, even amongst the crowd.'

'I saw the candlelight glint on the metal point of it, Your Grace. That attracted my attention and so I looked more closely. My eyes are very good, Your Grace.' She dropped a slight courtesy to him, a graceful movement and widened those very black eyes as though to display their excellence.

'And the other ladies? What did they see? Your Grace?' The cardinal gave a courteous wave of his hand towards the king's sister. She seemed to me to hesitate, but then she shook her head.

'And the other young ladies?'

Again heads were shaken. It would have been difficult for anything as small as an arrow to have been noticed in the confusion. Oranges flying from the fists of *Ardent Desire* and his men would have meant that the ladies would have been continually ducking below the parapet. I looked tentatively at Bessie Blount. I would have a word with her afterwards, I promised myself and then eyed Gilbert Tailboys. He averted his head and would not meet my eyes. I would leave him until afterwards, too, I decided. If Edmund Pace had been blackmailing those whom he was paid to instruct, then it might be difficult to get anyone as shy and as diffident as Gilbert Tailboys to speak out in company.

'It was difficult to see anything, Your Grace, because of wearing those masks with our names scrolled on to them.' Thomas Seymour spoke up from his place on the bench. 'That's right, isn't it, Francis? I had *Malebouche* written across mine and Francis had *Straungenes*.'

'That's right, Tom. It kept slipping over my eyes. I couldn't see a thing.' Francis was a sincere type of boy.

'And you, Edward, Your Grace?' The cardinal addressed the Earl of Derby with his usual gentle amusement at using the title of this rather grubby-looking boy. 'And George Vernon,' he went on without waiting for an answer. 'None of you saw anything amiss?'

'No, Your Grace.' They chorused their reply with an air of relief. Boys of that age, I had noticed when instructing at law school, have a poor grip on truth and like to be sure what their elders want of them before vouchsafing any information. They might tell a different story to a different form of interrogation, but now it was out said in front of all. They had seen nothing untoward.

'So it appears that only Harry Percy and Mistress Anne Boleyn saw this arrow in the hands of James Butler,' mused the cardinal. He had, I noticed, not asked any public questions of Gilbert nor of Thomas Arundel. I was glad of that. The younger boys would be more carefree in their answers. Gilbert was a worrier and might well have hesitated and stammered over his answer. And from what James had said, both Gilbert and Thomas were involved in bribing the dead man. I looked across at the cardinal and he lifted his head, raised his hands and spoke directly to the king's serjeant.

'Is there anything you wish to say, Master Gibson?' he enquired. 'Well, we must let you make your enquiries. Goodness, you and Master Rushe will be busy! Thank you all for coming, and I hope you enjoy your afternoon, Tennis, tilting, archery, cards, books, chess, boards, balliards, all that my poor house can offer is at your disposal. Master Cavendish, you will look after our guests,' he said to George, raising his voice so that everyone, crowded into his room could hear him and George immediately went and opened the door and waited there like an eager sheepdog ready to usher them out. The king's serjeant, though, stood stolidly by the table and did not move and John Rushe, the cardinal's man hovered uneasily beside him.

'We have your permission to take statements, Your Grace.' This was in response to a sharp look from the king's serjeant.

Cardinal Wolsey patted him on the upper arm of his black velvet doublet.

'Not just my permission, John, my orders. Summon who you will. I look forward to reading your script. I'm sure that you will both find the truth.'

'And Master James Butler.' Now the king's sergeant pushed forward.

It was time for me to play a part. I didn't have to act. Even I could hear the edge of anger in my voice.

'Your Grace, my client, James Butler utterly denies having anything to do with the unfortunate death of the instructor of the wards, Edmund Pace. He denies having in his possession on that night a wooden arrow, bodkin-tipped, the arrow which caused the death, he believes it to be one which he lost last week when aiming at a duck flying across the moat. That is all that my client wishes to say about the affair, at this moment.'

'You will let the serjeants have that statement in writing, won't you, Hugh? Well, thank you, everyone, you may go now.'

James was the first to leave. His lame leg went unevenly down the passageway outside and then George ushered out the crowd, all of them merrily clamouring for cards, and for balliard balls and other amusements. I glanced through one of the five-paned windows that were set high above the wooden panelling. The sky was a leaden grey and small crisp flakes of snow floated down. George would be kept busy finding indoor occupations for the guests.

Alice, to my amusement, had not left with the others. She put down her embroidery carefully on a bench and came over to the cardinal's side. He shook his head at her indulgently, but pulled a seat forward so that she could sit with us. His manner to Alice was paternal, but I often thought that if, like the Irish bishops, it had been the norm to have a consort, she would have made an excellent wife for him. As his ward, she played a part in entertaining his guests and kept him amused by her sharp wit.

'James was in a hurry,' she observed to me, 'do you think that he wants to be first in line for Mistress Boleyn's favours?'

'I doubt it,' I replied. 'Not if she is trying to get him hanged. I'm not an expert on love affairs, but that doesn't seem to me to be too friendly.'

'Are you a married man, yourself, Hugh?' asked the cardinal.

'Divorced, Your Grace,' I said cheerfully.

He shuddered and Alice laughed. 'Don't let the king hear you say something like that,' he said. 'He's very pious, our prince. He believes in the sanctity of the church laws and marriage, you know, is one of its sacraments.'

'Well, we're a bit different in Ireland. Our law grants divorce very easily.' I said the words casually and as he seemed to want to postpone the discussion about James's possible guilt, I continued in the same light tone: 'I've written it into the marriage contract and if that stands and Mistress Anne gets tired of our James she can walk away with all that she brought to marriage and at least half of the goods which she has helped to make, half the value of the wool that has been carded and spun by her even though sheared by her husband ...'

'Ancient laws!' The cardinal chuckled. 'I don't see that lady out tending her sheep, or carding and spinning wool. Perhaps a little embroidery.'

'And, of course, she can sign bonds and can divorce him if he fails to give her a child.'

'Hush!' The cardinal looked around uneasily as if the king were lurking behind the arras, or had his ear clapped to the keyhole of the door. 'Tell me,' he said hastily, 'why did you divorce your wife?'

'It was the other way around, Your Grace. She divorced me.'

The cardinal's eyebrows asked a question.

'She suspected that I loved someone else,' I explained. 'She thought we were not suited and she was right. We divided everything up according to the law. She's happily married to someone else now. She has two little daughters and adores them. I am godfather to one of them, just as Your Grace is godfather to Bessie Blount's son, little Henry Fitzroy.'

'And you, you must marry again, a handsome fellow like you. You must have a son. Or perhaps,' said the cardinal, carefully steering the conversation away from the king's illegitimate boy, 'you do have a son that we don't know about. Strange things happen in Ireland, do they not? Stephen Gardiner says that it is a godless place.'

'If you say so, Your Grace.' I didn't want to talk about Stephen Gardiner. I didn't like the man much. 'Now about this matter,' I continued. 'Is James under suspicion purely on the word of Harry Percy and of the lady? If so, I think that is on shaky grounds. It's obvious from the way that they look at each other, that pair, that this is a love at first sight, for the boy, anyway.'

'As Boccaccio says: *Love with his darts dwelt within the rays of those lovely eyes.* He wants her for those beautiful black eyes,' put in Alice.

'And she?' queried the cardinal.

'I'd say that she sees his vast acres of estates when she looks into his eyes,' Alice suggested demurely, and the cardinal chuckled.

'He seems very in love with her,' I put in.

'You're not thinking that Harry Percy planned to kill my instructor of the wards, just in order to free Mistress Boleyn of the Butler match are you, Hugh?'

'Not planned,' I said slowly, 'but perhaps on the spur of the moment, the notion came to him. That was an opportunist murder, Your Grace, it could not have been planned. No one could have known that the man would position himself just behind the arras cloth and no one could have foretold that he would fall dead without attracting the notice of any of the hundred or so people in the hall. You were there, yourself, Your Grace. As well as the king and his courtiers, the ladies-in-waiting and the pages, there were also the servants, the musicians, the gentlemen ushers, the yeoman, the marshals and perhaps some of the kitchen staff. It was an amazing matter that a man could be shot, fall down dead and not a single one of all those people would notice.'

'An act of desperation, perhaps,' suggested Alice thoughtfully.

'Desperation,' mused the cardinal. 'I'm not sure that I know the meaning of the word. There is always something to be done, is there not? Of course, boys are a bit different, aren't they? God bless my soul, I must by now have had dozens of boys go through my hands, and the strange thing is that many, many of them did quite unpredictable things, things that were incredibly dangerous, incredibly foolish and … and, well, just incredible.' The cardinal sighed, shook his head and held the ring he wore on his fourth finger up to the light. It was of gold and the stone, an oval-shaped turquoise stone, held by small golden clasps, was big enough to cover the entire lower end of his finger.

'Why should James wish to kill the instructor of the wards?' I asked the question abruptly. I didn't like the direction that the conversation was taking.

Alice and the cardinal looked at each other.

'I did mention to you that there was a rumour that the instructor of the wards was blackmailing some of the boys. The matter was investigated by my sergeant-at-arms, but was found not to have substance, at the time,' added the cardinal and he looked at me meaningfully. John Rushe, good fellow that he was, would be no match for the cunning instructor of the wards. I was worrying, though, that others knew of the dead man's reputation as a blackmailer.

I recovered my senses and presented a blank face to him. 'Nothing much in it, Your Grace. The odd crown to keep the man silent about a few boyish escapades. If he had any real worries, James would have confided in me. I have been part of his household since I was a young boy. My father was Brehon to the Ormonds in Kilkenny Castle. If James had been in any trouble when I arrived he would have immediately looked to me to sort it out for him. I knew James in his cradle.'

'Perhaps.' The cardinal sounded sceptical but, as he often said, he never argued with lawyers or Irishmen. It was one of his favourite jokes when I was present. He got to his feet. 'Now I must visit the queen. I'll leave you to sort out this affair.' He ambled gently towards the door. There would be something else to come; I knew him well enough for that. The cardinal always kept his important messages for the last. A little piece of information, just thrown over his shoulder …

'Have a word with George,' he invited. 'He's a young man himself. He would be able to tell you what went

on after the banquet. All that sugar, all that marchpane –
makes me want to drop off to sleep, but it seems to give
energy to the young. And, Hugh, I can't afford to delay
too long in this business. A murder committed probably in the presence of the king himself. Luckily he will
be busy with the ambassador and his train this week,
but by next week, say by next Monday, I will need to
be seen to have taken some action. I have the affair of
the Bishop of Carlisle to see to, also. But that gives you
five days.'

And then he was gone, closing the door softly behind
him. He was a man of his word. I would have this time –
these remaining five days with as little interference as he
could manage, but after that there would be no saving of
James, unless I could come up with another name, could
make a good legal case for another person to have fired
that fatal arrow.

'Come down to my room,' said Alice when the noise of
his footsteps had died away. 'We'll be more private there.

I followed her out of the room and strolled by her side.

'My little Lily hears me,' she said as she opened the
door and an excited squeal of barking hit our ears. The
small dog shot from the arms of a lady-in-waiting and
she picked it up, stroking the soft white fur and gently
pulling at the pure gold ears. 'White and gold; I had to
name her Lily,' she had said to me when Lily and I first
made friends.

'James is in bad trouble, Hugh,' she said when we were
alone.

'He didn't do it. It would have been a crazy thing to
do. James is not like that. Kill a man on the spur of the
moment by firing an arrow in the presence of the king

and the nobility. That's the act of an irrational man and James is not that. I'll get him out of it,' I said confidently.

'The king's serjeant will want to prove that he did it.' Her voice had sunk to a low murmur, but it held a warning note and Lily gave a small quiet growl and then wagged a responsive tail as her mistress told her to be quiet.

'Why on earth should he want to do that?' I asked.

She fondled the dog for a minute.

'Because he is bribed or intimidated by St Leger,' she replied. 'I saw them together, just before you came in. They had their heads together. You mark my words, a proposal has been made and has been accepted.'

I thought about this for a moment. Alice was a sharp observer. She had a habit of sitting quietly in the background, seemingly immersed in her needlework, but in reality taking in all the nuances of words spoken and unspoken, and absorbing all of the expressions. It was one of the reasons, I often thought, why the cardinal was reluctant to part with her, was happy to allow her to reject possible marriage offers.

'And, of course, if James is convicted of a murder, then his father's claim to the earldom of Ormond is very much weakened.' I could see the significance of a link between St Leger and king's serjeant.

'And St Leger's is very much strengthened,' pointed out Alice. 'After all, he is the son of the elder daughter of the late earl. Thomas Boleyn is the son of the younger of the two. He only came into the picture because, in the first place, he is the king's ambassador and King Henry likes to reward those who are in his eye. And secondly, unlike St Leger, the Boleyns still had an unmarried daughter and Cardinal Wolsey thought it a good idea to settle the matter peacefully.'

It was a shrewd analysis and I thought about it. Alice always knew the intricacies of every line of nobility. What she did not say, but what I knew well, was that the cardinal was fond of James and thought the match with young Anne Boleyn would be a way of giving the boy an earldom.

'As long as the matter does not end in James dangling from a noose,' I said grimly. But that was a futile remark. I needed to concentrate my mind on this murder.

'That was a strange way to murder anyone, wasn't it, Alice?'

'Almost like a piece of stagecraft, wasn't it?' Alice had read my thoughts. 'You don't think that our Mr Cavendish, George, the gentleman usher, had anything to do with it, do you, Hugh?'

'It's a tempting thought,' Despite the seriousness of the matter I could not help smiling. 'The ultimate in entertainment for the king. After all the Romans entertained their emperors by flinging Christians to the lions, didn't they?'

On another occasion Alice and I would have had fun with this notion, but now I had not the heart to pursue it. This talk of St Leger was worrying me. I gnawed the knuckle of my middle finger and thought about it. This murder just did not make sense. I wished that I had been present when the body was found.

'Shall I send for John? I think we need to know what's going on.' She was always responsive to what was not said. At my nod, she tinkled a small silver bell and the little dog barked vigorously until a lady-in-waiting appeared at the door. The household, including Alice's brother, took their attitude to her from the cardinal's manner and I was not surprised when John appeared within minutes. Alice fixed her eyes on the fire, stroked Lily and left her brother to stand facing me.

'John, where's the body? I want to see it.' I asked sharply. The more I thought about it, the stranger I found this arrow business.

'The king's serjeant is looking after it.' There was a note of evasion in his voice

'Looking after it!' I repeated. 'What do you mean?''

Alice's hand ceased stroking the little dog. Her eyes were fixed on her brother and her eyebrows rose. He looked at her hastily and then back at me.

'Master Gibson has taken over this matter; you have to understand that, Hugh.'

'Although this is Hampton Court, not one of the royal palaces. What does the cardinal have to say to that?' I said. I was beginning to get angry.

'You know what he would say, Hugh. *Everything that I have comes from the king.*' Alice's voice had a note of warning. She would not allow anything to be said against Cardinal Wolsey and so I changed my tack.

'This is a very strange affair, John. Can't you see that? If James wanted to send an arrow through Edmund Pace's heart, then why not shoot him from a window, or out in the Wildernesse one day. It must have been sheer chance and a most unlikely thing that it was not instantly noticed that a man fell down dead in front of a hundred people.'

'But he did.' John was stubborn.

'It appears that he did, John. There's a difference.' Alice placed the little dog on the floor beside her skirts and took up her embroidery. 'I agree with Hugh. It seems most unlikely that he was shot in front of the king, his court, and almost the whole of the cardinal's court. Hugh, why don't you go and have a word with George, as the cardinal suggested.'

I went at her bidding. John would be stubborn with me, but would be acquiescent to his sister. She had a better chance with him.

3

George was carrying a box filled with twelve glistening balls of ivory when I met him. I took it firmly from him, opened the door of the Balliards Room and deposited it into the hands of Tom Seymour. I had a quick glance into the room. No sign of James, though the room was full of young men. And one lady. Anne Boleyn was draped gracefully across the window seat, her long fingers sliding up and down a silver-tipped balliards stick, as though gently caressing it. And beside her stood Harry Percy.

'They'll be happy now, George.' I shut the door firmly before his anxious face and took his arm and walked him down the gallery. Few of the guests had left and there were people everywhere. I steered him towards a window seat and felt that he was glad to sit down. His face was very pale and his large eyes were anxious. I had once met his father, the clerk of the pipe at the court of the exchequer, a man with a look of a bulldog, but George must take after his mother. There was a gentle refinement about his face, a delicate mouth and his hair, worn rather long, had a slightly feminine curl to it.

'How is the courtship going with Margery Kemp?' I asked and saw his face relax and the lines of tension smoothed out. He looked very young, not much older than James or Harry Percy. It was a good match, fixed up by the cardinal. Margery Kempe, the niece of the lawyer, Thomas More, was an heiress and a very pretty and gentle girl. I listened to her praises for a few minutes and then steered the conversation around to James.

'A shame about that foot of his,' I said with a sigh. 'I suppose last night he had to stand out while the others danced after the sugar banquet was over. The cardinal was telling me that they all seemed very energetic.'

'Including His Grace, our king, of course.' George smiled happily at the thought. He had told me once that he took this position as he had a burning desire to meet great men.

'Oh, whom did the king dance with?' I asked idly. I didn't want to get onto the Anne Boleyn question too quickly.

'Mistress Mary Boleyn, I should say Mistress Mary Carey, one of the ladies-in-waiting, the pretty one who acted the part of *Kindness* in the pageant, the wife of Will Carey.' George always knew who was who in court circle. He could be quite a bore when he explained intricate matters of cousinship, so now I seized on his words quickly before he could tell me who Will Carey was.

'That must have made her sister jealous,' I said.

'Well, no.' George frowned slightly. 'She was occupied.'

'With Harry Percy?'

George looked at me sadly. 'I'm afraid that they are in earnest, Hugh. I watched them last night. I've seldom seen a pair of young people more in love.'

'Doesn't matter,' I said brazenly. 'We'll find James a nice girl over in Ireland. His mother would fancy one of her own clan, one of the Fitzgeralds, or so I've heard.'

George looked relieved. 'It was the way they clasped hands when they came together in the dance and once I saw him, young Harry, touch her cheek. He had such a tender expression. He touched her cheek, just with his forefinger.'

'And she?'

'She moved close. And she pulled off her mask and just smiled into his eyes. It brought a tear to my eye.' George gave a sentimental sigh. 'It's sad,' he said. 'But I don't think that the cardinal would like that match. I believe that all the papers have been signed for Harry Percy's match with Mary Talbot, the Earl of Shrewsbury's daughter. His Grace won't be pleased if there is any flirtation with Mistress Boleyn, and yet, you know, Hugh, the two of them there, they made such a handsome young couple, he smiling down at her, and she looking up with those lovely dark eyes of hers. And when they finished a dance, she dropped him such a curtsey. It was for all the world as though she said to him, in body language, *I am yours!* I couldn't take my eyes off them,' finished George in a romantic style, and I stared at him uneasily. This was bad news. I had not thought of the lady being so smitten.

'And they danced together, one dance, two dances …'

'All night,' said George. 'I'm afraid that they were together until the very end of the evening and it was an evening that went into the small hours of the morning.'

'And now she is in playing balliards with him.'

George grimaced.

'Probably holding his arm to make sure that he hits the ball in the right direction.' The mother of the maids should be looking after Mistress Boleyn a bit better, but that was none of my business. I was never a man to beat my head against a stone wall. From what George said about the pair of young lovers, I thought it would be difficult to make either admit to a lie. I would try something else, gather some other witnesses.

'Have you seen Gilbert?' I asked.

'I saw him going down the paved passage towards the kitchens a while ago.' George's anxious face lit up with a smile. Gilbert's fondness for marchpane was well known and the other boys teased him about it. He had probably gone to see whether there were any leftovers. I got to my feet, glancing out at the snow, which was thickening now.

'I'm sorry, Hugh,' George thought about it for a moment and then did not quite know what to say. 'I'm sorry,' he repeated. He was a nice fellow, this George Cavendish.

I clapped him on the shoulder. 'We have a saying in the Brehon Courts of Ireland, a triad, one of the truisms that young scholars memorise and it says: *There are three doors through which truth is recognised: a patient answer, a firm pleading, appealing to witnesses.* You've given me a patient answer, George, I've made a firm pleading and now I must appeal for witnesses. I'll leave you to your duties and see whether I can find Gilbert.'

★★★

There was no sign of Gilbert looking for snacks when I pushed open the kitchen door. The enormous room was relatively quiet, only the wood yard boys wheeling the flat-topped barrows into the main kitchen were still busy. All of the dinners were finished, the boys were washing up in the sculleries, the leftovers were being distributed by the almoner, and the chief cook himself was chatting with the clerk of the kitchens.

'Leave me some number ones to get the fire hot later on.' Master Beasley interrupted his conversation to turn towards the wood carriers and then saw me.

'Come in, Master,' he said cordially. 'Come and taste my wafers. I hear you didn't attend the sugar banquet last night.'

'I'm not much of a sugar man,' I said. 'Give me some of your quails and a good flask of wine and I'm happy.' There was a woman in the kitchen, I noticed. That was unusual. Master Beasley wouldn't normally have a woman around his pots and pans. She looked at me with a slightly annoyed glance and said firmly: 'Stale eggs, Master Beasley, not fresh.'

'I don't suppose that you will charge me for stale eggs, will you?' She said the words in an assured fashion to the cook as he came back with six and he grinned at her. They appeared to be old friends. There was something flirtatious about her manner to him, and perhaps something fatherly in his manner to her.

I wondered who she was. She spoke with a strong accent, Flemish, I guessed. The cardinal had quite a few Flemish working in his household, musicians and engravers. The people from the Netherlands were in the forefront of the new learning, the new art and architecture, and above all the wonderful tapestries that were of such huge importance to the court households. The glittery court of Henry VIII moved from palace to palace in order to cleanse the living quarters and to allow for the thorough cleaning of the rooms and the tapestries moved with them, making for instant warmth and instant colour once they were hung on the walls.

Many of these Flemish artists had come to work in London. I had never seen this girl before, though. Moderately young. About the same age as Anne Boleyn, but very different in appearance. Very soberly dressed, a black gown with a high-necked chemise beneath it, her blonde hair tucked into a white linen cap, no jewellery. No apron, either, so she could not be a confectioner or maker of pies. All of the cardinal's kitchen staff were ordered to wear an apron when in the kitchen, the rules were very strict: neat, clean clothing, covered with a linen apron.

'And the almond shells, you remembered to reserve me your almond shells?'

'Nicely baked, just as you ordered. Plenty of them, too, after all the marchpane that was made from the almonds. A chessboard, if you please. And thirty-two little men. Did you see it?' He cocked an eye at me and I nodded. There had been great excitement about that chessboard. But the cardinal had given it to the French ambassador and that was the end of the hopes of all the young gentlemen of the cardinal's court.

'Magnificent,' I said and the cook looked gratified.

'And the fish spine?' asked the young lady.

'Don't worry. I saved some perfect fish spines for you from the Ash Wednesday dishes for the queen. Not one of them broken. She has good carvers.'

'And three pounds of flour, one half pound of salt and a dozen fresh eggs, oh and some sugar, little, little bit of sugar,' she finished rapidly while I wondered idly what dish could be made from these diverse ingredients.

'We'll have to charge you for those,' said the clerk of the kitchen, coming forward from the desk. 'And sugar is very expensive. Four pence a pound.'

She grimaced slightly, but handed him her purse and he took the money from it, entered the amounts into his account book and asked her to sign it.

A beautiful hand. I admired the elaborate flourish of the S. Susannah Horenbout. Probably Flemish, yes, the name sounded like it. She stored her goods carefully into the basket she carried, gave a polite curtsey and left. The clerk of the kitchen nodded at Master Beasley and then followed her out.

'Who's she?' I was intrigued. The curtsey had been that of an equal, not a woman who made pies and sold them to the kitchen.

'She's a painter, works with her brother, he makes pictures for the cardinal. She often comes in here for her stores, mixes her paints and glues with these sort of things, eggs and flour.'

'And even the backbone from the queen's fish.'

'That's right.' He gave a shrug. 'They lodge in one of the workshops, near to the gate. The cardinal thinks highly of her work, has got her to illuminate a book for him and they say it was she who did those roundels in the gallery, those Roman emperors, not her brother.' Master Beasley held a flask beneath the tap of a barrel that supported and was partially obscured by a large copper pan. He filled the flask and then poured out two mugs of wine. Good stuff, I noticed, tasting it and wondering whether the clerk of the kitchens had taken a reckoning of that barrel.

'I was looking for Master Tailboys.' I shifted away from the icy draught from the wood yard arch and settled myself on one of the stools. 'Someone saw him around here,' I added, savouring the taste of the wine and then taking another mouthful.

'Here, have some of these. Sin and shame to waste them on those beggars at the gate. Good bit of brawn would be more in their line. But these are very nice. I made them especially for the king last night and I saved some that were not eaten.'

'Delicious,' I said. The thin juicy pieces of beefsteak were wrapped around olives and the olives themselves were stuffed with a buttery mixture of breadcrumbs and herbs. Even cold they were very tasty. Hot, they must have been superlative. It was no wonder that the king had put on weight since I had last seen him.

'Haven't seen a sign of Master Tailboys. He didn't come in here, but then he wouldn't when he saw old sourguts here, checking on every crumb that came into the kitchen.' Master Beasley swallowed some more wine.

'Perhaps he has gone to the confectioner's kitchen?' I didn't want to get the cook started on complaints about the clerk of the kitchen. This was a great new innovation of the cardinal. He was appalled at the huge cost of food in the royal kitchens in King Henry's palaces, George Cavendish had told me, and so he was trying out a new system in his own kitchens. The clerk checked in all food, doled it out to the kitchen and then checked the food served and tried to make sure that all leftovers were either eaten by the servants or else given to the almoner for the beggars who came to the gates of the palace.

'I'm sorry about your young gentleman.' Master Beasley chewed on one of the tasty meat parcels and swallowed some more wine to wash it down before he continued. 'Wish I never spotted that shoe. Didn't like the man much at the best of times. Hand in glove with that fellow who has just gone out.'

'Really,' I commented. It would be interesting to hear the views of the cook, a man who heard all the gossip in Hampton Court. He gave a grunt now, but said no more, waiting until another load of wood was added to the main fireplace. All three fires seemed to be well banked down now, each with a talshide of number one logs arranged neatly on a trolley, ready for when the fires had to be resurrected for cooking the supper.

'Terrible draught from that archway; I'm surprised that you don't get the carpenter to build a door across it,' I said to fill the minute while the boys, well-trained by Master Beasley, carefully swept up pieces of bark and wood dust from the tiled floor.

'You wouldn't if you were the cook, instead of just being a lawyer. You know what would happen without that draught? Well, the fires would smoke and smoulder and what would His Grace, or one of those tame gentlemen ushers, say to me then? If you've got a hundred pounds of beef to boil up, or fifty chickens to roast on a spit, well you need a good fire to roar up that chimneys. So that's how we keep it. Cold feet and hot head, that's the life of the kitchen worker!' Master Beasley drained his mug of wine and went across for a refill.

'There's a few bits and pieces for you lads under that cloth,' he said to the boys when he returned. 'Now be off with you all and make sure you check on the fires a good hour before I start the supper or I'll hang you all by the heels in that chimney.'

The boys went off chuckling, pushing their barrows in front of them and Master Beasley settled down for a good gossip.

'Yes, not a nice man, that instructor of the wards. Long nose, he had, and was forever poking it into other people's business. I had a feeling that he was hounding that young fellow, Master Tailboys.' The cook cast an inquisitive eye at me and I responded by draining my cup.

'Good stuff, that.'

'Have some more. The fellow who delivered the stuff got that barrel in here on one of the wood barrows before the clerk came down from his office. He has a window looking down so that he can see the deliveries arriving at the gate, but then, of course, he has to go down the stairs.' The cook chuckled. 'That stuff came in with a good few number six talshides heaped around it. We had it unloaded and stuck in a dark corner before you could say Jack Robinson. But to go back to young Tailboys. I heard him stuttering and stammering one day out in the paved passage. I was up above in the confectioner's kitchen, just up above the pastry ovens, and I looked down and saw the lad hand over a small bag to Master Pace. I'd swear, by the way he held it, that it was heavy with coins.'

I reflected on this for a while. I had to admit that it would be most unlikely that Gilbert Tailboys had anything to do with the shooting of Master Pace. Unlike James he was not a good shot and he was a nervous, irresolute type of boy. To shoot a man on the spur of the moment in the presence of the king and his court, not to mention the cardinal and his household, that took a boldness …

Or utter despair. I drained my cup and got to my feet.

'Great place this, good wine, good food, great gossip,' I said with a grin. 'Thanks, Master Beasley. I'd better be off now before the snow gets worse.'

I needed to find Gilbert Tailboys.

The confectionery was locked up, as were the saucery, the spicery and pastry offices, all their staff having a rest before the work of making supper had to begin. I went back downstairs, along the narrow passage and out through the gate. The moat looked dark and murky, and here and there were thin skims of ice. Some of the yeoman were drilling with muskets on the gravelled ground beside it, so I turned back again. No sign of him in the card room, although Bessie Blount looked up hopefully when I pushed the door open. No sign of him in the balliard room either. Only Harry Percy and Anne Boleyn were left in there and the lady gave me a bad-tempered look from her very black eyes. Nothing to do with me, my lady, I said to myself as I closed the door, I'm only a lawyer. I just draw up the deeds. We could find a good wife for the young man over in Ireland and she might suit him better than this Frenchified young lady. I doubt that James cared much for the title. Piers Rua, his father, well, that was a different matter. He had become used to being referred to as 'the earl'.

At last in desperation, I opened the door of the chapel and went into the dark, incense scented building. And there, under the stained-glass window showing the martyrdom of St Thomas á Becket, knelt Gilbert. I moved silently up and stood at some little distance from him. His beads were in his hands and he passed them through his fingers.

He did not look worried or even distraught. He knelt very upright, his eyes fixed on the tabernacle. His lips were moving. For a moment I could only hear an indistinct murmur, but then I distinguished a few words repeated over and over again. Not the *Pater Noster*, nor yet the *Ave Maria*, but two words '*gratias ago*', 'I give thanks'.

After a couple of moments I stole back to the door, opened it soundlessly and then shut it with a bang. Gilbert looked around and I came forward with a smile.

'Praying for the dead?' I enquired and took a seat in the window arch. He joined me there after a moment's hesitation.

'Not really,' he said after a moment.

'You're relieved he's dead. I'm not surprised,' I said. 'He was a man who liked to hold power over people.'

He gave me a startled glance. 'You, too?' There was a query in his voice.

'He had a way of worming out secrets. I know that about him.' I made the pronouncement without looking at him and I could sense him wondering whether to trust me. I held, after all, no official position at Hampton Court. I had only arrived a few days earlier with instructions from Piers Rua to make sure that the marriage contract between Anne Boleyn and his son James was acceptable to Brehon Law as well as to English law. Piers had steered an adroit route through the laws and the customs of both countries; though his father was a descendent of the Earls of Ormond, his mother was Saibh from the Irish clan of the O'Cavanaghs and Piers Rua had picked up a great respect for the native Brehon law from her. However, the earldom was dear to him and he wanted his son to follow in his footsteps. And of course, when I arrived James had welcomed me boisterously. I had been the youngest person among his father's household and we had always been good friends. Gilbert now showed no fear of me and I proceeded to probe cautiously.

'No, he won't be mourned, will he, Master Pace? Even made himself unpopular in the kitchen and that's a great mistake in any household.'

My light tone seemed to give him confidence. He turned his face towards me.

'Did he tell you about me?'

'Who, the cook?' I knew it wasn't that, but, as with a nervous dog, it would be better to allow him to approach me. The boy's face was strained and anxious.

'No, Master Pace. He swore he wouldn't tell, that he wouldn't tell anyone. I just wondered.'

'You can talk to me about anything that worries you,' I said. 'I'm a lawyer, you know. People pay good money for my advice, but I'll do it free for you as you are James's friend. I won't tell anyone, but blackmail has a habit of spreading. It would be good for you to have someone to approach if anyone tries to blackmail you again.' What was it that the cook had said about the clerk of the kitchens and the instructor of the wards? *Hand in glove with that fellow who has just gone out*, that was it.

'He saw me once. I'd been very tired. I was very worried. I was afraid, afraid about things.' Gilbert gulped heavily, but I didn't move, just waited and did not look at him. It was very dark in the chapel. The red glass within the cresset in front of the altar sent out a warm glow from the perfumed oil, but little light. We were quite private.

'I fell down and when I came to my senses, he was there. He was standing over me, looking down at me. I tried to pretend that I had just fallen and stunned myself, but he knew better. You see, you see,' the boy's voice stumbled. 'You see …' now it sunk to a mere whisper. 'I had lost control of my bladder. That happens, you know. My hose were drenched.'

I knew instantly what he was hinting at. 'You suffer from epilepsy?' I made the enquiry in a cheerful, uncon-cerned way and I sensed rather than saw him look at me. 'Nothing to be ashamed of about that, you know. It's supposed to be a sign of intelligence, of greatness. Julius Caesar suffered from it, you know, according to Tacitus.'

'Really, I didn't know that.' There was a moment's silence and then Gilbert said: 'I was afraid that I was going mad. Just like my father. Did you know that? Did you know that my father is a lunatic? That's why I am a ward of the cardinal's. He manages my father's estate.'

'There's no problem there.' I threw as much certainty as I could muster into my tone of voice. 'Don't worry, Gilbert. The two things have nothing to do with each other. The chances are that you take after your mother.' I knew nothing about Gilbert's mother, or his father, either, but it seemed to have been the right thing to have said as his voice sounded very cheerful when he spoke.

'Well, she's full of common-sense, she's got her head on the right way.'

'And has she met Mistress Blount?'

'Yes, indeed. She liked the little boy, too. She advised me to petition the cardinal to have him until he was five or six years old. She said Bessie would miss him if not.

She said that King Henry himself remained with his mother and his sisters until he was six years old.'

'Good idea,' I said heartily. 'You're feeling better now, aren't you?'

'I felt better as soon as I saw that he was dead. The only thing is,' and then he hesitated, 'I feel bad that he forced me to tell a secret that was belonging to some-one else. He overheard me, you know, he overheard me say that I would never tell anyone. I even swore secrecy. And he overheard me and he forced me to tell.' Gilbert turned around and said with a deep intensity. 'I shouldn't have done it. I know that, but you see, he, Master Pace, said that if the cardinal knew about me having a fit, if he thought that I had inherited my father's madness, he would immediately cancel the marriage between me and Mistress Blount. He said that the money I had given him wasn't enough. I had to tell this secret. I knew that he would use it to blackmail … to blackmail my best friend, but I had to tell him. I had to tell him James's secret. He forced me into it.'

'I see.' I rose to my feet. My hands and feet were icy and I could feel my heart beat fast. A secret? After all, I tried to tell myself, that secret was only known to two people. But what if one of those two had told a third party.

'Bessie is playing cards, go and join her,' I said, hoping that my tone hid my feelings, but not caring hugely at the moment. I couldn't waste any more time on Gilbert. I would have to talk to James, whether he wanted to or not.

★★★

One of the things that I had always liked previously about Hampton Court was that it was more like a small town than a house. One could so easily remove oneself, get lost among the multitudinous rooms, passages, corridors and courts. A marvellous place to avoid a bore, but a terrible place to conduct an urgent search and today I swore at the place.

No sign of James anywhere. His servant in his lodgings had not seen him since before the hour of dinner. He was not in any of the rooms where the visitors and the people of the cardinal's household gathered so merrily, playing games, chattering, inserting the odd stitch into a piece of embroidery, burnishing a weapon, or whispering in dark corners.

And this morning I did not want to ask any of the servants, or to question any of the lounging yeoman, chosen by the cardinal more for their size than their brain power, but nevertheless gossips to the man. Master James Butler, the name was probably on all lips. And my frantic hunt would give rise to more rumours so I tried to move in a nonchalant way, while thinking hard.

I searched methodically, court after court and then stood and thought, staring absent-mindedly at the suite of the cardinal's rooms above my head. I could see the glowing windows of the rooms that I had already searched and the others were in darkness. Where could he be? James was a reserved boy. If he had troubles he tended to go off for a long ride. Or he would sit with his arms around his giant wolfhound, his face buried in the dog's flank, but Conbeg had died last autumn and James had not wanted to replace him until he was back home in Kilkenny permanently. And surely he would not risk his horse today in this weather.

Nevertheless, I headed towards the stables, surprising the stable hands who were comfortably playing cards by a red-hot brazier secure in the knowledge that no one was likely to brave ice-covered roads beneath a sky filled with snow clouds. James's horse, nicely brushed, dozed beneath a warm rug and with a nod at the lads, I left and went into the kennels, causing all of the dogs to bark excitedly as I opened the door. He wasn't there, either, as I could see at a glance and with a wave at the kennel staff I went back down the narrow passageway and when I emerged, glanced up at the cardinal's rooms. One of the windows which had been in almost darkness was now lit up. The library. James was not bookish, he took after his mother in his love of the outdoors, but today, feeling that every eye was upon him, he might well take refuge there. With a lightening of my heart, I went inside and climbed the stairs and opened the door softly.

The room was ablaze with light. It picked out the gold lettering on the book covers of dark blue, brown, tan. And the heavy chairs and tables etched black shadows on the polished wood of the floor. The library was lined with bookcases, each about the height of a man, and there was a row of candelabra on top of each one of them. Every single candle in each one of these had been lit, recently lit judging by the lazy curl of smoke winding up from a long taper thrown carelessly onto the tiled hearth.

Near to the fireplace there was a low, square chest covered in red leather and filled with small drawers, each with a gold handle. In front of this there was a girl, curled up like a kitten on a huge floor cushion of crimson velvet. One of the drawers was open, empty, showing the white silk of its lining, its handle glinting in the firelight.

The girl was reading the book that should have been on that silk and reading it so intently that she had not raised her head when I came in. It was easy to see who she was, though I could only see the back of her head. There was something about this girl, some grace of posture, some fineness of bone that none of the other court beauties could emulate.

'You are enjoying your book, Mistress Boleyn,' I said. She had become bored with the balliards, I reckoned. Not a game for a lady like she. Or perhaps Master Harry had been summoned by his tailor, or his armourer. And then, with amusement, I saw that she was reading some of Rabelais' bawdy work.

'Well, well,' I said affably. I pulled over one of the cardinal's padded needlework chairs and sat down quite close to her. She looked up with a slightly tightening of the lips and then returned to her book. Either she read French with great fluency, or she was pretending. I was inclined to think the former. There was a slight twitch of the lips from time to time as she came to a juicy part of the narrative and her eyes moved down the page in the way that a practised reader goes through a book.

I kept quiet for a few minutes, leaving it to her to break the silence, but she made no move to break to speak, but continued calmly and unselfconsciously to enjoy the book. I had not too much time to waste, though, and when a small chuckle escaped her, I decided it was time to open a dialogue.

'Queen Katherine permits her maids-in-waiting to read Rabelais, is that correct?'

She raised her fine brows, but did not look at me, deliberately turning over the page and allowing another smile to light up her face. She certainly had pretty teeth, tiny and pearl like, but beautifully shaped. Only when she had finished that page, did she pick up a book marker and place it carefully to mark the spot. Then she closed the book, replaced it within the drawer and looked at me politely.

'*Je vous dérange?*' she queried.

'Not at all. I am glad to have an opportunity to talk with you.' I replied in English. I had no time to waste. It was a bit of shock to find her reading Rabelais, but then she had served in the court of Margaret of Austria with her famous collection of books and then was under the care of Marguerite of Navarre. I had heard a lot about Marguerite of Navarre, sister to King François of France and about the book of stories that she wrote, and read aloud to her ladies in waiting. When the match between James and Mistress Boleyn had first been mooted, Piers Rua had chuckled over the rumours of this scandalous book and had wondered what the little Boleyn girl would be like.

'Do you miss France?' I enquired and was surprised to see that she had tears in her eyes. Very, very beautiful eyes, otherwise not as pretty as her sister Mary, or the buxom Bessie Blount but in her own way, seen like this, curled up on the cushion at my feet, she excelled them. Exquisite was the right word for her. She shook her head, wordless – less perhaps as a negative reply than to dislodge the tears from her eyes without having recourse to a handkerchief.

'You know, you and James could have a very good marriage,' I said. 'He's a very nice fellow. He would treat you well. You could have your own library of books in French at Kilkenny Castle. You could make the place beautiful.'

She pursed her lips with a moue of disbelief, gave a long look around the Hampton Court library, the pictures from Italian painters in their golden frames, the panels of exquisite needlework, framed in a lovely bluish green, aqua green wood; she looked at the candelabra of embossed silver and at the Turkish carpets on floor and tables. And then she moved her hands, quite flat, with the delicate fingers spread wide.

'It's beautiful here,' she said. 'It does remind me …'

'You can't marry the cardinal,' I said jokingly. But I knew what she meant. She would like to create, but I had been to the court of the French king and I knew that to create in that style would take a fortune that would far exceed whatever she could command as the wife of James Butler, even if he were heir to the Irish part of the earldom of Ormond. And, of course, the Earl of Northumberland was vastly richer than the Butlers, or should be at any rate.

'Hampton Court is a little like Mechelen. The brick, the patterns, it does remind me …' she waved her hands in the air.

'I loved France when I visited the court there about five years ago,' I said impulsively and saw her turn eagerly towards me. This girl had imbued the French belief in their own absolute superiority in every aspect of life, whether writings, buildings, paintings or sculpture. For her, everything French was perfect. Her only chance of happiness in this northern isle was to reproduce a little of what she had seen in France

'I would put a statue in the centre of this room,' she said speaking almost to herself. 'It would be a beautiful girl, the spirit of wisdom, perhaps, just as it says in the Bible. I remember the line; I've read it in Isiah. Or perhaps it could be that branch of fruit that came forth from Jesse.'

'You have read the Bible?' My eyes were widening. Not many girls read Latin.

'Of course! We, her maids, were helping Madame Marguerite to translate it, to turn the Bible into French. She is a great friend of Erasmus.'

'How old were you when you went to France,' I asked. Erasmus? I'm not sure this is the right wife for James. And the cardinal would definitely not approve.

'Twelve,' she said. She got to her feet gracefully, with a spring of young limbs. She shook herself a little, rather like a fastidious cat, examined her reflection carefully in the gold-framed mirror of polished steel and then went towards the door.

'Kilkenny can be lovely in the summer,' I said hopelessly. Unless I could turn this girl from the dizzy heights of a match with the eldest son of the Earl of Northumberland, then she would persist in the effort to incriminate poor James. And yet, in a way, I was sorry for her. Her mind was full of dreams. I had briefly met Margaret of Austria and could imagine her effect on a clever, ambitious young girl. And then to come under the influence of the most learned woman in Europe, Marguerite of Angouleme, of Navarre, for the next five or six years of her life. I was beginning to understand Anne. She saw herself holding court, writing poetry and stories, encouraging men of letters, commissioning artists, embarking on great schemes for building a splendid house, perhaps something like a minor version of Hampton Court, and filling it with tapestries and gleaming mirrors. Have a northern court, up there in Northumberland, a court as cultured and as brilliant as anything that the cardinal had achieved here in the south.

But my business was to save James, and if possible save the way of life mapped out for him.

'You could achieve a lot with the castle at Kilkenny,' I said. 'The grounds are beautiful and it has a beautiful river flowing beside the castle.' I added, but it was no good. Her glance slid away from me and I knew that I had lost her.

'You know that they will never allow Harry Percy to marry you.' It was my final shot.

She opened the door, smiled over her shoulder. 'You forget that I have now been rechristened *Perseverance*,' she said.

4

The king's serjeant was looking for me.

Three different yeoman passed that message to me, and when I was passing beneath the clock tower I met the man himself.

'I was looking for you,' he said unnecessarily.

'And now you have found me, Master Gibson,' I said pleasantly, but I was wary.

He ignored this. 'I need to question that young man, but His Grace says that you must be with him. Well, I must go by what His Grace says, but I will tell you to your face that I am not happy about this. In fact, Master, I'll have you know that at the moment, there is no other suspect. And, before you come to complain, I will tell you also that I have a man watching James Butler at the moment to make sure that he doesn't escape before I get my hands on him.'

'But you will remember that the cardinal has told you to make sure that I am with James before you question in him.' His news had momentarily left me without breath, but I rallied quickly. It was important not to allow the man to suspect how worried I was. Of course it would be important for the king's serjeant to make an arrest as soon as possible. News of this murder was bound to leak out and soon all of London would know about it. The king would not be a patient man, I surmised, and would expect instant action in the case of a murder reputed to take place in his presence.

'Why do you have to be with him?' he said aggressively. And then when I didn't reply, he turned his question into a statement. 'I don't see why you have to be with him. None of the other lads have a lawyer with them and no one tells me not to talk to them.' His tone was unpleasant and suggestive. I responded equally aggressively.

'And have you? Talked with them?'

'There's something going on,' he said abruptly. 'Young Master Percy – and Mistress Boleyn, of course – but of all the young wards, Master Percy is the only one who will admit to seeing James Butler take an arrow from his bag. But I can tell from Gilbert Tailboys that he is lying when he says that he knows nothing. He was stuttering and stammering and his face got red when I pressed him to make a statement. And the other youngster, young Arundel, he was looking guilty, too.'

'Perhaps the other lads should have a lawyer with them,' I said, my tone as unpleasant as his. 'I don't suppose that you bullied the Earl of Derby, though, did you? He usually has a servant or two hanging over him. George Cavendish tells me that he has five men attending on him.'

'No one saw the little Earl of Derby take a deadly arrow from his bag,' he said unpleasantly.

'Something my client denies,' I came back swiftly, feeling that rush of exhilaration that always came to me when defending a client at a court. 'Anyway, why on earth should he want to murder an instructor of the wards?

His schooldays are over. Soon he will be a married man and perhaps return to Ireland.' It wasn't a question of any instructor, though, I knew that, but hoped the serjeant did not. It was a question of this particular man, Edmund Pace, who was a blackmailer and that might be something that would supply a motive for this killing. It might hang James. I gave him a stiff nod and walked off.

I was worried about James, though. It was less than a week since I had arrived back to Hampton Court, but I had at the time thought he was different, older and more silent than he had been when I had seen him a few months earlier, in the late autumn, when I came across to discuss the possible marriage with the cardinal. Then, as now, James had been a great favourite with the cardinal, but then he had been boisterous and funny, joking with his fellow wards and swapping tri-syllabic metric poems with the court poet, John Skelton. He had seemed, then, to be very happy, excited at the thought of his marriage to Mary Boleyn's younger sister, who was at the French court. James had been thrilled at the idea that then, through this marriage, he would be heir to the Ormond earldom and there would be no more legal battles with English lords over his Irish inheritance. I had met Mary during my visit in November, newly married, very sweet, and thought that if her sister was like her, then she and James would get on very well.

That thought came back to me as I went again under the clock tower, crossed the Base Court and emerged through the great west gate. Mistress Anne Boleyn had turned out to be very different to her pleasant, easy-going sister and their brief meeting this first day of March when she was introduced to both of us by cardinal, before all the wards had got dressed for the pageant, had seemed to me not to go well. I remembered now how she had surveyed young James coolly from head to toe, dropped a polite curtsey, but then stood very silent and very self-possessed while he endeavoured, in schoolboy French, to make conversation about her journey from Calais to Dover.

Once again, I checked the stables, but James's horse was still there. This time, however, one of the stable boys noticed me and came forward, abandoning his pitchfork against a wall.

'Are you looking for Master Butler, sir?' He lowered his voice when he spoke the name and gave a hasty glance around. Already the news had spread that James was in trouble, was a suspect. 'I saw him go towards the butts, in the Wildernesse, an hour or so ago. Don't know whether he would be still there, though. It's terrible weather to be out if you don't have to.' He glanced up at the grey sky and the frozen snowflakes fluttering down now in greater numbers.

James was still there at the butts when I reached him, still sending arrows thudding against the wooden butt. But he wasn't alone. There was a man watching James. One of the yeoman, a tall fellow wearing the cardinal's mulberry livery. He looked cold, but he stood stolidly between James and the pathway to the road. The boats were tied up at the landing stage, but all were without oars and too big to be managed without half a dozen stout men to row, and, of course, one to steer. In any case, this one guard was twice the breadth of James who had not yet grown into full strength. I gave the man a pleasant nod. It was not his fault. He was only obeying orders and we stood side by side watching the incessant thud of the arrows.

'Run and get yourself a hot drink from the kitchen,' I said. 'Don't worry. I'll stay until you return.'

He hesitated and then looked up at the clerks' rooms above the works gate. There was a movement at the window and in a minute another yeoman was by our side.

'Just going to …' The first man jerked his head towards that jakes built on the far side of the gatehouse and the other nodded. I walked away feeling rather shaken. Two men to watch the boy. The serjeant must be very sure of his facts. I needed to talk with James. He must have been aware of my presence, must have heard me speak, but he did not look towards me. His face, despite the bitter wind, was white and his lips compressed into a hard line. I stopped by the hedge that screened the workshops from the shooting green. I would wait until the first man came back, I decided. Then I would propose that we all go into the warmth.

'Better leave him,' said a voice from behind me. 'He shoot his demons.'

I turned around and smiled at the Flemish lady, Susannah Horenbout. A tall girl: I wasn't used to women looking me in the eye, or almost, anyway. They said that the Flemish ate lots of butter and cheese and that made them big, both men and women.

'Have you eaten up all of your stale eggs and your charred almond shells?' I wondered whether her English would be good enough to understand the joke, but she smiled instantly, small white teeth between parted lips. There was a slight smudge of green paint on one cheek and her hair was more dishevelled than it had been earlier, one lock of pale gold had escaped from her linen cap and trailed down the side of her neck.

'Come and see,' she said. 'Come and see what I do with your charred shells. It is lucky for me that the cardinal's court eat so, so many sweetmeats. Pounds and pounds of almonds to make those pretty subtleties.'

I cast one more glance back at James. He did look as though he were battling with demons, and I doubted that he was in the mood to confide in me. For the moment, thanks to the cardinal, he was safe. Until Monday. Four days and the scant remains of this one. I cast a glance at the sky. Ash Wednesday. The snow clouds, leaden above the bleached fields and skeleton trees, were the colour of dead ashes and there was that almost hush in the air that presaged heavy snow. My hands were cold and my feet ached with the icy chill, despite the good leather in my boots. It was tempting to go indoors.

'You are a good friend of Master Cook,' she enquired as we walked side by side towards the carpenter's yard. 'But not a cook, yourself.' I could see her surveying my clothes. At home in Ossory I wore the traditional *léine*, and a jerkin in winter, covered with a lawyer's gown on formal occasions, but here, under my cloak, I was dressed in the customary doublet and hose, topped with a leather jacket.

'No, I'm a lawyer. *Rechtsanwalt*.' I knew no Flemish, but reckoned that she would know German.

Mistress Susannah Horenbout smiled at that, but made no comment, just opening the door of one of the lodgings and beckoning me to follow her up the stairs when she had closed it behind us. She and her brother would have their living quarters downstairs and their workshop upstairs where the light was better, I guessed. I had been to one of the carpenter's shops and he had that arrangement. The large room that she ushered me into was just under the roof, cold, despite the fire. It took up the whole space under the roof and there were windows on both sides, north and south. Even on this gloomy day there was plenty of light.

'The almond shells, different now,' she said with a laugh, and pointed to a pestle and bowl in the middle of the table. The bowl was white and it enhanced the soft deep black of the thick mixture it contained.

'Just burned almond shells and pure spring water with a little size added,' she said.

'And then you have a nice pot of black paint! And what about the fish spine, the fish spine from the queen's own plate, what did you do with that?' She had a lovely smile. I was glad that I had slightly overacted my surprise.

'Ah, come and see.' She led me across the room to where an oak panel was covered with paint. It was the sea, lovely waves in ultramarine and flecks of white. There were the folds of a fishing net, just outlined in charcoal for the moment, and there were fish darting in and out of the net. Some had been painted, some were just charcoal outlines. But one stood out, just in the forefront of the picture. The backbone and ribs of the fish skeleton that she had got in the kitchen had been gilded and were glued onto the sea background and while I watched, the girl took a very small brush, just some hairs, probably miniver, stuck into the point of a chicken quill, and delicately coated the gold with a different green from another small pot.

'When that dries, I will put another coat and then another and in the end the gold backbone will be just a faint memory in the depths of the fish,' she said, and I smiled with pleasure. There was something about this picture that made it like a puzzle. At first glance it was turbulent waves, a net and some fish, but then as you looked, here and there, lurking beneath the green-blue of the waves, were shellfish, tiny fronds of seaweed, a hint of coral, a dark spike of rock.

'This will be the apostles fishing in the Sea of Galilee when Jesus calls them. It is for the cardinal's room. It will be a full wall telling a story. Many, many panels to cover his walls.' Delicately she smeared some more green onto the seaweed frond. And then she said without looking at me. 'What is the matter with James?'

So she knew James, well enough to call him James. Not Master Butler, but James.

'How do you make that green? It's so bright, so vivid.' I wanted to know the answer to my question, but I also wanted a little time to think.

'You pour some verjuice or vinegar over a piece of copper. Leave for a day, or even two.' She was waiting for an answer to her question while I silently counted the number of different greens that I could see in her picture.

'Did he kill that man, the instructor of the wards?' This was even more direct.

'No, certainly not.'

'I heard that there was a body. My brother told me that the carpenters had measured it. They were making a … a box for it. Stiff as board, they said.'

There was a mask on the table and I picked it up. Just like the one that James had been sporting last night.

'Did you make these? How do you do them?'

'But yes, easy. Just grind up a bit of ochre, some tailor's chalk together, a little bit of Armenian clay, this to stiffen the paper. When the paper is dry, I go a little silver powder get, left over from making ornaments and cups of silver, and I mix that with a little mordaunt and then the paper paint. When it is dry, I make the masks. This one was for me to try.'

She picked up the mask and placed it against her face. It had two ovals for the eyes to shine through, covered her cheekbones and nose, but not her mouth, and it scrolled up to a peak on the outer edge of her blonde eyebrows. It intrigued, but could not conceal and I immediately shelved one notion that I had that someone else, wearing a mask, might have been mistaken for James. This mask would hide nobody's identity. In any case, his red hair would make it a certainty that he would be recognised.

'And then with a brush, I write the names on them, just so.' Seizing the brush she dipped it into the small pot of black and wrote without hesitation, the word 'Brehon'.

'That's what James calls you. The Brehon. He tell me that you are a judge. He was happy the last time you came. But …'

'But not this time.'

She did not disagree with the statement, but after a moment said thoughtfully, 'He worries about something.'

'Tell me about last night. Were you there, at the pageant? Did you go to see your masks, take them over to the great hall, perhaps?'

'I went to the great hall, gave them over to the gentleman usher, Master George Cavendish, sixteen masks as he had desired; the king, His Grace and the gentlemen from the court bringed their own masks. He told me that I could watch if I pleased and he invited me to come back and to watch the dance after supper, after the sugar banquet. He said that it was planned that all would be masked until the king commanded that they should be removed.'

'And how did you enjoy watching … did you notice anything?' I changed my general query. This was a girl with a sharp eye and one that would notice small details.

'I noticed the king paying a lot of attention to Lady Mary Carey.'

'But not to her sister, Mistress Anne Boleyn.'

She smiled and her smile said: that's what you want to know, isn't it?

'No,' she said, her face becoming grave. 'No, Mistress Anne danced with Master Harry Percy for the whole evening.'

'Did you think that upset James?'

She considered this for a moment. 'I think it annoy him. But he danced with Mistress Anne Browne, the lady who played the part of *Pitie* and I think that he, your James, was happy with her. She admired his red hair and I saw her reach up and touch it. He smiled and laughed, then, but when he looked across at Master Percy and Mistress Boleyn, his face was very angry.'

That was quite valuable evidence. One could not imagine a boy who had murdered a man a few hours ago would have been annoyed at being deserted by the lady who was due to be betrothed to him. It would be more likely that he would have gone off to bed, pretending to sulk at being deserted.

'Where were you standing to watch the dance?' I smiled at her. It seemed a shame that such a pretty girl should have had to watch other girls dance with young men.

'By the arras, that was in the beginning, but then one of the yeomen moved me away just because I was touching the tapestries. I wanted to look at the flowers on the border; it's a skill that I don't have, but I would like to do some small pieces, perhaps the cardinal's coat of arms. But then he told me to go away and so I moved over beside the table with the refreshments. I could see the dancing very well. It was very beautiful. The girls were all in white. Your Anne Boleyn looked well with the lace scarf, they call it a caul, I think, wound like, like a crown across her brow and her dark hair that shine out underneath it.'

'And dancing with Harry Percy.'

'That's right,' she said. 'And he so dark, too. A handsome couple. He had a jerkin woven from silver thread. That was the way with the young men and ladies, silver and white, like moonbeams. But these two, well, you could tell that they were in love, the way that he looked down so tenderly and she looked up at him and then when everyone took off their masks, she smiled like an angel.'

'Tell me about the arrows, was it you that made the arrows for the boys to shoot?'

'That is correct, and the bags.'

'And the bags.' I was surprised at that. Without taking much thought in the matter, I had assumed that the boys had used their own arrow bags.

'I show you.' She went swiftly to a large chest with a hinged lid. It had come to England with the brother and sister, I reckoned. The grain and colour of the wood was unfamiliar.

'Here,' she said, picking out a neat package and undoing it. 'Here are the eight bags: one for each of the cardinal's wards. See their pageant names are written on them.'

The little arrow bags were beautifully stitched, the names written in gold, in that same elegantly curving script that I had seen on the masks: *Dangier, Disdain, Gelousie, Vnkyndenes, Scorne, Malebouche, Straungenes* …' Suddenly, I noticed something. I picked up the bag marked '*Gelousie*'.

'There are some arrows left in this bag,' I said.

'Just pieces. I pick the pieces from the floor of the great hall when all had gone to their sugar banquet. There was no one around. The servants and carpenters were carrying away the wooden walls of the *château* and picking up the orange and the dates, but I take these.' She sounded a little hesitant and there was a slightly troubled expression on her face which had not been there a moment earlier. 'They would be swept out, Master Brehon. They would be no use to anyone else. I use those small leather particles, crumbs, to build up a relief on friezes, like in the queen's chamber. By the time that they are painted or gilded, then …' she was talking fast now, but I interrupted her.

'There's a whole arrow here. Someone did not fire all of his arrows.'

She made no comment. James, I knew, had been *Danger*. He was the oldest, then it was Harry Percy for *Disdain*, Thomas Arundel, I knew had been given *Unkindness* because he had lamented that the Howard girl would never marry him if he was called by that name.

Jealousy must have been Gilbert Tailboys.

I would have to make sure about that, but it was a puzzle that an arrow had been left over.

'Was it in this bag when you picked up the pieces?' I asked and after a moment she nodded. That made sense. She found the bag with the arrow in it and then used it to store the other pieces.

But why should Gilbert Tailboys have one arrow left over? The boys had been practising this assault on the king and his men. Every move, according to James, had been scripted by George Cavendish and he, together with the instructor of the wards, had taken them through their part in the proceedings. The eight young wards had been told when to fire and where. If I remembered rightly, all of the last of the arrows were to be shot off just at the very moment that the king scaled the battlements and seized the first lady in his arms.

'Who was rescued first by the king?'

'It was Lady Mary, the sister of Mistress Anne Boleyn,' she said in her precise English.

I nodded. 'Anyone fire an arrow after that?'

She shook her head. 'No, all the boys dropped their arrow bags on the floor and started to tear off those strange cloaks they wore. And the ladies threw some of the comfits and the orange to them as they came up to the wall of the *château*. Everyone was laughing and shouting and all was very gay.'

'And then?'

'And then all went into the great chamber next to the hall. There was a banquet laid out for them. I gathered up what might be useful and then I went. When I was going out, Master Cavendish reminded me, very kindly, to come back and watch the dancing and suggested that perhaps I should bring a few spare masks back with me just in case some had been trodden on, or got torn. He said that the ladies and gentlemen would continue to wear their masks during the banquet and for the dancing, and until the king gave a signal. I told him that I would also bring my brush and my paint so as to paint the name on it.'

'And did anyone require a replacement, a new mask?' I had to wait for a few moments for her answer.

'It was Master Tailboys,' she said then. 'He dropped his mask when the king seized Lady Carey in his arms. That is what he told me.'

I pondered on that. Why should Gilbert drop his mask at that moment? Who was Lady Carey to him? It was not as though it had been Bessie Blount who was the focus of the king's attention once more. According to the cardinal, when King Henry tired of an amusement, he seldom went back to it again, and this, I gathered from the cardinal, included ladies. The king, apparently, had not slept with Bessie Blount ever since she had borne his child, or, as the cardinal put it, more delicately, His Grace had ceased to frequent her company.

'And James, did you notice anything about him during the storming of the *château vert*?'

'He shoot well, even with little toy arrows, he shoot very well indeed,' she said promptly. 'I see him aim at an orange on the floor and the arrow fell beside it. It did not, not stick in it,' she finished after a brief search for a word.

'So you were watching him.' I began to think that this girl might be very valuable to me as a witness, but she read my mind and shook her head.

'Not all of the time. No, there was more to see. I have never been so near to a king before. He is very, very magnificent.'

'So he is.' I brought her back to James. 'And where did the rest of James's arrows go? Who did they hit?'

'Just the boots, or in the air between persons.' Her reply was prompt, but unless she could swear that she had her eyes on James all of the time, it would be of little use in a court of law. She had gone back to her fish and placed another layer of green over the gold outline, very, very delicately, managing with her tiny brush of miniver hair to leave minuscule slivers of gold untouched. I wondered whether I might be able to pick out that fish when the whole of the cardinal's room had been covered with the painted panels, and then thought that I was unlikely to see the finish of this work of art.

'Farewell, Mistress Artist,' I said. It was time that I got back to James. He had had sufficient time to have shot his demons.

'Farewell, My Lord Judge,' she said and then laughed. She did not curtsey to me, but held out her hand as though we were friends and I took it and pressed it lightly.

'I will see you again, I hope,' I said and went down the stairs, not thinking about James, for a few minutes, but of this interesting Flemish woman called Susannah.

But when I came out, there was no sign of James. The butts were deserted, his arrows had been plucked from the greensward and the yeoman, who was supposed to be in surveillance, was happily exchanging insults with a barge-load of lively Londoners who were unloading some boxes. As I hesitated, the clerk of the kitchens came scurrying down from his office above the gate and the cook appeared through the archway, neatly garbed in a new white apron.

'Now for heavens' sake don't take all the straw from around them. The sugar will take in the moisture from this damp air and it will weep and the cones will be spoiled.' Master Beasley made his complaint in the weary tone of one who knows that he will not be listened to. The clerk continued to lever up the cover.

'Well, we'll waste it then, and if anyone complains, I'll refer them to you,' said the cook emphatically. 'One of the gentlemen ushers was talking about the amount of sugar used. I told him to tell the cardinal that used is one thing, spoiled is another. That last lot of sugar was so damp that many of the subtleties just broke down and had to be thrown away.'

The clerk hesitated. The cardinal, whose mind, I noticed, loved new knowledge and new problems, was a formidable figure to the kitchen clerks now that he was taking such an interest in the running of the kitchen. The involvement of the gentlemen ushers had meant that the clerks' work was being checked, too.

'Look, why don't you just take the box into the weigh house and weigh it,' said Master Beasley impatiently. 'There should be ten sugar cones in there and each of them will be anything up to fourteen pounds. Now if this box weighs more than 140 pounds then we're all to the good and these fellows can get on with their delivery for Westminster now that the tide has turned.'

There was still no sign of James but I reckoned that he had gone off to his lodgings. He would be tired and cold. Let him have a glass of wine and a manchet of bread, and he would be feeling more himself. Then I could talk to him privately and find out exactly what Gilbert Tailboys had been hinting at.

So I followed the clerk to the weighing house. The box weighed 160 pounds, to the cook's satisfaction.

'Well, there you are then, and don't say that the straw makes a difference because we all know that it weighs next to nothing. All right, lads, you be off, take the tide and do your delivery, come on, young Dick and Matthew, take one end each and if you drop it, then I'll boil you alive in the big cauldron in the boiling house.'

I followed them in obedience to a slight jerk of the head given by the cook.

'Do you know, I've never seen a sugar cone,' I said loudly. 'It's just honey in Kilkenny Castle.'

'Honey wouldn't make subtleties. These sugar cones are the stuff for marchpane. Come and see them.' He lowered his voice. 'Now that we've got rid of old sourguts we'll have a little piece, you and I, just to make sure that it is good.' The cook led the way to the confectionery. I could see his point about not opening the box until we got there, because the air in that place, heated through the floorboards from the pastry ovens below, was warm and dry. Once the straw was removed, the ten cones shone like white marble and Master Beasley, helped by a man in a green waterman's cloak, lifted them one by one onto a slatted shelf.

The kitchen boys, too, were given a tiny pinch, carefully scraped off with the edge of a sugar scissors, before they were sent off to check that the wood yard boys had brought in some more number one talshides to get the fire burning hot for the supper.

'Not too much for me,' I said hastily as he took up the scissors again. 'I'm a man for the wine, not for the sugar. So that's what you use to make subtleties like that magnificent chess board that I've been hearing of. You mix the sugar with crumbs of almond nuts, that's right, isn't it?'

'And here are the moulds.' He reached up to the shelf above him and took down the shapes hollowed out of pewter. 'See these are for the figures: castle, knight, bishop, king, queen and pawn.' And then, without looking at me, he said very low: 'Your James is in trouble, Master Brehon. They are all after him. They want to make sure that he is the one who swings for this murder. I heard them in the clerks' offices. The serjeant is hand-in-glove with that lot, you know. James is a stranger, not like the Earl of Northumberland's son, or Master Arundel or any of the others who come from the nobility around here. They would want to pin this on him. If I were you, I'd try to get him out of here. The cardinal is fond of him, they say, but – Lord, bless my soul – the cardinal has a lot on his mind. He comes and goes, might be away from here for a few months on end. He'll leave the matter to his serjeant-at-arms.'

I nodded, but said nothing. He had told me no more than I had been thinking myself, but I was dismayed to find that the serjeant's suspicions were common knowledge.

'Take him this. The young like sweetmeats.' The cook took a piece of marchpane from the moulds box, wrapped it in a napkin and handed it to me with instructions to keep it warm and dry. 'And don't let the clerk of the kitchens have a sight of it or I'll be out of a job,' he warned.

I placed it inside my pouch just beside my knife and went to the door, leaving the cook and his helpmate behind me. The wood yard boys were wheeling loaded barrows in through the archway to the kitchen, but I dodged around them. I would waste no more time, I vowed. I had to tackle James and I had to find out the truth. I had already turned towards the butts when I heard the shouting and one voice amongst them that I knew well.

'I've got a sword and I'll use it!' It was James's voice.

5

It was a crowded scene. Sir George St Leger and his men were on the pier, the wood yard workers, kitchen staff, clerks, yeoman, servants and workers scattered on the grass lawns, were shouting, gesticulating and many running in different directions. Out in the centre of the river four barges, each laden with building materials, stone, cement, wooden doors and panes of glass, made their slow way towards Hampton Court and a small, swift boat rowed by one man shot out from a small stream and turned neatly in the direction of Westminster. The cardinal's barge was on the river, also. The usual crew, helmsman, oarsmen, but no passengers, none but …

And then I saw him, I saw James standing beside the helmsman of the cardinal's barge. His arm was held stiffly above his head and the sword glinted despite the grey sky. The barge had come to a stop, mid river, but now it began to move again, the men moving the oars with slow reluctant sweeps.

I forced my way through the crowd, ruthlessly pushing and thrusting myself between the crowded figures. I was not the only one. A man with a green doublet, not one of the cardinal's men who were all dressed in mulberry and gold, overtook me, brutally slashing open a passageway

with the stock of a matchlock gun. The other men on the
wharf fell back for him leaving the route open. He passed
the matchlock rapidly to St Leger, who lifted it unhesitatingly to his shoulder.

'Stop that boat,' yelled St Leger, 'stop it, I say or I fire.'

'Get out of my way, or I'll kill you,' I grunted to a man
who had put a hand on my arm. The pier was crowded
with St Leger's men. I savagely punched one of them in
the ribs as he, also, tried to stop me mounting the wooden
landing stage. St Leger now had the heavy matchlock
securely balanced and had aimed it at the barge.

Once again the barge slowed to a stop and had half-
turned so that its prow faced the bank. Now I was near
enough to see the faces of the rowers and of their helmsman. All had turned towards the St Leger and his deadly
weapon. This time James's voice was audible.

'Get on men, there's no danger.'

St Leger's answer came within a second. 'I'll fire on the
count of three!' But he wouldn't. I tried to tell myself that
as I punched and kicked my way through the crowd.

But I was too late. I was halfway along the pier when a
shot rang out. Men jumped back. The cold still air stank
of gunpowder. I could see the seated oarsmen on the
barge, every head was down to the level of their knees.
The helmsman was no longer visible and neither was
James and for a moment my heart stopped.

'You murdering villain; I'll see that you swing for that,'
I roared at St Leger. The crowd between him and me had
fallen to the ground, each fearing to be killed – it was not
unknown for these guns to spew out death to all around
them. In a moment I was by his side and had gripped

him by the collar of his shirt. I grasped the matchlock, wrestled it from his grip and flung it into the water.

'Who gave you authority to shoot one of the king's noblemen?' I could hear my voice bellow out in the sudden silence that had followed the explosive shot. Three swans further down the river had risen into the air, trumpeting an alarm and a flock of crows that burst from the riverside willows rent the air with their raucous cries.

He faced me. 'I gave the man fair warning,' he said. I said nothing in reply but my breathing slowed down. Floating on the river, just below where the swans circled, was a white form, long neck outstretched. These guns were notoriously inaccurate. James was very contemptuous of them, saying that one good archer would always be worth ten gunners. Still, I was not going to call St Leger's attention to his victim.

'You've killed the helmsman,' I said with purposeful brutality, pointing to the empty seat in the prow. The cardinal's barge wavered in the water and its prow swung around. It was not the only one; the barge carrying the unpainted doors seemed rudderless also. There was a loud crack as the cardinal's large, heavy passenger barge hit the smaller one and seconds later the icy water was covered with brown slabs of wooden doors, each floating like a miniature barge. The man in the skiff paused, seemed to edge a little nearer, perhaps to give assistance, or perhaps with thoughts of towing one or two of the doors to his home. The cardinal's barge lurched dangerously. The helmsman rose up from the floor and snatched the tiller and then James, with a hasty glance back at the wharf went over the side of the barge. Two seconds later I could see him spread-eagled upon one of the floating doors.

I put my two hands to my mouth and yelled as loudly as I could.

'Ahoy, there, you in the skiff. There will be a sovereign for you if you pick up that man and take him to Westminster.' By now I had recognised the fellow. He was the man in the green cloak who had been in the confectionery helping to put away the sugar cones. He would have seen me there with Master Beasley and would know where I would leave his reward. At least I hoped so and held my breath for a moment until I saw the skiff approach the floating door. Once I had seen a hand outstretched, I turned on St Leger to distract his attention, hurling every insult that I had heard in the kitchens or stables of Hampton Court.

'You murderous dog! You filthy, bloodthirsty fool! I'll see you flung into gaol for that! I'll see you hung for murder!' I yelled the words at him. And then to one of the yeoman, I shouted, 'send for the cardinal's serjeant-at-arms. He's with the Lady Alice in her rooms.' And then I turned back to St Leger, resolved to keep his eyes on me and away from the river until John arrived.

'Don't think you can get away with this, St Leger. There's a law in this land and it's for you to obey as well as others. Wait until the cardinal hears that you fired on his ward.' The men from the cardinal's barge would report Master Butler's escape and how he had been picked and ferried down river up by the man in the skiff, but they had not yet turned the boat around towards the wharf. I had to rely on them waiting for orders before they made a move. In the meantime, I would keep St Leger's attention on me.

John, good fellow that he was, came at fast run, only slowing down when he reached the wharf. I saw him smooth a hand over his mouth and jaw as he came towards him. I was running out of insults and had just called St Leger 'a base scullion' and 'a bottled spider' – an expression which I had overheard one of the watermen use.

'What's all this about, gentlemen?' John might not be as quick-witted as his sister, but he was well used to brawling noblemen. I cast a surreptitious glance down the river. There was no sign of the skiff. A crowd had gathered, including Colm, my servant, and Padraig, James's. I smoothed my expression.

'This gentleman has tried to kill Master James Butler by aiming and firing his matchlock at the cardinal's well-esteemed young ward.' I laid a heavy emphasis on the last words. Cardinal Wolsey was not a patient man and few of the courtiers ever dared cross him.

'James Butler has been accused of murder and was now trying to escape.' Even to St Leger, himself, the words sounded weak and he flinched slightly when the cardinal's sergeant-at-arms stared at him incredulously.

'You fired at him!'

'He was trying to escape' he repeated. His voice was truculent, but he betrayed his uneasiness by the hand that endeavoured to smooth his bushy thatch of iron-grey hair.

'Escape from what?' I put in. With satisfaction I could hear that my voice now sounded calm and judicial. James, by now, would be well on the way to Teddington where he would meet the ebbing tide. That light skiff would travel quickly with the north-westerly wind behind it.

'Master James Butler was not under arrest,' confirmed John stolidly.

St Leger gulped. He looked around, but there was no sign of the king's serjeant so he had no backing. 'What about my valuable gun?' he spluttered. 'This man deliberately threw it into the river.

'An unfortunate outcome,' I said blandly. 'Of course it is the duty of any good man to make sure that murder is not committed. You were trying to shoot the son of my employer, the Earl of Ormond.'

I saw a crimson tide of anger spread over his narrow face at that. There was something wolf-like about that face. Despite its smooth skin, the alert and hungry eyes and the prominent side teeth beneath the tuft of bristling grey hair had a menacing appearance. I faced him, unafraid, but very aware of the threat that he posed to James.

'Send for the king's serjeant,' he said abruptly to one of the yeoman.

'No need,' said John mildly, but with a quick glance at the yeoman, a very quick glance, but it was enough to keep the man rooted to his spot on the wharf. 'No need, at all,' he repeated. 'You are at perfect liberty to depart. Thanks to the quick thinking of this gentleman here, no harm has been done.'

And then John deliberately took me by the arm and turned away. The yeoman on the wharf and even St Leger's men drew back respectfully as we marched together back towards the gatehouse.

'Better go and see Alice. She'll have heard of the fuss and will be waiting for a report,' he said with a grin and, as he predicted, Alice was waiting for us when we came into her rooms. There was a flagon of wine on the table and three of her favourite glasses.

'Well, Hugh, what have you been up to this morning?' she said lightly. 'What's this story that my maid tells me?'

'He drowned St Leger's gun and was just about to drown the man himself when I arrived in the nick of time.' John was in better humour than he had been for days. It occurred to me that it must have been very irksome for a man in his position to be compelled to hand the conduct of a law and order case over to another man. 'Goodness knows how much that matchlock cost St Leger,' he added with a slightly malicious chuckle. John, I guessed, had worked out that the king's serjeant's continued involvement in the matter of the death of the Hampton Court instructor of the wards stemmed from St Leger's interest in convicting the heir to the Ormond estate in Ireland of the crime of murder. Any serjeant would not have been human if he had not bitterly resented this. I hastened to take advantage.

'Serve him right. He was trying to fire at James,' I explained and he gave a secret smile, pulling at his beard.

'I think I'd better go and have a word with Master Gibson,' he said, putting down his empty glass upon the table. 'It's only right that he should hear of this affair involving a member of his court. Tell the whole story to Alice while I am gone.'

Alice was her usual decisive self. 'I'm sure he's safe if that man was a friend of the cook's. And, you know, Hugh, it's just as well that he has gone. Let him stay away for a while,' she said as soon as I had finished the tale. 'While he's around you are worrying about him all the time. You'd do him a better service finding out who committed the murder rather than hovering over him like a nursemaid, or losing your temper with king's serjeant, or with St Leger. Now calm yourself. Sit down there and hold Lily in your arms. She is a dog who knows how to relax and she'll teach you how to relax.'

'Edmund Pace was a blackmailer; I've found that out for sure,' I said slowly, sinking down onto the cushioned chair by the fire and accepting the small, warm dog onto my lap. I hesitated for a moment wondering whether to talk to her about Gilbert. I had no wish to get the boy into trouble, although I considered that he had as good a motive as James would have if it were true that Edmund Pace had wormed that dangerous secret out of him about James.

'The instructor of the wards blackmailed Gilbert Tailboys – forgive me if I don't tell you why,' I began.

'I suppose you mean about him having fits,' said Alice with a quiet smile. 'The cardinal knows all about that. He didn't think it was of any importance. He thought – you know how optimistic a man His Grace is – well, he thought the boy would grow out of it. We had a chat together about it and I pointed out that Gilbert's anxieties would be less when he was set up with his own household. His worries about his father would then retreat into the background.'

I thought about this for a moment. It did not, in my mind, change anything. The boy was distraught with anxiety and could have been driven by fear into taking action.

'He had one of the toy arrows left over in his bag,' I said. Alice, like myself, knew well how carefully choreographed the whole pageant had been. She had even attended a dress rehearsal so that she could report to the cardinal that all was well.

'I still can't see him doing something like that. And if it is improbable that James, or Harry Percy, shot an arrow to kill a man in the presence of king and court, then I would say it is out of the question that a boy like Gilbert would have that sort of nerve,' added Alice.

'I've been thinking about that,' I said. 'It is, as you say, improbable that anyone would take such a chance, almost impossible, but what if the man was not killed then? What if he were shot later on, shot when all the festivities were over and the body carried into the hall when it was empty?'

'Why? Why run the risk of transferring a body? Why not just leave him where he fell?'

'There's an easy answer to that,' I said readily. 'You agree that it is more feasible for the shooting to take place after the pageant was over. But if that was what happened, well, the body could have been moved to avoid incriminating the murderer.'

'I see what you mean,' said Alice. 'Master Pace went to someone's lodgings, tried some blackmail, the victim takes his bow from behind the door and aims, then fires.'

'Or better still, retires into the other room and then fires through the open door. Much easier to do than to stick a knife in a wary man.' I thought about this for a moment, testing the theory for possible flaws. 'The only drawback, I suppose is that both Harry and Gilbert are quite slight in build, not come to their full strength, as yet. I wonder whether they would be able to carry a body from their rooms to the hall.' James was broader and stronger than either and his lame foot, while it made him ungainly, never seemed to stop him carrying heavy weights. I decided not to mention that, or to reveal the dangerous secret which could make my employer's eldest son very open to blackmail.

'Perhaps,' said Alice thoughtfully, 'there might have been two of them. Harry and his friend Thomas.'

'Or Harry and the Lady Anne,' I suggested. 'She's a good archer, you know. I've seen her pull a heavy bow.' I thought about it for a minute and smiled to myself at the picture in my mind. Yes, it would fit with what I had observed of the lady. 'What about this for a possibility? The Lady Anne and Harry Percy are in his rooms, discussing ... Rabelais, perhaps ... a knock comes to the door. Anne retires to the inner room, overhears the blackmail demand, coolly takes down the bow from its hook, fits to it an arrow from the box, perhaps selects one with the initials JB, which Harry had picked up and meant to return to James. Anyway, our intrepid young lady comes to the door and with a steady hand shoots the blackmailer stone dead and then decides to throw the blame from the man she does want to marry, onto the man she does not want to marry and helps Harry to carry the body to the hall. I'd say that the plan was hers, wouldn't you?'

'Ingenious,' said Alice thoughtfully. There was a crease on her brow as though an unwelcome thought had occurred to her. I began to wonder what was worrying her.

Aloud, I said, 'And knowing that he was a blackmailer, well, that opens up the field doesn't it? Edmund Pace could have visited anyone's rooms after everyone had retired for the night. It could be anyone.'

'It could, indeed,' she said readily. 'I could be on the list myself. Who knows; I may have a secret lover over there in my closet. And you know how good I am with a bow.'

I ignored that. 'You see, at law school we teach the scholars to look for motives for murder under greed, fear, anger, or jealousy. Well, the dead man's nearest relations are living somewhere in Cornwall, and, in any case, I don't suppose that he was particularly rich, so 'greed' drops out. 'Anger' is a possibility. 'Jealousy', not, I would say. I don't think he was a ladies' man. I saw no sign of it.'

'So we come back to fear. Fear of being found out, fear of a secret being discovered. Someone was driven, by an extremity of fear, to kill the man.'

'That's right,' I said quietly. 'I think if I probe I may discover that he was blackmailing all of the wards and many of the cardinal's staff.'

'But, of course, you are looking at others, also, are you not, not just members of this household, members of the court?' She put a few stitches into her embroidery and held it up to the light of the lamp above her head.

I smiled. It was a pleasure to see how quick-witted she was. She had brought me neatly back to St Leger. I thought that I knew why. There had been a shade of worry on her face. John was her young brother and she was motherly towards him. Still, St Leger was a more likely guess.

'I've had a word with Master Cavendish while you were away, Hugh,' she continued, reading my thoughts. 'He's in charge of the arrangements at table and he has promised to put me next to St Leger during supper. John will be with us, also and that will be good. He has a great memory for the spoken word.' She put in another few stitches while I said something appreciative about John. He came to the door just as I finished and Alice greeted him with the news that I had just been singing his praises and was sure that he would find the truth more quickly than the king's serjeant.

'Master Gibson is most upset about the flight of young James,' he said in reply. 'I must tell you, Hugh, that he thinks it is a sign of guilt.'

'Or a lack of trust in justice.' I sent the rejoinder whizzing back to him and he lifted a hand in acknowledgement, just as though we were knocking balls across a tennis net.

'It's a puzzling business,' he said, sinking into another fireside chair. 'I just do not know how it could have happened right under my own eyes.'

'We were trying to make a list of people who might have disliked Master Edmund Pace.' Alice put in another couple of stitches, avoiding my eyes.

John gave a gruff laugh and passed his hand over his head. The ripe cornfield gold of Alice's locks was, in him, transmuted to a pale sandy colour. He grimaced slightly.

'A very long list,' he said. 'Give me a name and I'll give you a motive.'

'George Cavendish,' I said promptly. It was the least likely name that I could come up with and was meant as a preliminary.

'Could be,' he said thoughtfully, seeming, to my surprise, to take it seriously. 'George is a bit of a lady's man, in a quiet way, of course. Master Pace could have found out something about him and be threatening to tell Mistress Kempe about it, but no, it has to be one of the wards. They were the only ones with bows and arrows in their hands.'

I ignored that piece of nonsense. Time enough to face John with the real situation once I got a chance to view the body. 'Harry Percy, then,' I said promptly.

James considered this while Alice eyed him protectively like a mother with a not-too-bright child. 'Young Percy is very keen to fasten the blame onto James,' she prompted.

'I suppose that Harry Percy could have a motive,' said John slowly. 'I overheard some talk after the Earl of Northumberland's last visit. It appears that he is not very fond of his heir and is thinking of one of his other three sons as the next earl. The king likes second sons. And, of course, it is very important that the Earl of Northumberland's heir should be a strong, reliable man. It would only take one more report of gambling debts for young Harry to lose his inheritance. If Edmund Pace was blackmailing him, he may have gone a step too far.'

'And, of course, Mistress Anne Boleyn might have encouraged him, seeing it as a way that she could get out of this marriage arranged between herself and James Butler.' Alice nodded her head encouragingly at her brother, but did not explain my theory.

'And I've heard rumours that young Tailboys suffers from black bile. Gives him fits,' said John morosely. 'I could probably find out something about Thomas Arundel, too if I tried. Funny family, that.'

I decided to open attack and distract him from poor young Gilbert. 'You know, John, there's something very strange about this whole affair. I'd like to have a look at the body. There's something puzzles me. I don't, I can't …' I looked at his face, expecting to see a stubborn look, and surprised an expression of alarm. 'I was thinking that the murder might not have happened until after the evening was over. After the dancing. It seems impossible that someone shot him with an arrow in front of the king and the court. When the sugar banquet was finished, perhaps. Did everyone go off to bed then, John?'

'Mostly,' he replied. The look of alarm had intensified. Perhaps he just didn't like matters to get too complicated. He shook his head like a dog shakes its ears before resuming. 'I waited for a while to make sure that there was no trouble and then I went off myself. Some courtiers went off with the king to play cards, were at it for half the night, I heard that from the king's serjeant. He said that they finished at dawn and then the king went off with a small riding party and the others went to bed.'

'And St Leger?'

'He was playing cards, but he sought his own bed after the king had departed.'

Alice gave me a quick look and I knew that she had read my thoughts. It had, indeed, crossed my mind to wonder whether St Leger had set up the whole business to discredit James, but it seemed unlikely.

'More a matter of seizing an opportunity,' she said aloud and smiled sweetly at her brother's puzzled face.

'You mean that James seized the opportunity when he had a bow in his hand and saw that he had a real arrow in his bag,' he asked.

'Yes, and perhaps he's insane or just plain stupid.' I was getting tired of this. The cardinal's serjeant-at-arms was not as bright as his sister, but he wasn't stupid, either. Surely what was blindingly obvious to me should have occurred to him by now. And if it had, why was he not doing something about gathering evidence instead of deferring to Master Gibson.

It was strange how he appeared to have accepted that ridiculous notion that the instructor of the wards had been shot during the pageant.

'I think that I should have a word with cardinal,' I said, and was meanly glad when I saw the expression of alarm come back into his eyes.

6

I did not see the cardinal until suppertime. He was busy entertaining the queen, I was told. I was invited to dine in the chamber that evening and would be placed beside the queen. George came to break the news to me and to offer, tentatively, the loan of a very ornate rose-pink jerkin embroidered in gold which I turned down on the grounds that it would suit him and his blonde hair better than a dark-haired Irishman like myself and, since Mistress Margery Kempe would be present, then George had to look his best. The gentlemen-ushers took it in turns to dine at the cardinal's table, and tonight was George's turn. He was lit up and excited at the thought, still new enough in his position to find life in the cardinal's court exciting.

'You don't feel festive. Yes, I know; you are worried about James, aren't you, worried that your employer will blame you. But never mind, the queen and her entourage may leave tomorrow morning, and if they do then you will get an opportunity to talk with the cardinal. He is a man who can always give good advice.' George patted my arm with such an expression of commiseration that I knew the news of James's flight had spread through Hampton Court.

I made sure that I was early for the supper in the dining chamber. Even so, most of the gentlemen had already arrived and the cardinal was there, also, making easy conversation with Lord Mountjoy, but keeping a close eye on the preparations as the carvers stood by with their enormous napkins slung over one shoulder and knotted at the other hip and the trays of knives of all sizes ready in front of them. The boys with the ewers and towels at the entrance to the chamber had already arranged themselves in a neat row, standing still as statues. It was a magnificent display, a room full of light. The flames from the tiers of candles arranged on every surface were reflected in the silver trenchers, knives, spoons and cups at each place setting and in the goblets and plates that were ranged on the buffet by the wall.

The queen and her ladies arrived punctually and the cardinal hurried down the room to escort Her Grace to her place. Queen Katherine, I gathered from George, was unlikely to speak to me, beyond a greeting and few polite words. The cardinal would keep her fully occupied.

'I've put Lady Willoughby on your other side; she's very pleasant to talk to, speaks good English,' whispered George in my ear, as the cardinal took a bowl of rosewater from one of the boys and held it out for the queen to tip her fingers in.

Lady Willoughby, who had once been Maria de Salinas, had been in England for over twenty years. Once we had exchanged a few remarks about the weather, I glanced down the table to where Alice was chatting to St Leger and wished that I could be with them and making some progress in solving this strange case. Moodily I cut my manchet in the regulation four neat slices. The silver plates were lined with a thin circular wooden platter so I could cut down viciously on the small loaf in order to relieve my feelings as I glanced down at one of the lower tables and saw the smug, self-satisfied face of Master Gibson, the king's serjeant-at-arms, sitting beside Alice. He supposed, doubtless, that the murder of Edmund Pace had now been solved. He had, I heard from my servant, sent a boat off as soon as he heard the news. At the moment he probably had men out scouring the streets and lodging houses of Westminster looking for James. I dipped a piece of bread into the bowl of pottage to be shared between the four of us: Lady Mountjoy, George, Lady Willoughby and myself. This allocation of food into 'a mess' for four, or in the case of royalty, one or two persons, was an English custom that we did not have back in Kilkenny, but I was well used to it by now. We had in front of us a pie baked into the shape of a salmon, but once the pottage was consumed that would be removed by one of the servers and carved into neat slices and our portions placed in front of us. The service was superlatively good at the cardinal's table.

'That was a very sad and terrible occurrence to happen at the end of such a pleasant evening.' To my astonishment the queen addressed me just as I had dipped my spoon into some walnut sauce. Despite her thirty years in England, she still spoke with a Spanish accent.

'I understand that it happened in the middle of the evening, Your Grace.' I hoped that it wasn't the wrong thing to contradict the queen, but she looked a sensible woman as she vigorously cleaned her spoon with a piece of bread. She mopped her lips with the napkin draped across her shoulder and said in a motherly fashion:

'Try the greensauce. It's better for the digestion than walnuts. Mint and parsley, both very good for the stomach.'

Obediently I helped myself to some of the mint sauce and cut a small slice of baked frumenty and porpoise for myself, taking it with the left hand and placing it on my plate, according to the custom. It smelled delicious and I hoped that the queen would turn back to the cardinal and allow me to enjoy it in peace. Even during days of fast, like Ash Wednesday, the cardinal served magnificent food. I would have to pop into the kitchen afterwards and congratulate my friend Master Beasley.

'Eat,' she commanded and watched me carefully as I picked a small cube up between my right forefinger and thumb. I chewed and waited. There was a slight frown on her brow.

'I understood that it was a brawl after the evening was over,' she said.

I let that go. I should have been more careful. The cardinal always had a reason for what he said. I had never known him to utter a hasty word. A brawl after a night's jollification was acceptable. To kill a man in the presence of the king himself might be a crime worse than murder. It could, perhaps, be designated treason and if James were to be convicted, he would be hung, drawn and quartered. I replaced my knife on my plate and sat back feeling suddenly slightly sick. The queen showed no sign of a loss of appetite, but helped herself to some of the pickled crabmeat that was served splendidly garnished and piled high in a bright red crab shell. There was a great buzz of conversation. It had begun to snow heavily outside and broad stripes of eerily pale white light from the windows fell across the side tables. I thought of James, out there in the cold, and clenched my hand beneath the starched tablecloth.

'You must have some of this rysmole, I insist, Master Brehon. Your Grace, your visitor from Ireland is not eating well.' The queen held out the dish of rice, ground almonds and ginger and I carefully wiped my spoon a second time on some bread and took some from the dish shared between herself and the cardinal.

'I have an affection for the Irish, you know,' she said pleasantly. 'My nephew, not the emperor, but his younger brother, the archduke, he loves the Irish. His ship went ashore at a place called Kinsale and he was very kindly treated. He was very taken by the young girls, there and their fine linen smocks.' Her eyes twinkled a little and I smiled back. The traditional *léine* softened by much wear and washing would be very much more revealing than the stiff formality of the boned and corseted court clothing worn by the young ladies that the archduke would meet in Spain or in England. The queen must have a good relationship with her young nephew if he had confided this piece of information to her and I could see amusement in her eyes but then they sobered. 'I'm sorry to hear that young James Butler's name, or so I understand from one of my ladies-in-waiting, has been connected to this affair. And our good cardinal so wished him to be betrothed to Sir Thomas Boleyn's younger daughter.' She sighed heavily, fiddled for a moment with the silver spoons and forks laid out in front of her and then turned to me in a confidential manner, tilting her heavy, square-shaped hood towards me so that it made a barrier between us and the rest of the table. When she spoke then she slightly lowered her voice.

'It is all so difficult when there is not a male heir,' she said, and there was a note of sadness in her voice. 'This affair of the Ormond inheritance, just two daughters, equal heirs of course. The eldest girl, Anne St Leger, was a lady-in-waiting to me at one time. She inherited her mother's fortune many, many years ago, all the land in Devon. That is her son, Sir George St Leger,' she nodded in the direction of St Leger whose bushy beard was now angled towards the ear of the king's serjeant. 'Margaret, I did not know so well. She married Sir Thomas Boleyn. I have his two daughters here in court with me: Mistress Mary Carey and, of course, Mistress Anne Boleyn who may, we hope, change her name to Butler.'

'Mistress Anne Boleyn,' I said with a certain amount of spite, 'does not seem to want the match.' I looked down the table. The young lady had initially been placed between the thirteen-year-old Earl of Derby, promoted to the cardinal's chamber in the absence of James, and Thomas Arundel. She had, as I watched, instantly swapped places with her pliable sister and was now smiling up into the face of Harry Percy. Her very black eyes seemed to glitter in the candlelight and the boy was not eating, just gazing down into the flower-like face tilted up towards him. As I watched, I saw his hand go to the pulse in his throat and pull impatiently at the lace-edged neckline of his shirt as though he felt stifled. 'She may, I suppose, wish for better,' I said, watching the heir to the Earl of Northumberland bend his head to drop a kiss on the lady's hand.

'Nonsense,' said the queen stoutly. 'She will do as she is bid. This is a good match. My dear old chamberlain, the

Earl of Ormond, God rest his soul, would be pleased to know that two branches of his family were to be united like this.' She sipped meditatively at her white wine and I took a vigorous swallow, feeling, somewhat more hopeful than I had felt for hours. And the cardinal's wine, as always, was superlative. A deliciously rounded white wine from Burgundy. I took a tiny sliver of salmon pie between my left finger and thumb, dropped it on top of the rysmole on my spoon and swallowed. Excellent. I turned to the queen.

'A secret and unlawful killing is not something that James Butler would ever do,' I said emphatically.

'But why is he involved. Explain it to me.' The queen had now turned her back on the cardinal and was giving me her full attention.

'The man was killed with an arrow and the arrow was marked with James Butler's initials.' I looked at her carefully. She did not appear to be too shocked, so I added, 'But he didn't do it; I feel sure of that.'

'But these arrows …'

'Yes,' I said hastily. 'The arrows were toy arrows, would not kill a fly, but a real arrow was used in the killing of the instructor of the wards. James didn't do it,' I reiterated firmly.

'And yet his name is on the arrow.'

'Another reason why I know that he is innocent, Your Grace.' Her whole attention was on me and I made the most of it while the cardinal chatted with the Duchess of Suffolk and her husband, Charles Brandon. 'James is a clever boy, Your Grace,' I said earnestly. The cardinal will tell you. *Wise and discreet*, that's what the cardinal says about him. Why shoot a man in the middle of a crowd of people with an arrow marked with your own initials? Some one used that arrow on purpose. Someone wanted him to take the blame.' I kept my voice low, but looked straight into her eyes. For a Spaniard she was very fair, with light-coloured eyes and her hair, though turning grey in streaks, was of a reddish brown shade.

'And there is something else,' I said emphatically. 'I remember seeing in Ireland, a day after a battle, dead bodies with arrows in their hearts, lying around the fields, seeing bodies piled on carts and still the arrows remained even after the bodies lost their stiffness. But the body in the hall, Your Grace, apparently its arrow fell out almost immediately, although, according to reports, it was stiff as a board.' I took a deep breath. 'The physician here at Hampton Court is an old man and he has seen little or no violent death, Your Grace. It worries me. I'm finding it impossible to get permission to view the body.' I had no wish to offend the cardinal who had been so kind and so hospitable to me, but this was an opportunity that I could not miss. 'I was wondering whether ...'

She turned away from me for a moment, frowning slightly. One of the gentlemen ushers came forward and deftly refilled her silver cup with wine. She sipped it med-itatively and then put it down and turned to the cardinal. 'We talk of the death of your instructor of the wards. Has the body been examined by a doctor, Your Grace? Does he give a time of death?' She listened politely to his reply and nodded many times. He spoke low and into her ear so I could not hear him. And then after a while she said in her authoritative tones. 'I will ask my own doctor Dr Ramirez, to examine the body, if you wish for that, Your Grace. Only with your permission, of course. This, of course, is an affair of great importance and may cause a terrible scandal.' She listened to his reply, her head nodding vigorously and then she turned back to me.

'Well, that is settled. Now eat some of those shrimps. They are very good and you will need your energy. Later I will introduce Doctor Ramirez to you and you can talk over the affair with him. You will find him to be a most intelligent man. He is Spanish.' She gave another one of her nods then as though she had said the last word about this doctor's intelligence and discrimination. 'We must find out the truth about this matter.' She directed her glance down the room. Harry Percy and Mistress Anne Boleyn had both leaned towards the salmon-shaped pie, which was now, like ours, neatly cut into bite-sized portions. Her left hand and his met together mid-air. For a moment they stared at each, their fingers intertwined and then they released the grip. The boy was blushing. There was a three-tiered candlestick, filled with nine candles, quite close to him and his face and eyes glowed in their light. She, Anne Boleyn, was quite self-possessed. With dainty finger and thumb she picked out a morsel of salmon and without transferring it to her plate, or even to her right hand, she parted her lips and, still keeping her black eyes fixed on the boy's face, she placed the piece of salmon within her mouth and then slowly and caressingly, she licked her thumb. A parting of cherry red lips, a flash of white teeth, and a glimpse of a pink tongue, all lit up by the tall candelabrum in front of her, and in a minute she had lowered her eyes again to her plate. I found myself thinking of the marriage contract that I had drafted so carefully, all the clauses that took care of the wife's property and of the husband's property, of each partner's right to divorce. I might as well tear it up and throw it in the fire when I went back to my lodgings. There would be no marriage for Anne Boleyn with James Butler. A very much bigger fish had swum into the lady's net. From beside me I heard a sharp click of the tongue as the queen gave vent to her opinion of her maid-in waiting's conduct.

'In our country, Your Grace, we have a legend that Finn McCool, a giant from ancient times, burned his thumb on the magical Salmon of Knowledge. For ever afterwards, when he wished to know anything, all he had to do was to suck his thumb.' I made the remark in a neutral tone of voice and I kept a smile on my face. It would be important not to arouse any suspicion that James Butler had been pressurised or in despair in any way. After a minute, the queen giggled, an attractive sound and I began to think that I liked her much better than her mercurial husband.

'My daughter Mary, she is six years old now, but when she was a baby she used to suck her thumb,' she confided.

'Well, there you are, Your Grace. The cardinal tells me that she is the wisest child in Christendom,' I said lightly.

'And you, you are a judge, a judge in Irish Law, is that not right.' Queen Katherine was one of those women, just like my Aunt Saoirse, who always like to find out everything to be known about a man when she meets him.

'That's right, Your Grace. Whenever I get a chance. My father is a judge and both my uncles are judges, also. We are a legal family, the Mac Egan family. I qualified as a Brehon from the law school, but I haven't found a position as Brehon to any great lord. My father is Brehon to Piers Rua Butler, James's father, and I do work for him. Sometimes I do some teaching in our legal school, sometimes I work in a court as a lawyer, and occasionally as a judge, sometimes I go abroad as an envoy to the earl, as we call him. I have no settled position.' I found myself pouring out all my troubles to her as though she were, indeed, my Aunt Saoirse. 'And I am thirty years of age,' I finished.

'You will find a position,' she said. 'Why don't you stay here and qualify as an English lawyer. You could attend lectures at Lincoln's Inn, like our cherished Thomas More, so valued by the king. And there is our dear cardinal, here. He is involved in so many legal matters and he can do with good legal advisors. Ireland is, will be, of great importance. You could be an advisor to him. You would enjoy that, wouldn't you?'

'I would find that very interesting,' I said cautiously. It was true. I enjoyed the society, the sharp wits here at Hampton Court. And the cardinal's wine and food were both superlatively good. Kilkenny Castle had appalling food, and appalling wine until I had started to take a hand in the ordering of it and riding down to the port myself to make sure that we got the barrels that had been paid for. James's mother, Margaret, was a woman who loved gardens, loved the outdoor life of horses and dogs, but she had no interest in food and each new cook seemed worse than the last. I enjoyed everything about Hampton Court. The new building work that the cardinal was undertaking was fascinating to me. I had been to Italy, to Spain, to France, and to Burgundy, had seen the wonderful rebirth of the old civilisations. The New Learning, they were calling it. The cardinal was rich enough to employ artists, paints, stonemasons and designers from Italy and from the Netherlands, rich enough to buy pictures and tapestries. This house of his at Hampton was going to be a palace to rival any king's establishment. The queen's suggestion that I should attend lectures in the Temple Inns in London was a good one. It probably would not take me long to pass the examinations – I had a very good memory, had been trained in the Irish law from the age of five years. Of course, I didn't like the English system of justice, especially the savage punishments, but then I could fight on behalf of those wrongly accused and save them from a terrible death, perhaps, and also influence my colleagues into a contemplation of an older and more merciful law. In any case, I had enjoyed the position of an *aigne* – a defending lawyer, I mentally translated – more than that of a Brehon or judge. I imagined myself standing up in the Star Chamber at Westminster and making an impassioned speech on behalf of some poor person threatened with the axe or disembowelment. All London would come to listen to my speeches. I could perhaps make a real and vital difference in the law system of this country.

And then the thought of Westminster reminded me of James and I turned back to the most powerful woman in England.

'I've known James Butler since he was a small child and I have never known him to lie or to misuse his strength or his position,' I said earnestly. 'I do believe, Your Grace, that he is wrongly accused. And,' I added, 'the cardinal will tell you that James is *wise and discreet*. These were his very words, Your Grace. A *wise and discreet* man would not shoot down an enemy in public with an arrow marked with his own initials.'

'Then you must find out who did this deed,' she said briskly, almost as though she were sending me off to fetch something from her rooms. She turned back to the cardinal, speaking to him earnestly and in a voice too low for me to hear what she was saying. George, good fellow, was keeping Lady Willoughby happy by questioning her about her three-year-old daughter, who was, according to her proud mother, the most stubborn child in England. She had named her after the queen and I pondered for a while on her majesty, Catalina of Spain, now Katherine of England. The cardinal had said to me that all her ladies-in-waiting were devoted to the queen – that was, of course, the ladies-in-waiting that she had brought with her from Spain, and people like Margaret Pole, daughter of the Duke of Clarence, the present king's great-uncle. And I looked down again at the pale oval of Mistress Anne Boleyn's face. She was wearing a gown of red silk that shimmered in the candlelight and her dark hair was gathered loosely into a gold net and it perfectly framed the pale oval of her face. Perhaps attracted by my steady gaze, she glanced up towards the top table, the candlelight flashing a gleam from those very dark eyes. It was at the queen that she looked and there was none of the usual deference of a lady-in-waiting to be observed in her expression. Instead she wore a defiant look. As a child, Anne had been sent to the court of Margaret of Austria, whose motto was '*Groigne qui groigne: Vive Bourgogne!*' This young lady might well have the motto: '*Groigne qui groigne: Vive Boleyn!*'

The cardinal was on his feet now. A Latin grace. I wondered whether he believed in it any more than I did, but he made a splendid show, bowing his white head and his sonorous voice uttering the Latin words: '*Agimus tibi gratias, omnipotens Deus, pro universis beneficiis tuis, qui vivis et regnas insæcula sæculorum,*' he prayed, energetically making an enormous, wide-armed sign of the cross over everyone and then leading the way to the bottom of the room where the sweet course of the meal was laid out. This was 'the void', an emptying of the room, an opportunity for the sewers to remove the dishes, and the leftovers, fold up the linen tablecloths, remove the trestle tables and leave the room ready for dancing or for music. I left Lady Willoughby chatting happily with Lady Mountjoy and made my way over towards Alice who was stowing some gingerbread away in a napkin.

'For my little Lily. She does so love gingerbread,' she said aloud and then as I exclaimed loudly and threatened to fetch the sergeant-at-arms to deal with this theft, she said very low: 'He has been promised to be bailiff and keeper of the wood and park at Ewelme in Oxfordshire.'

'Disgraceful!' I said and gave her a smile. That was interesting news. St Leger was a hanger-on of the king's best friend, Charles Brandon who held lands in Oxfordshire. This post would be a valuable position for the king's serjeant, yielding a good income. No doubt more would have been promised. I left her and went in search of Master Gibson. He had a smug, self-satisfied expression to his face.

'I wouldn't eat any of those wafers, or that sugary, spiced wine, either, or else I will definitely beat you at our next game of tennis,' I warned him in a good-humoured way.

His eyes narrowed as he nibbled a caraway comfit and swallowed a draught of Hippocras. We had first played tennis in a doubles match with John and myself against him and young George Boleyn. Later we had sought each other out and the odds were even between us both so far.

'And so our little bird has flown,' he said. His tone was aggressive, but there was something else shown in his eyes as they rested on me, a certain satisfaction. He was glad that James had flown. It was an obvious sign of guilt and would save him from the trouble of proving his guilt.

'Well, you know what boys of that age are like,' I said lightly. 'James was at Westminster attending on the cardinal last week. He made a friend there at the court. I understand that she is a pretty young lady.'

His lips parted in a sneer. 'And so he didn't flee, is that right? He didn't go to Westminster out of fear. He went to meet a young lady, that's what you say, is it? Not because he was afraid of being arrested.' He shot out the final words in a tone of vicious triumph.

'I'm sure that he did not fly for any reason. I'm certain that he trusts to your justice,' I said evenly. 'You will, of course, be busy during the next few days taking evidence from all who were present, the cardinal's servants, workmen, and women,' I added, thinking about Susannah. 'I suppose you and your clerk already have reams of paper piled up with witnesses' accounts. What with the music in the background and the shouts and the laughter and fruit and comfits flying to and fro it must have been a most confusing scene.'

That slightly disconcerted him. I could see from the eye that he turned on me that he was mentally going through the new legal handbook about dealing with a murder.

'I think that I have a fair idea of what happened,' he said cautiously.

'Of course you are far too experienced a man to jump to conclusions before you have all of the evidence,' I said affably.

It was like one of our games of tennis. I had chipped a ball to his backhand, now he volleyed it back across the court.

'A judge,' he observed, 'would assume that the flight of a suspect was an admission of guilt.'

'Oh, did you inform him that he was a suspect? It was understood that James would only be interviewed in my presence.' I sent the ball winging up to the penthouse roof and he responded awkwardly with an aggressive side sweep.

'Everyone knows that James Butler shot that arrow through the man.'

'It will be impossible to have a fair trial if the serjeant in charge of the case has already announced his views to all and sundry.' It was perhaps an unfair shot; I had sent the ball into the tambour and it rolled along the floor, unreturnable by him.

'I didn't …' he began, but then was interrupted.

'Excuse me, Master,' murmured one of the gentlemen ushers to me, 'Her Grace, the queen, wishes to speak with you.'

I smiled with triumph at the serjeant. 'I must go; Her Grace is very interested in James Butler. It's only natural, I suppose, since she was so fond of the late Earl of Ormond.' Anne Boleyn was nearer in blood to the late chamberlain than James, of course, but I could see that that serjeant was slightly shaken by this so I left him quickly. He would have noticed, the whole table would have noticed, my lengthy conversation with the queen during supper. The king's serjeant could easily find himself in the wrong if the queen complained of him.

'Your Grace!' I snatched off my cap and bowed low. She was talking to a tall man of about my own age and height, no darker than I. The queen introduced him as Doctor Ramirez.

'I have been in your country for seven years, Master,' he said in careful English when I greeted him in Spanish. 'And have studied at Oxford University.' And then a smile broke up the severity of his thin, clever-looking face. 'But do take the opportunity to practise your Spanish, if you wish, Master Brehon,' he said.

I laughed a little at that. 'I think we might get on better in English,' I said. 'My Spanish is limited to negotiating for good barrels of wine at the harbour of New Ross in Ireland. We get lots of Spanish ships there.'

'I am speaking to Doctor Ramirez about this sad and terrible affair,' said the queen, ignoring this frivolity. 'It's been such a dreadful business for the poor, poor cardinal.'

'And not too nice for the man who was shot, also,' said Dr Ramirez and I found myself warming to him. We exchanged grins.

'So you talk together, both of you and you work out what has happened.' The queen's voice made an order out of her statement and we both bowed as she turned away and greeted Lord Abergavenny, enquiring after his younger brother, the king's friend, Sir Edward Neville.

'I hear that the cardinal mistook him for the king, when they were both masked,' she was saying, laughingly, as we moved away and I wondered how such a serious and intelligent woman could put up with all the silly and childish games that the king spent his evenings playing.

Still that was none of my business and I turned my attention to this Spanish physician who was looking at me with interest.

'You are a lawyer, yes? You have studied the law, is that right?'

'Since I was five years old,' I replied and he bowed respectfully, but with a glint in his eye which amused me.

'And this death? I have just this evening come here to Hampton Court. My wife has been delivered of a child, safely, and I come to ask Her Grace to so graciously condescend to be a godmother to the little girl. She will be called Katherine. So of this death, I know nothing.'

'Happened in the hall, yesterday evening during the Shrove Tuesday Pageant,' I explained. 'The body of a man was found the following morning, this morning and he had an arrow stuck in his chest. He had fallen behind the arras.' I searched for the Spanish word. '*Tapiz*,' I said doubtfully and he smiled with a flash of white teeth.

'They think that he was killed some time during the pageant because the body was completely stiff when it was found at ten o'clock the following morning,' I explained and he nodded thoughtfully, suddenly grave again.

'I can see the body?' he enquired and once again I warmed to him. He did not waste time asking questions or making explanations. I had a poor opinion of the cardinal's doctor who seemed to me to spout a lot of nonsense about humours and phases of the moon. He had been fairly perfunctory about his pronouncement on the time of death. Could he really be so sure?

'Yes, of course,' I said briskly in reply to his request. 'Come with me.' I led him down through the room and

towards the table where the sweetmeats and the wine of
Hippocras were set out. He knew nobody in that assem-
bly, I noticed. People greeted me and then looked at him
without recognition.

The serjeant had a tasty, very thin wafer in his hand
when we approached.

'Her Grace would like Doctor Ramirez to view the
body of the dead man,' I said briskly and waited while
the serjeant snapped the wafer in half and then placed
both pieces into his mouth. He drained the hot spiced
wine from the silver cup, holding it, not by its stem, or
even by its base, but wrapping his fingers around the
waisted centre of the vessel, almost as though he needed
to conceal his face for a moment. He was thinking hard;
I knew that, but I waited confidently. There was no way
that he could disobey an order from the queen herself,
and even if he went to check with the cardinal, if he had
the temerity to do that, well, he risked a severe repri-
mand if I were speaking the truth. He didn't trust me
though. We had played too many games of tennis against
each other to have any illusions about our partners.

'The body,' he said slowly, lowering his cup back down
onto the table. 'I don't think that I should …'

'Let's go,' I said briskly. I saw his eyes go towards John
Rushe and watched him decide not to involve the cardinal's man.

'I'm not sure …' he began.

'Shall I ask Master Rushe where it has been stored?'
I enquired, though I knew where the body had been
placed. My servant, Colm, had told me that the body
was, by the cardinal's orders, placed in the underground
cellar of the fish house. The wood yard workers cut ice

from the moat every winter and stored it beneath the fish house, within layers of sawdust, readily available to keep valuable fish, such as salmon, cool until cooked. No doubt the coroner had been informed, but probably told to come on Monday when enquiries would have been made. Cardinal Wolsey was not a man that any coroner could gainsay. I waited confidently. The serjeant gazed at us for a few long moments, defiantly took two more wafers, but then led the way towards the door to the yards in silence. Dr Ramirez followed and I stuck close to him.

There were several lanterns placed on the table near to the door and I took a taper and lit three of them. Like everything else at Hampton Court, they were fine lanterns, made in the new style, six-sided with panes of glass rather than the old-fashioned horn. In silence the serjeant and the doctor took up their lanterns and we went outside, braving the weather and, in my case, swallowing down the nausea induced by the thought of having to inspect a dead body.

And then I thought of James, alone and desperate, wandering the dangerous streets of Westminster as the snow fell and I resolved to make sure that this Spanish doctor had a chance to help.

7

There was a harsh chill to the night air and it hit us as soon as the door was opened. I recoiled momentarily when the north wind, whistling through the buildings, robbed me of my breath for a second. It was no night to be out-of-doors. There were no moon or stars to be seen and the torches, stuck into their iron holders outside the kitchens and the sculleries, flickered wildly in the freezing snow-laden gusts that swept down the narrow passageway between the buildings. How was James faring?

'Hurry up,' said Master Gibson roughly. 'Let's get this over and done with.'

I held up a hand to shelter the candle inside my lantern and felt my feet slip slightly on the icy surface of the pavement. I deliberately slowed down. Let him break his leg if he wanted to. I allowed him to go ahead of us until he reached the place where the fish was stored.

'Friendly sort of man,' said Dr Ramirez to me in an undertone as the serjeant, with a muttered oath, put down his lantern, produced a large key and inserted it into the door of the fish house. He went in first, made room for us, and we waited while he locked the door behind us. There were plenty of boxes piled up in the fish house, filling the shelves on the walls, all of them full of fish, ready for tomorrow's Lenten cooking. I wasn't keen on the smell of fish in the best of times, but this place was so cold that there was very little odour apparent. Master Beasley, I knew, was very particular that his fish should be fresh. He would not tolerate fish that had begun to smell. There would be trout, lobster, crayfish and salmon for the cardinal's table and for the yeoman and the servants there would be plentiful supplies of cod, ling and eels.

And downstairs, beneath all these foodstuffs, lay the body of a man.

The cold was intense and the sawdust beneath our feet in the cellar was frozen into hard lumps, as though the dust had been transmuted into its original wooden substance. There was no smell. I held up my lantern. Stone walls, whitewashed with lime, piles of sawn ice blocks heaped one on top of the other around the sides of the walls. In the centre were two trestles and on them the body of the dead man, the instructor of Cardinal Wolsey's wards, lay stretched on a marble slab. Not as handsome as a silver-scaled salmon, but looking remarkably life-like, though his short beard was more unkempt than in life and his ruddy cheeks were bleached to the colour of parchment. He was wearing, I noticed, his best apparel. It was mulberry in colour, as befitted a member of Cardinal Wolsey's household, but his doublet and jerkin were made from silk velvet and his hose were woven from the finest wool. I gazed down on him. In the light from our four lanterns every detail showed. In the centre of his jerkin was a flat, dark patch of dried blood.

'You say that the man had been examined by the cardinal's doctor.' Ramirez's voice sounded puzzled and his Spanish accent was stronger than usual. I turned to look at him. He had placed his lantern on the marble slab, close to the dead man's chest.

'That's right. Well, he declared him dead. Said he had been dead for over twelve hours. *Rigor Mortis* that's what he called it. He said that the man must have been killed during the pageant as it would take twelve hours for him to stiffen like that.'

'But didn't he examine him? Look, the man is in his clothes.'

'Well, as I was telling you, he was stiff as board when we picked him up. Nothing could be done with him then. We had to get him out of the hall. Feel him. He's still stiff.' The serjeant put down his lantern by the feet, then tentatively gripped the dead man's sleeve and tried to raise the arm.

'*Jesu!*' Dr Ramirez made the exclamation with an air of a man barely keeping grip on his patience. He drew his knife from his belt, grabbed a handful of the dead man's clothes, just where the frilled collar of his fine linen shirt showed above his doublet. He brandished the knife and with one quick slash ripped the layers from neck to waist. Impatiently he tugged at one side and I shifted Master Gibson out of my way and folded back the other side. The fabric was stiff with frost and it remained open, almost as though it were a door set ajar. The doctor gazed intently for a moment and then rapidly drew his knife down the dead man's chest. The flesh parted reluctantly and there was a gleam of bone.

'I need a better knife, some more knives. Fetch some from the kitchen. Good strong knives. Sharp. Get the cook to sharpen them.' He snapped out his orders without looking around. The king's serjeant turned his head towards me, but I ignored him. Master Beasley, the cook, normally went early to bed so that he was up and waiting for the fresh food deliveries before six in the morning. He would not be happy to be roused from his first sleep. In any case, although I owed it to James to try to find out as much as possible, I had no obligation to assist the serjeant. And I wanted to have a private moment with this Spanish doctor. There was something strange about that small hole in the middle of the man's chest; it confirmed what had occurred to me earlier, but I might be wrong and I didn't want to say any more, in the presence of the king's serjeant, the man who was already convinced that he knew who the murderer was. I kept my lips closed until he had left.

'The arrow was bodkin-tipped,' I said tentatively when the serjeant's footsteps on the cellar steps had ceased to echo. I heard the door slam and the sound of the key turning. He had locked us in, or locked others out. A cautious man.

'Arrow, where is the arrow?' The doctor glanced around in a slightly theatrical fashion.

'He was shot with an arrow,' I said.

'And where is the arrow?' he asked the same question, but in a different tone of voice, more like a teacher instructing a pupil. I smiled to myself. I had not mistaken my man.

'It fell out when they went to pick up the man.' I watched his expression carefully. 'So I was told,' I added. 'I was not there. I heard about it later. The cook had been called into the hall to be publically thanked by the cardinal for the magnificent supper that he put on for the king and his court and then when he was going out, he noticed a shoe sticking out from behind the arras and when they lifted the body, then the arrow …'

'Yes, yes. And the man was stiff.'

'That's right.'

Ramirez looked at me. 'My friend,' he said gently, 'you are not stupid. I hear you are a lawyer. Tell me again what happened.'

I grinned with pure pleasure. '*Me dice*,' I said in Spanish. '*Muchos, muchos testigos.*'

His stern face puckered to a smile. 'How many?'

I pictured the hall and the crowd who would have been dining there, the men who would have been serving.

'About a hundred witnesses,' I said aloud.

He held up two fingers and counted solemnly on them. 'One: a hundred peoples lie,' he said bending back his forefinger. 'Or two,' he bent the middle finger, 'the dead body lies.'

I laughed. '*A hundred peoples lie* – dead men do not lie.' I pointed to his second finger and he grinned, his eyes gleaming and his teeth flashing in the light from my lantern.

'But we wait,' he said, lifting a cautionary finger. 'We wait. No guesses. Just facts. It's science we need, my friend, Master Brehon.'

'Call me Hugh,' I said. 'Everyone calls me Hugh, even the cardinal. And when I am back home in Ireland there are so many of the Mac Egan clan, all of them lawyers, that I am always Hugh. And this isn't the first time that I've been involved in solving a secret murder. I know all about gathering the facts.'

'You have investigated murders? You do work like that in your own country?'

I nodded. 'A Brehon is like a mixture of a serjeant-at-arms and a judge. We hear witnesses, investigate the circumstances of the crime and then we pass sentence. But,' I said very firmly, 'we don't hang men or behead them or hang, draw and quarter them. We give them a chance to become a good member of the community again. They pay a fine, a very big fine, lots of silver, or many cows, mostly with the help of their family or even the whole of their clan.' I struggled with the explanation. Soon I would see the look of scepticism on his face. Then would come the exclamations: *'But what stops people murdering again! Doesn't the Bible tell us: "A life for a life"? Surely a fine is not a proper compensation for a life!'* but, to my surprise, Ramirez just said crisply:

'Good. What's the point of two deaths? And a sorrowing widow left penniless.' And then he went back to cross-questioning me. It occurred to me then, that, though our professions were different, we shared a liking to accumulate as many facts as possible and to get them straight before making any guesses.

And so, in the event, I asked no questions, just patiently gave as many details as I could. The body, I related, was discovered in the Great Hall, lying behind the thick screen of the arras or tapestry. The time of discovery, if it were at the end of dinner, was probably about almost eleven o'clock in the morning. Yes, there would have been a fire in the hall at that time. No, it did not burn all night. The dangers of fire were too great. It might be left banked down and smouldering, but certainly not blazing. And in the morning one of the wood boys or a kitchen worker would wheel in the wood from the kitchen and get the fire going in plenty of time for the first dinner sitting at ten o'clock in the morning. The hall, I told him, could get very cool if the fires were not kept up. It was a big room.

'Why the kitchen?' He was a man who liked to get all the details straight and I explained about the damp in the wood yard and how the bundles of faggots and of talshides were left overnight in the main kitchen so that they would be warm and dry for relighting the fires in the morning.

'And so the hall would have stayed warm, but not very warm all night.' He was talking more to himself than to me.

'Not too warm, more cool,' I said thoughtfully. 'It's a very big room. I remember the first time that I came to Hampton Court, last autumn, James showed me the hall – it was a few hours after supper and it had already cooled down. It's got all those windows and that high roof. I can see what you mean. It helps with fixing the time of death. In cool air the body would not stiffen too quickly.'

'This pageant, what time it was?'

'About six o'clock,' I said promptly. 'Supper was at half past four as usual and then they started to get ready the hall, the carpenters were bringing in the walls of the castle as soon as the tables were cleared away. I went into the small chamber beside the hall and I was busy writing, but I could hear all the voices, the music and thuds, of oranges, I suppose.' I opened my mouth to ask a question, but then shut it again. This was a man of science.

'And the onlookers?'

It was not really a question, but I knew what was in his mind.

'I'd say that most of them would have been looking at the king and his courtiers who were making the most noise, throwing the oranges and dates and comfits,' I said. 'They were wearing masks, but of course everyone knew who the king was, so most people would have been looking at him. Some may have been looking at the ladies, peeping over the turrets of the castle. They looked very pretty with their lace gowns and white lace scarves. But as for James and his fellow wards, I don't suppose anyone much looked at them. They had been warned to fire their arrows – just little twig-like things – at the floor, although I don't think they would have harmed a fly – just leather mâché, you know. Now that I come to think of it, I believe that I noticed the fire was very low when I peered in. With all the people there, the steward or one of the gentlemen ushers probably gave orders to allow it to die down in case the hall got too hot. The king, they say, feels the heat.'

'Master Gibson arrives back!' Ramirez's ears were quicker than mine. He had heard the click of the key in the lock before I felt an icy draught sweep down into the already freezing coldness of the cellar. The man had locked us in and looked at him with fury. I said nothing, though. He was looking bad-tempered and there was no point in starting an argument. No doubt he had suffered the rough edge of the cook's tongue. He thrust a leather sheaf of different-sized knives at the doctor. There were plenty of them, two or three of each width, and of different lengths. There looked as though there were about a dozen knives, but the sheath was small enough to be held in the left hand.

Dr Ramirez sorted through them quickly, picked out the largest and handed the sheaf back to the serjeant.

And, then unhesitatingly, just as butcher would do it, he slashed the man's chest open.

There was no blood; I was thankful for that. The flesh had the texture of old meat and was pale in colour.

All except one small spot, not much bigger than a man's finger, where there was a dark incision, going deep into the body.

'See, Hugh, he found the heart.' Ramirez ignored the serjeant. 'Slipped his knife in between the ribs, to the left side of the sternum.'

'The arrow went in there.' Richard Gibson peered through the space between us.

'Master Serjeant, if an arrow went in there; the arrow would stay there unless you pulled it out straight away. And if you pulled out a bodkin-tipped arrow, then the wound would be …' he hesitated for a moment, seeking a word and then said tentatively '… would be frayed. But if you did not pull it out straight away, then the muscles would clench it hard and while the body remained stiff, it would certainly not fall out.'

'You're trying to say that the man was not killed with an arrow.' Master Gibson gave a short, incredulous laugh.

'A small, small knife, very thin, that killed him. Not like any of those knives here.' The doctor gave a cursory look through the knives slotted into the sheath. 'Perhaps not a working knife. A secret weapon. You see them in Europe, in Italy, Spain, Netherlands, Austria … There is one in the hand of a youth in the tapestry in the cardinal's dining chamber. Our murderer, my good serjeant, plunged a thin, sharp knife into the heart of this dead man. And then,' Ramirez raised a finger, 'and then he pull it out again, hide the body behind the tapestry and poke the arrow in the wound.'

'Someone tried to make James Butler appear to be the murderer,' I said. Hope began to rise. 'But who hated James enough for that?' I turned to Ramirez. 'When do you think that the murder took place?'

'Probably when the hall was empty,' he said promptly. 'It makes sense.'

'You made that up between you, didn't you, while you got rid of me on some excuse. I know perfectly well that James Butler killed Master Pace.' Gibson was choked with anger.

'How can you possibly know that?' I took a step nearer to him and looked down at him. 'Has someone employed you to find James guilty at all costs?' I could hear the menace in my voice and he heard it, too. He took a step back.

'I'm going for the cardinal's doctor. He'll give me his opinion, and I wouldn't be at all surprised if he says that you are talking nonsense.'

'He won't. Not if he has learned his profession.'

'And you have.' There was a sneer in the king's serjeant's voice. 'In Spain, I suppose.'

'And at Oxford. You can ask the queen about me if you wish.'

'Are we interested in who actually committed this murder, or do you just want to pin it on James Butler at all costs? Because if so, I warn you that you won't get away with this. I'll go to the king himself if necessary.' I allowed a threat to enter my voice.

The king's serjeant ignored that. He stared with frustrated fury at the dead man. 'I know that he was killed with that arrow belonging to your James Butler. I'll prove it if it's the last thing that I'll do.' He turned on his heel and went back up the steps again.

'And don't you lock us in here.' I yelled after him, but it was no good. A minute later the door clicked open, slammed shut and there was there was the ominous scraping sound of the key in the lock. I jumped to my feet with a curse, but it was too late. We were locked in.

'Damn him to death,' I exploded, but the slightly amused demeanour of Ramirez had its effect on me and I looked back at the corpse on the marble slab. The clouds must have cleared and the moonlight shining through the barred window of the fish house cast a square of striped light on the stone steps leading upwards.

'How long does a body take to stiffen after death?' I enquired, trying to keep my voice calm and my enquiry to be without any trace of emotion. 'I hate being shut up,' I said by way of explanation.

'It's variable,' said Ramirez. 'Sometimes it can be quite quick, but in a rapidly cooling room, it would probably take about twelve to fifteen hours.'

The pageant had finished at about ten o'clock. The players and audience had then gone into the cardinal's dining hall for their sugar supper. I had gone on writing, glad of the respite from the thud of the drum, the clash of cymbals and the wail of the flute. But of course there had been other sounds that followed, nothing that disturbed me too much. Voices, hammers demolishing the fake castle, a broom crashing against a stool or bench, a burst of laughter, an exclamation of surprise or pleasure – perhaps someone found an orange or a date to bring back to a sweetheart or to some wide-awake children. I hadn't minded those noises as I filled in the clauses about divorce, about the children of the marriage, and about the redistribution of the couple's possessions.

And then they had all trooped out, still laughing and calling to each other and there had been a short interval of silence. Perhaps Edmund Pace met someone in the empty hall, someone with a knife, a thin knife, a knife like the knife pictured on the Flemish tapestry in the cardinal's dining chamber. There was, of course, one person, who was there, carefully checking the floor for pieces of leather mâché. Had Susannah left by that stage? It would be worth going to see her again and I smiled a little at my feelings of pleasure at the thought.

'So it was likely that Master Pace was killed after the pageant was over, don't you think?'

'Most likely,' agreed the doctor. 'And there would have been blood. We should go and examine the tapestry in the hall. I would expect a wound like this to spurt blood from the heart.' Vigorously he rubbed his hands together and then began slapping his sides, alternating his long arms and stamping up and down on the frozen floor.

'Here he comes,' I said with relief. I was beginning to feel ill with the cold. I jumped up and down a few times and then began practising my backhand. Dr Augustine came in aggressively. He was probably about forty years older than the young Spanish doctor and his expression said that he was not going to put up with any lectures from the younger man.

'Nonsense, nonsense, of course it was an arrow. I examined the body myself as soon as it was found,' he said emphatically. 'That wound was conducive to an arrow incision, or at least it was before you carved the poor man up,' he said looking disdainfully down at the corpse.

'The muscles tighten around the weapon at the moment of entry,' said Dr Ramirez. 'The body is still stiff. How could an arrow just fall out? It's nonsense.'

'Nonsense, indeed,' snorted Dr Augustine. He turned disdainfully back to the serjeant. 'There's nothing here to make me change my diagnosis. The man was shot in the chest with an arrow. You have the arrow. You've seen the blood on it. And now I understand, Serjeant, that the young man has fled: a clear admission of guilt.'

'Or lack of faith in justice,' I said quietly, and they both glared at me.

'I must lock up this place. The body will be buried on Monday, after the coroner has seen it, but until then I can keep it here. I have arranged with the cook and the clerk of the kitchen that supplies of fish can be taken out in my presence, but until Monday I hold all the keys to this fish store. And I'd better return these.' The serjeant picked up the knife from the marble slab, cleaned it on a piece of frozen sawdust, replaced it into the sheaf, buckling it onto his own waist and then took the old man's arm and walked up the steps with him. I followed immediately. My toes and fingers were beginning to feel frostbitten. The two men went towards the lodgings in the clock court, but Dr Ramirez stopped at the door to the gallery steps.

'Let's take a look at this tapestry,' he said, and I followed him up. Most of household had gone to bed by now. Eight o'clock was the usual retiring hour in winter months; the wax guttered, unchecked, in wavy trails down the sides of the candles in the six-foot-high candelabra in the passage, although a few yeoman still stood around yawning. I kept my lantern in my hand, as did Ramirez. We would need these.

The great hall was, as I had expected, in almost total darkness. Only a faint glow came from the dying fire. It was, I noticed with interest, quite cold now that it was empty of people and the small charcoal fires that burned in iron braziers at the sides of the huge room had been carefully extinguished.

'Which tapestry?' asked Ramirez in a hushed voice.

I wasn't sure. There had been something about the arrow going right through the hub of a cart, but there seemed to be carts in both of the tapestries that covered the walls of the great hall.

'Probably that one,' I said pointing to the one nearest to the small side door. The cook would have been unlikely to have marched out beneath the ceremonial carved archway and through the great double doors at the end of the great hall. He was quite a shy man away from his kitchen. 'Yes, it's that one. See, there is a cart wheel near to the flower border there.'

We went across and I held the edge of the cloth while the doctor examined the hole, right in the centre of the hub. Quite a large hole, I noticed; the threads of the weaving had been torn or cut and the canvas that lined it had been pierced, also.

'Good shooting to send an arrow right through the centre of the hub!' I said the words sarcastically. By now I was quite convinced, and vastly relieved to be so convinced, that, wherever he had been killed, the instructor of the wards, Master Edmund Pace, had been stabbed through the heart with a knife. And afterwards, when the body was slumped on the floor, the arrow had been put through the heart in order to throw the blame onto James.

'No arrow could go through a tightly woven, lined tapestry like this, and then through a man's heart,' I said in a low voice. I was not an expert bowman like James but I was sufficiently experienced with a bow to know that thick heavy carpeting like this, even without the canvas backing, would slow down or stop any arrow.

'Surprising that the servants did not notice the body when they cleaned the room,' said Dr Ramirez.

'I'd say that they cleaned the place thoroughly last night after the pageant and then just mended the fire and perhaps flicked a duster around this morning,' I said. It was not surprising that the body had not been noticed by those entering for dinner, as an elaborate buffet, filled with shining cups and plates of silver and gold stood in front of the tapestry and its shadow would have darkened that part of the room. The body might have lain there all day if the cook had not spotted the man's shoe.

'So it looks as though he were killed after that happened. Perhaps he came in here late in the evening, just as we are doing now and he met his fate, met a man or a boy who had a grudge against him.'

'Fear, anger, greed, jealousy – I remember the *ollamh,* the professor in our law school, used to tell us to look for these motives when we were trying to think of a motive for a killing. And he used to say that 'fear' was the most potent.'

He said nothing, just looked a question, so I continued reluctantly: 'I believe that the dead man, Master Pace, was blackmailing at least two of the cardinal's wards, and possibly others as well. They were giving him money and other things for fear that he might inform the cardinal of their secrets.' Something occurred to me then and I added, 'Just the wards, perhaps, but it could be others in the household, what do you think?'

'It could be. Me, I like to keep to facts. Conjecture can be futile.' He sounded a little impatient, so I switched back to the dead body.

'He wasn't killed here, was he?' I asked, keeping my voice low in case one of the yeoman decided to eavesdrop.

He pursed his lips, perhaps reluctant to commit himself to an opinion, knelt down on the floor and moved eye and nose close to its surface. Then he nodded.

'No, no, no stains of blood, no smell of blood. The man bled, that's sure. He had a knife wound – we agree it was a knife, don't we? A sharp, slender knife. But he did not bleed here.'

'And the hole in the tapestry?' I studied it carefully, noting the way that the threads were not just cut but twisted. The canvas at the back, also. That had a rounded hole in it, not just a slit. 'Do you know, I do believe that these holes were actually made with an arrow, with the arrow, with the arrow that was found in the man's chest, what do you think, Ramirez?'

'Could be, I suppose.' He did not sound too concerned. His interest was more in bodies than in woven wool. The more I thought about it, the more I believed that I was correct in my guess. So the man was murdered, possibly in a different part of the great hall, perhaps by the cooling ashes on the hearth – fire would destroy any traces of blood. And then the body was hidden behind the arras when it had ceased to bleed. There would have been plenty of time. No one was disturbing us here; it would have been the same the night before. Once the Shrove Tuesday pageant was cleared away, once the banquet and the dancing had finished and all had gone to their beds, there could have been a secret meeting here in the great hall. Blackmailer could have confronted victim. It made sense that both would have stood by the fire. The hall cooled down rapidly when emptied of people for an hour or so. The blackmailer made an exorbitant demand. The victim pulled out a slim, sharp knife and plunged it into his heart.

And then when the blood had been cleaned – some soot and kindling rubbed into marks and then burned – another plan occurred to the killer – and here I was uncertain. James had said that he had lost an arrow one day firing at a duck that flew over the moat. Could it have been picked up with the intention of restoring it, placed in a pouch? It seemed strange that it had not been restored. But if it had been forgotten, then it could have been remembered suddenly when a dead man was lying in front of the killer.

But why try to implicate James in the murder?

Unless, of course, the murderer was driven to his first crime by fear, by blackmail, and the second, the conviction of an innocent young man, the death perhaps by hanging, drawing and quartering, by jealousy. If James were to be convicted of the murder of Master Pace in the presence of the king, then he would be sentenced to that terrible death. And it would mean that he could never marry Sir Thomas Boleyn's daughter.

And so there would be no obstacle in the way of another young man, already deeply in love with the charming Lady Anne.

8

I waited outside the chapel after Mass next morning in the hope of meeting Ramirez again. The queen, of course, was the first to leave. She swept down the steps on her way back to her rooms, but stopped to smile graciously at me and to invite me to come to see her in an hour's time, after she had broken her fast. I scanned the troop of household officers and ladies-in-waiting who followed her. The younger ones, perhaps less used to the queen's piety, looked cold and sleepy. Anne Boleyn yawned widely as she passed me and her sister pinched her arm admonishingly. Mary Boleyn, according to the cardinal, had been in the service of Queen Katherine since 1519 and would know all the queen's regulations and preferences. Her younger sister, though, did not accept the reproof meekly, but angrily threw off the admonishing hand and muttered something. I saw the queen look around and frown, but Anne seemed to take no notice. She just tossed her head, turned around to whisper in Bessie Blount's ear and gave me a contemptuous glance from her bold bright eyes. There was no sign of my new friend Dr Ramirez. Like myself he had probably slept in after the late night on the previous evening.

'The cardinal busy this morning?' I asked George when the procession had gone on its stately way.

'Gone,' said George with a sigh. 'Poor man. A message came for him early this morning. He has to attend the king at Richmond. He was in his barge by dawn.'

I had a momentary alarm, but then thought it over. It was unlikely that news about James would cause the king to send for Cardinal Wolsey so early in the morning. The death of the instructor of the wards would be of very small consequence to the King of England.

'France!' said George, his kind face reading my anxiety. '*Toujours La France*! It's always an anxiety. His Grace, our cardinal, is always at the treaty table.'

'Of course.' I nodded.

All the ladies of the court looked more cheerful and warmer when I arrived punctually in the queen's rooms. Like myself, they would have had some bread and wine and warmed their chilly toes by the fire in their bedroom. Dinner would be in less than an hour and then the afternoon would be filled with amusements for them. They made a pretty picture, sitting gracefully on large cushions or on stools, the gold threads on their gowns glinting in the candlelight, while they stitched industriously at small pieces of embroidery, holding the cloth stretched over a small circular frame and keeping their eyes down. Even the queen herself stitched an intricate design on to the cuff of a man's shirt with black thread.

'Your Grace!' I bowed deeply. She had a small brown monkey wearing a harness, sitting on the floor beside her, tied to her chair. She saw me looking at it, bent down and then stroked its little head and it looked up at her with large astonished eyes. I wondered if it was a baby substitute for her and felt very sorry. The cardinal had told me about the death of her children and I remembered hearing, when I was a young lawyer, the Earl of Donegal, straight from London, telling a story about a six-week-old son who had suddenly and unexpectedly died. I didn't like the monkey much, with its almost human-like face, and wondered why she did not have a dog instead. Still, I had to say something. It was expected of courtiers, and I needed the queen's approval.

'What wonderful embroidery, Your Grace can do,' I said hastily. 'I have seen nothing like that in Ireland.'

'It is the way that we work in Spain.' Her smile was sweet and it lit up her face. 'This is for the king's highness. I make all of his shirts.'

I almost said: 'Lucky man!' but decided it would be too familiar. I had spotted Gilbert Tailboys chatting to Mistress Bessie Blount over a chessboard and turned my gaze towards them.

'You play chess.' The queen's glance followed mine and then she said swiftly: 'Go and finish the game with Master Tailboys. Mistress Blount!' She had not raised her voice above the sound of the lutenists in the corner, but Bessie immediately jumped to her feet and hurried over to the queen and was presented with some sewing. Anne Boleyn, who was sitting on the windowsill, laughing with Harry Percy, received a similar summoning glance, but deliberately turned her face towards the window, rubbing moisture from one of the diamond-shaped panes with a long finger and gazing up into young Harry's face with a teasing expression. I passed them on my way to

Gilbert and paused for a moment, removing my cap and bowing to them both. Neither said anything and barely acknowledged the bow, but I waited. After all, Harry Percy and James had been pages together for many years in the cardinal's household. Did he feel any compunction that he had driven his one-time friend from shelter and protection?

'You've heard about James?' I asked him then and he nodded reluctantly, looking at Mistress Anne as though she were his master.

'When you saw that arrow …' I began.

'It was quite clear,' interrupted Mistress Anne.

'That's what puzzles me, you know,' I said confidentially to Harry. 'Let me just understand how it went. You saw James take an arrow from his bag – I understand that they were bags supplied by the household artist, that's right, isn't it? Not your usual quivers.'

'That's right.' Again the lady answered. Harry was very flushed. He suffered from bouts of ague; I knew that. Now he looked as though he were running a fever. I began to be sorry that I had not seen him when he was alone. He looked at Mistress Boleyn as a boy looks at a schoolmaster, hoping for approbation, but fearing a reproof.

'I've been at some of those pageants,' I said, injecting a note of confidence into my voice. 'I've watched them and I know how hard it is to see anything. People move, shadows are cast, candles flicker.'

'I have good sight and I was standing up on the dais, looking over the castle wall.' Her voice rose to a shrill note and I saw Lady Willoughby get to her feet and thread her way down towards us. I pictured the scene.

Candlelight picking out faces and hands, perhaps the white Milan lace on gowns and scarves, the silver flash from a mask. 'But a dark brown arrow,' I said aloud. 'How can you be so sure that it was a real arrow?'

'It looked quite different,' she snapped. She looked as though she were enjoying this keen encounter of our wits.

'But I have been to the artist and have seen the false arrows,' I said. 'They were, you know, Lady Anne, similar in colour, length and size to the real arrows. One difference only. They did not have a point, neither bodkin nor broad-headed, but they had a pointed tip, painted in silver, that must have been virtually impossible to pick out. So how could you possibly distinguish the real from the false?'

'Mistress Anne, the queen wishes to speak to you,' said Lady Willoughby from behind me.

I snatched off my cap again and bowed at the queen's favourite lady-in-waiting. She gave me a smile, but waited until Anne had swung her long legs from the window seat and had begun to move towards the queen. Then she gave me another smile and followed the girl.

I was glad to see them both go. Harry would be an easier target for my questions than the young lady. I gave him no time to think.

'This is all rubbish, Harry, you know,' I said roughly. 'You couldn't possibly be certain that it was a real arrow, not by candlelight, not with those crowds of people milling about. And if it were, wouldn't you cry out an alarm? How could you possibly risk the king being shot with a real arrow if James, by mistake, had fitted it to his bow? That's treason, you know, risking the king's life,' I said warming to my subject, though I was a little sorry when I saw the hectic flush on his cheeks turn to livid spots of colour. He was white around his mouth and at the side of his nostrils.

'Look,' I said more gently. 'I know what it's like. I remember when I was about your age and I was deeply in love with someone, married to another man. You'll get over it, Harry. You and James, you have to do what your fathers want you to do. You're both to be betrothed for reasons of state; you to Mistress Mary Talbot, daughter of the Earl of Shrewsbury, and he to the lady there.' I jerked my head towards where Anne Boleyn was reluctantly accepting a piece of sewing from the hand of the queen.

'I would have thought that I could have chosen a wife for myself.' Harry's voice was sulky, but my heart leapt at his words.

'Perhaps you might,' I said soothingly, though I doubted it. Things didn't work out that way, not for the heir to an earldom. 'But, Harry, take my advice, take advice from a man much older than you. Don't take on the cardinal or the king. If it comes to a joust, you are not up to their weight.'

He had not, I noticed, reasserted that he had seen a real arrow in James's hand on the night of the pageant.

'I'm commanded to play chess with Gilbert Tailboys; come and support me,' I said, throwing a careless arm around Harry's shoulders. He had not denied the charge that he could not possibly have noticed whether it was a real or a mock arrow. Let him admit it, admit that he was unsure in front of a witness, and I might have the beginnings of a defence for my poor James.

He shrugged me off, however.

'I know what you want; you want me to take back my words. I did see the arrow,' he said, his tone loud and emphatic. I saw the queen look across the room. She had no objection to young men coming in to chat to the ladies, to play cards, or chess, to sing to the lute, but she was a stickler for good order in her rooms. I didn't want her to think that loud voices followed in my wake and so I went across and sat down at the red and white chess board in front of Gilbert Tailboys.

'We'll start again,' I said after a cursory look at the board with its exposed king and underdeveloped pieces. 'Pretty girl, your future wife, Gilbert, but not much idea about chess.' Quickly I set up the board, giving him the white pieces, and within seconds our two king pawns faced each other across the centre of the board.

'I've been promised a barony,' he said as he pushed out a second pawn to eye mine.

'Worth a lot of bad chess play,' I said flippantly. I moved my knight. I would allow him to take the pawn; I could always win it back later, but I wanted him relaxed and in a good mood. I noticed that the Spanish doctor Ramirez had arrived and was bowing to the queen. I saw them laugh together and guessed that she was teasing him about his late arrival.

'The wedding will be at Easter,' Gilbert said, moving out his king's knight's pawn. 'Will you still be here for it? If so, you would be very welcome to attend. The king himself has promised to grace our nuptials with his presence.' He said the last words stiffly, as though someone had taught them to him.

The least he could do after making the girl pregnant, discarding her, taking her little son away from her and then marrying her off to a man she had never met before. I felt sorry for Gilbert. He asked so little and lived with the terror that his father's insanity would be inherited by him. I would handle him gently, but I had to find out what he knew, I resolved as I turned back to the chessboard. I recklessly sacrificed the opportunity to exploit Gilbert's weakness on the king's side and offered him another tempting little pawn. 'I'm not sure whether I will be still here,' I said. 'It depends on whether this coil around James has been sorted out. I thought it was all nonsense in the beginning but what you told me has made me a little worried.' I advanced a bishop and allowed it to hang uselessly in the centre of the board. He flushed guiltily and bent his head.

'I don't blame you,' I said. 'You were in a quandary. It's just that I wonder how James found out about the secret, the one that Master Pace held over his head; do you know who told him?' I said, keeping my eyes averted from Gilbert and fixed on the board. The music from the lutes was loud enough now to cloak my voice, but I kept it low as I asked the question.

'Well, you probably know the secret, James thought that you might, but he said that you didn't know that he knew.' He had missed the tempting little gift of my bishop while he formulated this convoluted sentence. His mind was on other things. Although I kept my eyes down, I could sense that he looked up at me a couple of times, while I was pretending to study the board. I looked away, studied the picture of a woven David playing a woven harp on the arras hung to cloak the wall beside us and observed him surreptitiously from beneath my eyelids as I waited patiently for Gilbert to make his move.

This time he spotted the defenceless bishop and snatched it triumphantly from the board. The coup brought a rush of words to his lips.

'He was furious that nobody had told him before now. At least, he said that he had been furious first when he found out, but then, afterwards, he was thinking about it when he was riding back from Bristol to London, when he had come back from a visit to Ireland with the Earl of Surrey …'

'And what conclusion did James come to?' Coming back from Ireland. I knew now the answer to my question as to who had told James the secret. I said no more, though, and contemplated the board. I considered using the new Spanish move of castling but it might be unfamiliar to Gilbert and I didn't want him to lose his thread of thought. I moved my queen instead. She might be a useful weapon.

'Well, he thought – this is what he said – he thought that you all were probably acting for the best when you didn't tell him. He said you might even have thought that it didn't matter. He said that under Gaelic law, under Brehon law that it wouldn't matter that much.'

Very true. But Master Piers Rua Butler might be the son of an Irish mother, might be a fluent speaker of the Irish language, might employ lawyers and judges learned in old Irish law, what we called the law of the Brehons, nevertheless, he was a hard, ambitious man who knew that fame and fortune were in the hands of the English monarchy and that English laws of inheritance would prevail when it came to his heir. The earldom was of huge importance to Piers. He had been unofficially known in Ireland as Earl of Ormond ever since the death of his distant relative Sir Thomas Butler.

And, under English law the secret certainly did matter.

'It was his mother, I suppose.' Savagely I baited a trap for Gilbert's unprotected castle. He would be better off away from court, I reflected. He had neither the stamina nor the guile for the dangerous life that was led by the favourites of kings. Let him take his Bessie, shut his eyes to her past and settle down in the country and breed sons. Perhaps Piers Rua would have been happier if he had stayed at Polestown and not laid claim to Kilkenny Castle and an earldom.

Gilbert stared at my red queen in a perplexed fashion. 'I don't know,' he said almost absent-mindedly. 'Perhaps it was his mother. Just before he came over to England. Perhaps she thought he should know.'

I tightened my lips and swept his castle from the board. This matter was very, very serious. The motive would be established if Gilbert gabbled about this to anyone other than me.

'Speak to no one else about this, Gilbert.' I kept my voice low and my temper under control. 'You will put a noose around James's neck if you betray his confidence.'

'I resign.' He tipped his king over and rose to his feet. His face had a stubborn, angry expression and I feared that I might have mishandled the matter. I did not follow him as he walked away and perched on the window seat beside William Carey and his wife, Mary, the amiable sister of Anne Boleyn, but stayed where I was, eyes down on the chessboard as though studying the position.

And then I saw young Tom Seymour. He should have been at his studies, of course, but the death of the instructor of the wards had left the four young boys at a loose end. The young Earl of Derby, Edward Stanley, was there with him. His mother had been a lady-in-waiting to the queen, and Her Grace was reputed to have a motherly feeling for this orphaned boy. And Tom Seymour, ever an opportunist, came with him.

But that was not what interested me.

Tom Seymour had a knife in his hand. A long, thin, very sharp knife. He was displaying it to his friend.

I started to go forward, but then stopped and waited. Dr Ramirez had finished his conversation with the queen and was bowing deeply and backing away from her presence. I waited until he came close to me. And then I spoke in his ear.

'See that knife, in young Seymour's hand.'

He looked startled, but I saw a flash from his eyes and knew that he had understood my meaning.

'Yes, that's right. Just like that.' He whispered the words in my ear while I considered the best way to handle this. Tom Seymour was quick-witted and sly. I did not want to give him any food for gossip.

And then, while we both watched, Tom, accompanied by young Stanley, strolled nonchalantly over to the side of the room. He gave a quick conspiratorial grin at his friend and then rapidly he sliced the penis from one of the moulded *putti* on the waist-high frieze that ran across one wall of the room. The little naked figures, I noticed, seeing the brown mark where the incision had been made, were formed from that same leather mâché used in the making of the mock arrows. It had been skilfully painted in a blue-white colour so that the effect was that of stone.

In an instant I had young Seymour by the scruff of the neck, standing right behind him so that my action went unnoticed by the others in room. He had the sense to keep quiet and I allowed him a few minutes in which to get really worried about what punishment defacing a frieze in the queen's own room would incur.

And then I said in his ear: 'Where did you get that knife?'

Tom Seymour was used to trouble. His gaze into my face was limpid, as innocent as the leather mâché *putti* themselves.

'Just picked it up in the long gallery, that's right, isn't it, Edward?' he asked his friend, who nodded hastily and turned a shade of puce.

'Go and play with the monkey, Your Grace,' I snapped. He was a fairly stupid boy, the Earl of Derby, but the cardinal, very conscious of rank, treated him with a great show of ceremony and I did not want to get into the cardinal's bad books.

Tom Seymour watched as his friend made his way awkwardly up the room towards the queen. His dark-skinned face was inscrutable, mouth well under control, eyes hooded, but I guessed that his mind was working fast. The small leather mâché penis fell from his hand onto the floor and he made an effort to cover it with his shoe.

'Pick that up,' I said. I released his neck, but took a firm grip of his left wrist. He bent down obediently, but there was a slightly scornful twitch of his lips as he turned towards me and politely offered the scrap to me.

'Put it in your pocket. And I'll have this.'

He made no move to resist as I took the knife from him. Ramirez, the Spanish doctor, was a man of my own size, a big man, also, and together we towered over him. Tom looked from one to the other. His dark brown eyes twinkled and he had a deprecating look on his face. I viewed the knife. I had thought so when I had seen it in his hand and now there was no mistaking it. On the plain ash of the handle the owner's initial had been drawn and then burned into the wood. There was no mistaking that elaborate and ornate S. I hesitated for a moment, but then handed it to Ramirez. My first duty was to James. I would cope with other considerations later on.

I glanced around. The little Earl of Derby, small for his age, and fragile-looking, had obediently gone to play with Queen Katherine's monkey and the spectacle of boy and furry animal provided an excuse for the ladies to abandon their sewing and cluster around, cooing and exclaiming. The queen's attention was fully occupied. She would not miss us.

'Let's go and return this knife,' I said to Tom Seymour, still keeping a bruising grasp on his arm. I could see by Ramirez's face as he examined the knife that he had seen its significance.

'You know the owner.' Although we were now outside the presence chamber and walking through the ranks of yeoman who guarded the entrance to the queen's rooms, he still kept his voice very low.

'I think so.' But I knew. I remembered then what had been in my mind when Ramirez had described the knife that had made the fatal incision into the heart of Edmund Pace.

9

Susannah opened the door as soon as I knocked. Her face lit up when she saw me and it gave me a pang to watch the full lips parting and the sapphire blue of her eyes warming with pleasure.

'This young man has something to say to you.' I pushed young Tom roughly with a hand between his shoulder blades.

'Sorry,' said Tom immediately. I guessed that he spent most of his time saying that word to the adults in his life. It popped from his mouth with an automatic ease.

'Sorry for what?' She looked from him to me at the dark Spanish face of Ramirez and then back at me again. Her own face grew suddenly serious, and I guessed that she had seen something in his eyes, some shock, some regret, perhaps.

'Come in,' she said, standing back and we passed in front of her and stood around awkwardly while she shut the door. I went to the window on the north side and looked out upon the busy scene. The boys from the chandlery were delivering bundles of candles to the lodgings: for everyone entitled to a *bouche de court* there would be one torch, one pricket, two sises, these candles which gave such a very pure illumination, and one pound of white lights. These would have been delivered to my lodgings by the time that I got back – and in the drive for economy commanded by the cardinal, the used candle ends would be collected and melted down in the chandlery to make new candles. Colm, in my absence, would have signed for everything, forming the English letters with pride in his skill.

'Is this knife belonging to you, Madam?' I heard Ramirez ask the question but I did not turn around. The clerk of the spicery, for some odd reason in charge of the chandlery, had turned up and was checking the amounts in the flat barrows. There was an argument going on about a torch over the door to the fish house. I tried to focus my attention on the scene below, but every nerve was strained to catch her response.

'Yes, it is.' She sounded puzzled. I had the courage then to turn around and to look at her face. The blue eyes were lightly widened, looking from Ramirez to the sulky face of Tom Seymour. There was no suggestion of alarm or tension in her face. I joined them.

'This young man seems to have borrowed your knife, Madam, to deface some of the *putti* on the frieze in the queen's chamber,' said Ramirez

'Deface …' The word puzzled her and she looked from him to Tom.

'He cut off their …' I made a quick gesture towards Tom's hose and she fastened her teeth into her lower lip. She took the knife gently from Ramirez and then made a sudden lunge at Tom.

'Then maybe I chop you!'

'What!' He was young enough to feel alarmed. His eyes were widely opened with a mixture of terror and astonishment and suddenly her expression changed. The hint of smile in her eyes vanished. She stared at the boy intently, dropped the knife, snatched up a piece of charcoal and went across to the wall to the wooden panels where a Palestinian lake heaved with fish. As we watched, she sketched in the face of Tom, the tightly curled hair, the widely opened eyes and as the swiftly drawn lines multiplied, the expression of stunned amazement and of terror came out. Now she no longer looked back at him. Everything was focussed on her drawing, on the inner picture that she carried on her mind's eye of his shock and astonishment. He was to be a model for one of the fishermen of Galilee; I could see that once painted his dark eyes and jet black hair would suit her picture, but the real skill was in the swift capturing of a fleeting expression of astonished alarm when the four fishermen were summoned by Jesus. Ramirez and I watched her at work, and I could see my own admiration mirrored in his eyes.

By now Tom had recovered his poise and had begun to think that nothing too bad was going to happen. His face had regained its normal, slightly sulky, slightly defiant expression.

'There!' Susannah put in a final stroke with the charcoal, a line above the left eye, hastily smudged to a shadow with a fingertip and then she turned back to us. The knife lay on the table and absent-mindedly she went to replace it, slotting it into a wooden block. There were, I noticed, several slots empty and some of the knives bore the inscription 'LH'. Susannah and her brother Lucas seemed to share their knives.

'Master Tom Seymour says that he found the knife in the hall. Or did he steal it?' I watched her expression as I said the words. Her face did not change in any way.

'No, I'm sure that he did not steal it,' she said. Her mind was still on the fishermen of Galilee and she picked up the tiny paintbrush and put another coat of verdigris over the gilded skeleton of the fish. Now it was almost indistinguishable from the other fish and yet the half-hidden glint drew the eye. I remembered the queen's advice to me, last night, to stay with the cardinal. I hoped that I might be still at Hampton Court when the carpenters fastened these panels to the walls of the chamber and the whole large picture sprang into life.

'You think that he is speaking the truth when he says that he just found it in the hall?' Ramirez was looking sharply from her face to Tom's.

She shrugged her shoulders, smudged another of the charcoal lines, looking from her picture back to Tom. Then she frowned as though the words had just penetrated to her brain.

'In the hall?' she said absent-mindedly. 'I did not leave it there.'

'And Tom would have no business in your room.'

'No,' she said. 'I have never seen, never noticed him before.' Then she seemed to remember why we had brought him to her room and her lips slightly twitched. 'That was very bad, what you do,' she said to him. 'You should not do a thing like that.'

'Sorry!' Tom was good at this sort of thing. I had noticed him before, getting himself out of trouble for borrowing Harry Percy's horse and on the occasion

when the instructor of the wards had threatened him
with a whipping for an unauthorised visit to the man's
own room in order just to borrow, as Tom said plaintively,
a glass of wine.

'But the knife, Madam, where did he get the knife?
Is he speaking the truth?' Ramirez brought her back to
the question. It did not unduly bother her. I could see
that. In fact, I thought that most of her mind was still on
her picture, but that, of course, could be what she wanted
us to think. It was possible that her mind was busy thinking of an excuse. I was inclined to believe Tom. She had
obviously not seen him before so he had not frequented
the lodgings that the Horenbouts shared.

'Perhaps Lucas took it,' she exclaimed and then to
Ramirez, 'That is my brother. But I don't think so. Why
would he? He has his own tools. He is working on
some glass now for the new summer banqueting house.
He would have no reason to take a knife to the hall. Are
you sure you find it in the hall?'

'I swear by the Mass,' said Tom.

'But the Mass did not tell you to ... to mutilate my
little *putti*; that was the devil that made you do that!' She
rounded on him with a sudden return to savagery which
made him take a step backwards. 'Now, you go to the
kitchen. Go to the cook and beg, beg on your bended
knees, for some more of that fish water and fish skins
that he bring me yesterday, fish soup he call it. Two pints
boiled and boiled and we make some glue. You, you will
stand there,' she pointed to the brazier basin set into the
stone counter by the north facing window, 'and you will
stir and stir until it thickens enough to make good glue,
or else ...'

He was gone in an instant and we heard his footsteps scuttle down the stairs. Susannah laughed.

'I have a little cousin like him back in Flanders, a little devil,' she said and then her expression changed. 'Why are you so worried about this knife? Has there been another death? James has fled. I heard that.'

This took my breath away for a moment. She said it in such a calm way, almost as though there were a connection.

'This knife.' Ramirez took the lead. 'It's yours, is it not?'

'Yes,' she said and she watched him carefully. 'Yes, that is my knife.' She gave a cursory glance at the initials on the handle.

'What would you use a knife like that for?' asked Ramirez.

She shrugged. 'Many, many things,' she said evasively.

'To cut paper, cardboard,' I suggested. And I was conscious of the feeling of betrayal, almost of treachery. James was my concern but I could not help a sensation of guilt. She seemed such a lovely girl.

'Perhaps.' Her eyes were wary.

'So you might have brought it to the hall in case one of the masks was damaged.' I hated myself for pursuing the matter, but then there was James. I had to make sure that he was not wrongly blamed in this matter.

She thought about it and shook her head. 'No, I did not bring it. Why? It would be useless. A knife does not repair. It cuts.'

'You think that young Tom Seymour took it from here, from your room here? Or does he the truth tell?' Ramirez rushed out the question, stumbling a little over the English words.

She took only a second to answer that. 'Oh, no. I don't think that he took it from here. I think that he tells the truth. He has never been here, not even when I was absent. I saw the way he looked around. He was amazed, astonished at everything. And then I frightened him. Boys of that age will tell the truth when they are frightened about what may happen to them. He did not betray that he had stolen it. No, I do think that he just found it.'

'So how did your knife get left in the hall?'

'Was the man killed with a knife, not with an arrow?' That was not quite an answer, but it deflected attention from her.

And then when neither of us answered, she said, 'It makes more sense if the knife killed him, not the arrow. I went into the hall today to see the tapestry. It will need mending, my brother tell me. I hope I might be trusted to do it. And I think to myself it does not make sense. A man behind a tapestry shot with an arrow. He bring down the whole hanging when he fallen is.' Her English was deserting her as her intensity grew and she sounded worried.

'It may be,' I said carefully, 'that the instructor of the wards, Master Edmund Pace, was killed not during the pageant, but after it. When the hall was empty,' I added and watched the delicate colour in her cheek fade.

'Not when I was there,' she said. Absent-mindedly she snapped the stick of charcoal that she held and then put it aside.

'I think that I should tell this, but my brother said that we should keep out of trouble. That serjeant, the king's man, is a bad enemy to have, that's what my brother say.'

Why was the serjeant so eager to fasten the murder onto James? Susannah was on the verge of speaking. She glanced again up at the sketch that she had just done. I could tell that she was itching to get back to it, to paint in the face, to make the large brown eyes luminous with excitement and fear at the summons from the man on the shore, the sacred Jesus of whom they all had heard. It was going, perhaps, to be her masterpiece. She looked at the panels for a long moment. And then she looked back at me with resolution on her face.

'There was no man there, no man lying behind the arras, when I was there. I tell you that I stay behind to pick up pieces of arrows, scraps that had fallen, everything is of use to us artists; I even made a mosaic, once, you know, from pieces of eggshell! So everything that I find, I save. But before I leave, then I go back to the hanging. I felt it in my hand, I touched it. I examine the canvas that lined it, if there might, per chance, be a hole in the canvas lining there so that I could look behind it and see how the sketches were made, back to front … And I tell you that there was no hole, and what is more, there was no man there and the hole, the hole that is now in the centre of the wheel of the cart, that hole was not there when I looked.'

I took in a deep breath. 'That is very valuable evidence, Mistress Susannah,' I said. Even if it was true that under English law an accused man was guilty until he could get twelve honest men to swear that he was not present when the crime was committed, nevertheless, surely the evidence of this girl would be enough to clear my poor James. I turned to her, and I knew that my face wore a wide smile.

But she shook her head. 'It will not work,' she said. 'My brother is right. I should not have said this. The serjeant will not believe. He will not believe what I say.'

'Then I'll go to the cardinal,' I said hotly.

She shook her head again. 'He will not believe either.'
She looked into my face with a very straight, very direct
expression. 'You see,' she said, 'James and I were lovers,
once only, but that was once too many. And he, the serjeant, he knows all about it. Master Pace, the instructor
of the wards, he tell him. If you go to the cardinal, the
serjeant will tell him all about that affair and I might be
sent away from Hampton Court. I do ask you,' she said
with her eyes steady upon my face, 'not to disgrace me.'

Oddly my immediate reaction was one of anger. What
did that young fool James think he was playing at? What if
the girl had got pregnant? What did she see in him, anyway?
He was nothing but a boy. But my second thoughts were
sad. The girl was right. This would not be the way. I had
a feeling that I would have to fight hard to get James
acknowledged as free of guilt, that it might, perhaps be an
impossible task. The king's serjeant–at–arms was in the pay
of St Leger. He would strain every nerve to have the heir to
the Ormond earldom declared guilty of murder.

My anger and jealousy died down. James was in very
serious danger. The serjeant had Dr Augustine under his
thumb. Like all stupid people, the good doctor would be
reluctant to admit that he might have made a mistake
about the cause of death. Once again I turned my mind
towards getting the boy out of England. Even if the king
demanded that he be tried in Ireland, Piers Rua could, as
he had often done, set up a court with a Brehon as mag-
istrate and the verdict and punishment, if the crime were
to be proved, would be under Irish law. It would cost
Piers Rua a large sum of money, but James's life would
be safe.

I got to my feet. There was nothing more to be gained here. I was reasonably convinced that Tom Seymour had told the truth and that he had picked up the knife in the hall.

'We'd better go,' I said abruptly to Ramirez. And then, even more abruptly, to the girl, 'Where is your brother?'

'Gathering willow twigs for charcoal,' she said instantly. 'You will probably find him at the bakehouse now. They will have finished baking the bread for suppertime and they will allow that the charcoal can be baked overnight in the warm ovens.' She had understood that I was going to check on her story. Her manner was quite unlike her earlier easy-going and frank way of speaking. Now she was stiffly self-possessed and her eyes were hard. 'You can *verifieren,*' she added.

Ramirez took a polite leave of her, but I said no more. It was barely worth seeing the brother, but I followed my Spanish friend through the carpenter's yard and towards the enormous bake house. By now the chet loaves and the manchets had all been baked for supper and, swathed in towels, were being carried in wicker baskets towards the kitchens.

I recognised Lucas Horenbout instantly. Very like his sister, tall, Flemish-looking, the very same blue eyes, the same blonde hair. He did not look at Ramirez, but eyed me warily and I knew instantly that he had identified me.

'Yes,' he said. He had an iron casserole in one hand and its lid in the other. The basin was full of small pieces, each about four inches long, of willow twigs. I looked at them with a feigned interest.

'Your sister told us that you would be here,' I said. 'You are going to bake these twigs.'

He was wary, but he followed my lead. There were many bakers and kitchen boys around.

'That's right,' he said. 'The ovens are still piping hot. These casseroles will stay until morning and then the twigs will be turned to sticks of charcoal. If we are lucky!' and then he added with shrug, 'And if we are not lucky, well, we try again tomorrow morning after the dinner.'

We waited in silence as he handed the iron casserole over to one of bakers and slipped a coin into the man's hand, and then as he turned to go back, we fell into step, one on either side of him.

'We've been talking to your sister,' I said after a minute and then as his suspicious eyes flashed towards me, illuminated by the torch still burning on the corner of the carpenters' yard, I said hastily, 'We wondered about a knife found in the great hall. The knife had her initial on it, the letter S.'

'And …' He sounded hostile and I hastened to put him at ease.

'As you know, there was a man murdered there and we were anxious to know whether someone could have stolen the knife. It was found by a boy, Master Tom Seymour, one of the cardinal's wards, but he denies that he stole it. He says that he just picked it up in the hall. Your sister,' I said, with an eye on him, 'does not think that the boy stole it, but she wondered whether you might have borrowed it for some work in the hall.'

'I have no work in the hall.' Like his sister, his voice, under stress, became more Flemish and the smooth v sound in the word 'have' sound much more like a sharp Flemish '*haf*'.

'So you can't tell why the boy should have picked up, in the hall, the knife with the letter S engraved on its handle?'

'No.' His voice was curt and unwelcoming, but I persisted.

'Your sister, like you, has no idea why one of her knives should have been found in the hall.' I watched him carefully, but his lips were compressed and his eyes, hooded by drooping lids, were fixed on the shadows at our feet.

'I'm not sure why you are so interested in this knife, Master Lawyer. I understand that the man was killed by an arrow, by one of the young wards of Cardinal Wolsey,' he said and his eyes darted a sudden glance at me. A moment later they were, once again, fixed upon his feet, but we had just passed beneath a flaring torch and I had caught the sudden gleam from those pale blue eyes so like his sister's.

'There is no evidence as to that, no real evidence – what triggered this supposition was false information,' I said, keeping my voice as calm as I could.

'Well, I'm afraid that I can't help you. I haven't the slightest idea of how my sister's knife came to be left in the hall.' He turned from us abruptly then, crossing the carpenter's yard on the diagonal and seconds later I heard the door click.

'Suspiciously uncooperative,' said Ramirez.

'Or perhaps he just doesn't want his sister mixed up in a scandal,' I said, remembering what Susannah had said regarding her relationship with James. I could not blame the brother for not wanting his sister's name tied to this murder.

'Well,' said Ramirez, 'we don't seem to have got too far, today, after that interesting evening yesterday.' He sniffed the air, full of the sweet smell of newly baked bread. The wine, ale and manchet allowance for each of the lodgings was being trundled down the narrow passageway on these narrow flat barrows and the pungent smell of wood smoke rose from the tall brick chimneys with their twisted patterns outlined with icy traces of sleet.

'Time for a snack, a glass of wine and a quick rest. See you at dinnertime,' he said.

'I'll see you,' I responded, lifting a hand in farewell. It was, I supposed, all a bit of game to him. To me, it was of vital importance.

I gazed after him resentfully for a moment and then went in search for Gilbert Tailboys. He was, according to George Cavendish, at the tennis play with Thomas Arundel and Harry Percy, so I went off to join them.

Harry, stripped to shirt and hose was on the court and opposite was Thomas Arundel. For a moment I could not see Gilbert Tailboys, but then I spotted him in the 'dedans', the netted window where the spectators sit, and often lay bets on the match.

And beside him, in the 'dedans', was not Bessie Blount, but Anne Boleyn. I had to look hard to make sure of that, as the two shoulders were touching and the two heads were so seductively together and the girl's mouth was by the boy's ear. But there was no mistaking the outline. Only Anne wore the French headdress, delicately shaped to the head like a crescent moon. Today she wore a dark veil and in the gloom of the 'dedans' it merged with her black hair and formed a frame for the faultless pale oval of her face.

I watched for a moment. No one had noticed me. The two boys continued to thunder shots at each other, the heavy cork-filled ball ricocheting off the walls and roofs and striking targets. I withdrew into the shadows and made my way around the back of the tennis-play and crept softly into the 'dedans'. Neither Gilbert, nor Mistress Anne heard me. Harry had just hit the grille and was shouting aloud in triumph, his voice echoing again and again around the hall.

In a few moments I had crept into the seat behind Gilbert. I could see the back of his head, and the faultless profile of the lady as she spoke softly into his ear.

'Harry says that you are such a good friend,' she was saying sweetly. 'But, of course, you could not be a friend to a person who had committed murder, "*Les yeux hautains, la langue menteuse, les mains qui répandent le sang innocent* – hands that shed innocent blood" that's the English of what the Bible says, but the king's sister, a very learned lady, she translated it into French for us, and I think in French. They are very striking words, are they not? It would be a terrible sin, would it not, to try to protect someone like that? It would be something that you would have to confess, Gilbert, confess to the cardinal himself, perhaps even to the pope in Rome.' She seemed struck by that idea and repeated, 'You might have to go to Rome, and then, of course, you would no longer be able to marry Bessie. The king would find another husband for her.'

Gilbert turned a worried profile towards her. Down on the court Harry declaimed that the game was his, but neither of the pair in the gallery even looked in his direction. Gilbert stared at the young lady as fascinated as a snake faced by a mongoose.

'It takes courage, I know,' she whispered, 'but I could help you.'

What was she trying to do? I wondered about that, but not for long.

'Harry, Master Percy, says that you know why he did it. You know what drove James Butler to that terrible murder.' She took a scrap of lacy handkerchief from within her sleeve and dabbed at her eyes.

'My father wants to force me to marry James Butler, to marry a man who has murdered someone. I'm scared, Gilbert, Master Tailboys, I mean, I am so frightened. If a man has murdered once, he will murder again. I have heard that said.'

Mistress Boleyn had dropped her affectation of inserting French words in amongst the English ones. Now she was fluent and persuasive.

'I could not sleep last night,' she said in a voice that had a moving quaver to it. Once again she touched the handkerchief to her eyes. 'I was thinking that if I ever angered him after we married that he would murder me. He will murder me in my bed, perhaps. And I would be over in Ireland, hidden away from my family and my friends. He would murder me and hide my body in one of those bogs that they have over in Ireland. I would be never seen nor heard of again and if my family inquired, well he would tell them that I had run away with a wild Irishman.'

She gave a realistic-sounding sob at this terrible picture and I smiled grimly to myself in the darkness.

'Don't!' Gilbert's voice was husky with emotion. It was just as well that Mistress Bessie Blount was not nearby. His hand stole out and covered hers.

'I know, I know, I should be strong, but I am so frightened, Gilbert.' This time she did not change the name to 'Master Tailboys' but said his first name sweetly and seductively, pronouncing it in the French fashion, *Geelbare*.

'Harry says that you alone have the evidence to convict this murderer. He says that you know of James's terrible secret, that you know why he was being blackmailed and why he had to take life away from that man.'

'Good match, isn't it?' I said heartily from behind them. This was a conversation that should not allowed to be continued. Whatever about Gilbert's discretion, there was no way that I would trust to Mistress Boleyn. This projected match with James Butler was spoiling her chances of a possible union with the heir to the Earl of Northumberland. But not the strictest father could expect his daughter to marry a man accused of murder, so the lady was taking steps to get her freedom. I leaned forward and looked from face to face.

Meanly, I enjoyed the start that both of them gave. 'Good shot,' I yelled down as Thomas Arundel sent a ball crashing against the tambour and the angled buttress deflected it across the court. I was deemed enough of an expert to render my interference more of a compliment than an annoyance and Thomas, an amiable fellow, raised a hand with a slight bow in my direction.

'Yes,' I continued blandly, 'they are both playing well. You are interested in tennis, Mistress Boleyn?'

She cast me an annoyed glance from her black eyes. 'Certainly,' she said shortly.

'Or is it more exciting in France?'

'I suppose it's much the same game,' said Gilbert awkwardly after a long minute of silence from the lady.

'I do not like to talk while watching,' she said then.

'Really? Goodness, I must apologise. I thought that you were already talking. Did I make a mistake?' I saw Gilbert flush at my words, but Mistress Boleyn stared stonily ahead. The match was drawing to its conclusion. Harry Percy was out of condition or had been drinking too heavily the night before. Even from this distance I could see that he was pouring sweat, continually stopping to wipe his face, and when Thomas sent a shot down the floor of the court Harry just stepped back awkwardly and it skidded fast and low and struck the corner of his racquet.

'My point,' said Thomas triumphantly. 'Game, set and match.'

Without a word, Mistress Boleyn got to her feet and went back out through the door. Gilbert and I were left together in the semi-darkness, and neither of us said anything as we watched her come towards young Percy. She picked up a linen towel from the table and carefully, almost as gently as a mother, she mopped his face. He took it from her with a smile. The door opened, casting a broad stripe of light along the wooden floor and causing the candles in the man-sized candelabrum to flicker dangerously, and Harry's servant came in. She went away, then, but not before I had glimpsed a very tender look on her face. Everything within her, love, ambition, a dislike of having her course through life mapped out for her, everything, I realised, was pushing her to repudiate the projected betrothal with James Butler.

And she was a very strong-willed young lady.

I waited for a moment, watching while Harry towelled himself hastily, pulled on his fresh shirt, thrust his arms into doublet and then jerkin and rushed off. Thomas's servant now arrived and supplied him with towels and a clean shirt. He got dressed in a more leisurely way and then he went out also. The trumpeters sounded the warning. Supper would be in half an hour. It was time for all to get ready, but Gilbert did not move. He sat very still and gazed straight ahead.

'I wasn't going to tell her, you know,' he said.

'I'm sure that you are too good a friend to put a noose around James's neck,' I repeated my words of earlier as I got to my feet. I wished that I were sure of that. He had been, I reckoned, on the verge of betraying the secret, but perhaps I did him an injustice. It would, however, be no harm to remind the boy of the consequence of yielding to the lady's questioning.

10

The queen was to have supper in her own chambers this evening and she had invited the cardinal to share her meal. The rest of the guests from the court and the cardinal's household dined together at the first sitting in the great hall. George was in charge, very flushed with the excitement of his promotion and totally unable to quell the un-Lenten-like atmosphere of fun and of excess that gradually arose as no quelling glances were sent from the high table. Voices grew louder, servants scurried around, yeoman of the pitcher house were kept busy refilling cups and glasses. Harry Percy, Gilbert Tailboys, Anne Boleyn and Bessie Blount were on the high table. They formed one mess just across the tablecloth from me and I studied them anxiously. Gilbert was getting very drunk and I feared that it was not good for him. I knew very little about epilepsy, apart from a mention in Suetonius of the epilepsy that afflicted Julius Caesar, but I hoped that this excessive alcohol would not bring on another fit. Anne Boleyn was tempting him to drink more and more. She almost seemed to be flirting more with Gilbert than with Harry and I could see that Bessie was fast moving from a forced expression of amusement to tight-lipped anger. Once everyone rose to partake of the 'void' in the cardinal's room next door and allow the table in the great hall to be re-laid for the household officers, I went forward to meet the four of them.

'Just a minute, Gilbert,' I said, catching him by the arm and drawing him back. Mistress Boleyn gave me a quick glance from her black eyes, which I met with a bland smile. She put the tips of her fingers on Harry's sleeve and went forward with him. Again there was that swift upward motherly glance to check that he was well. He smiled down at her and there was a great sweetness in that smile. I began to see what they saw in each other. People are complicated. He fell in love with her milk-white skin, her black eyes, her swaying and graceful figure; she, I reckoned, originally may have been attracted by his position as the heir to the mighty earl, liked the warm colouring of his cheeks, the curl of his brown hair, but then his helplessness would have pulled down the barriers. Mistress Anne Boleyn had a pretty face, a sheaf of midnight black hair, a gorgeous figure and an alluring voice, but under all of that she had a strong nurturing instinct.

And Harry, poor fellow, disliked by his own father, was a lost boy in need of the tender care of a mother.

I looked after them with a tinge of pity. There would be no possible future in that romance, no matter how much the lady personified *Perseverance*' as she had done in the pageant of *Château Vert*. Life would have been easier for both of them if they had been boy and girl on neighbouring farms.

Bessie, with a contemptuous glance at Gilbert, hurried after them and I was left with an intoxicated boy drooping from my grip.

He was not the only one who was drunk. Queen Katherine's physician, Dr Ramirez was singing a quite impolite song in Spanish and as I passed him, he reeled and almost fell over, just saving himself by putting an arm on my shoulders.

'My friend, my Irish friend,' he hiccupped. 'We put our brains together. We …' he waved a hand.

'That's right, old fellow,' I said soothingly. 'We're friends. We'll have a game of tennis tomorrow. Just before dinner. That's the best time. I'll see you on the tennis play then.'

'No. Have to go tomorrow. Go home to wife and baby. Got something to tell you, first. Got idea. Heard something about you when I in the bayne tower was. Bathing very good for braining.' He giggled hysterically at this piece of wit and I managed an indulgent smile. The boys folding the tablecloths grinned at each other and then smoothed their faces when they saw me look at them.

'You talking to Her Grace, Queen Katherine, about St Leger and the king's serjeant …' The words seemed to erupt from his mouth and then he stopped and began to look very pale. I was relieved. Goodness knows what he was about to say. I interrupted quickly before he could resume.

'Now you go and have some of that nice Hippocras. Ramirez. You will enjoy that. You know how they make it, do you? I've been in the privy cellar,' I went on, desperate to stop him talking about St Leger. The Spaniard had a penetrating voice, even more so when he was drunk. 'You must go down there, one day, Ramirez. Go down to the privy cellar. It's the place that is used for sweetening and spicing wine to make hippocras. They say that it's good for the digestion, so go and have some before you get sick,' I babbled on.

'Yes, but, my friend, you are a judge, not a wine groom. Listen to me,' he stared at me owlishly.

'Yes, yes,' I said soothingly, but raising my voice to drown his, 'and, you know, Ramirez, the spices are put into a filter-bag. It's shaped like a cone and it's made from some sort of felted woollen cloth and they pour the wine and sweetened wine back and forth through the spices until the wine is clear. You'll love it, Ramirez.' I was running out of ideas to keep chattering and stop him blurting out things about St Leger. I was relieved when one the queen's gentlemen ushers, a man called Juan de Montoya came to my rescue, taking Ramirez by the elbow and leading him away, leaving me with my own burden, as Gilbert drooped heavily from my supporting arm.

Ramirez would have a headache in the morning and probably not feel too well. I wondered whether he would remember what he wanted to tell me about St Leger and the king's serjeant. Well, he was a doctor so he probably had some sort of medicine that would make him feel better. I had more important matters to see to. Firmly I steered Gilbert away from his friends, Thomas Arundel and the four younger boys who had been allowed the treat of dining at the high table this evening, and got him out in the fresh air. It was snowing slightly, the frozen flakes drifting down, clinging to the red brick walls and powdering the fountain courtyard at our feet. The fountain had been turned off during this cold spell, but the water in the basin had a thin skim of ice over it and the flakes fell softly on this, linen-white against the pale grey.

I wondered whether to walk Gilbert around for a while, or whether I should get him straight back to his lodgings and hand him over to the care of his servant. I decided that would be best. He had looked very green, but now as I examined him under the wavering light of the torch I could see that a faint trace of colour showed in his cheeks. Best to get him home before he decided to go back and join the alluring Mistress Boleyn again.

'Come on, Gilbert, let's get you into bed and you can have a good sleep.'

'Secret. What's the secret about James Butler?' muttered Gilbert.

'There is no secret. Gilbert, do you hear me? There is no secret.' I hissed the words into his ear. There seemed as though no one was around on this sleety evening, but I still spoke very quietly and hoped that the intensity in my voice would penetrate through the fumes of wine. 'Say nothing about James. If anyone asks you, say you don't know.' I took a firm grip on his upper arm and marched him towards the steps to his lodgings. I knew them well. He was housed next door to James and when I had got rid of him I went in to have a word with Padraig.

'Not a sign, not a word,' he said as soon as I put my head around the door. He looked strained and anxious. He and James had grown up together in Kilkenny. I had a picture in my mind of them both at about the age of ten, bare-footed and covered in mud, just back from a fishing expedition in the River Nore and slinking into the kitchen to see what was left over after dinner. I scrutinised him carefully. I would have thought that James, if he planned to escape back to Ireland, would have found some way of letting Padraig know.

'And his horse?' I asked.

'Still in the stable. Eating his head off with oats. I'd better take him out for a gallop soon if himself doesn't turn up.'

We stared at each other for a few minutes, each trying to guess what the other knew. Padraig was the first to break the silence.

'We'd better get him out of this place, Brehon,' he said. 'The cook, Master Beasley, was having a quiet word with me. He says to get him out of the country and back to Ireland. He thinks that the king's serjeant means business and he's a man who knows all the gossip. I'd say that there's more known in the kitchen about what's going on in Hampton Court than there ever is in the clerks' offices.'

He was right, of course.

'Keep James's horse in good condition,' I said. I looked around the room. Bread, ale and wine were piled up on the table. The boys who brought the *bouche de court* every morning and every evening were still supplying the lodging for man and master. 'Useful stuff, bread,' I said. 'I remember when the Earl and myself were going up visit the Earl of Tyrone, the country was in such a state of unrest that we took loaves, baked hard, and then when we were hungry we dipped them in ale.' I saw him nod and knew that he would set to work immediately, placing the bread in the covered iron pot that stood on the hearth. Once well-hardened, it would not go mouldy and would be perfectly edible when dipped in ale or wine.'

'I've got a good cheese here, too,' said Padraig with a grin. And I've taken in the saddle bags and the leather bottles. I have them all ready for when you give the word.'

'Good man!' I left him then and wandered out again. The second dinners would have been served by now and the kitchen staff relaxing after their labours.

'Tired of the fish, are you?' Master Beasley greeted me with a knowing grin when I came into the kitchen. 'Still hungry, I suppose.'

'We don't have all this fasting over in Ireland. Well, yes, Ash Wednesday, Good Friday … not the whole forty days of it.' I was not, in fact, hungry. The meals at the cardinal's table were, for a person like myself who liked to play tennis, far too engorging. But I welcomed the opportunity to talk to the cook. The kitchen was a very welcoming place with the three huge fireplaces throwing out warmth and light.

'I always say that there is nothing like meat. And, of course, if your conscience don't trouble you, well, why should you worry? In any case, the serjeant says that all who live under your kind of law in Ireland are doomed to go to hell so you might as well enjoy this life while you are here.' Surreptitiously he extracted a chicken leg from under a covered dish and I nibbled at it with an appearance of huge enjoyment.

'Why does the serjeant say that I'm going to go to hell?' I enquired, sounding, to my satisfaction, quite at ease. A cup of the cook's own private supply of wine had appeared and I tasted it with appreciation.

'He says that murderers should be hanged and that by your law they are only fined. Mind you,' the cook lowered his voice. 'I think that it's a hard law we have here. Many a decent man or woman have dangled on the end of the rope. There are reasons for killing some-one. And sometimes it can be a good reason. A man can kill another man to defend himself, to defend his property or his life itself. A woman can kill a man because he rapes her or tries to rape her.' He looked sombrely out of the window.

'Men can be beasts,' he said unexpectedly. 'When my daughter was a young woman I used to tell her to carry a sharp knife when she walked the streets, a sharp, thin knife, no weight, no bother. "You'll get me hanged," she used to say. "I'd prefer to pray."'

'Or scream,' I suggested. I wondered what Master Beasley's daughter looked like. He was a massive man, himself. As tall as myself, but very much broader.

He shook his head. 'I used to say to her: "Scream or pray all you like, but have that good sharp knife in your hand and be prepared to use it."'

Reflectively I bit the remaining meat from the chicken leg with my front teeth and washed it down with some more wine. What was he trying to tell me? Warning me not to investigate too deeply into this matter of the death of the instructor of the wards. Did he know something that I did not? No women worked in the kitchens at Hampton Court, not even in the pastry or the confectionery. The queen's ladies, of course, had been present, but they were carefully chaperoned and there would be no question, no possibility of rape by such as Master Edmund Pace, a middle-aged and rather ugly man, on whom these young ladies would not even think of bestowing a glance, not to mind a conversation.

But there was one woman who worked within the walls of Hampton Court. And she had in her possession a sharp, thin knife just as Master Beasley described it. Susannah Horenbout might be considered by the instructor of the wards as fair game. She worked for her living as he did. She visited the kitchens often; that was obvious. Most of the materials for her paints and her glues came from there.

And in between the larders, the boiling house, the kitchens, the saucery, the spice house and the bakery were small dark passageways. A girl could easily be seized in a doorway by a man who was stronger than she and who was determined to have his way.

'It is a cruel law,' I said curtly. I didn't want to think about the picture that he had evoked. I had to clear James, but when I reflected that it might be at expense of hanging another my mind quailed.

I might, of course, manage to get James out of the country and back to Ireland, back to the land known as the Pale, but that wouldn't finish matters. The English were still nominally in charge there. And their deputy, the Earl of Kildare was continually at war, not just with the native Irish, but with his cousins, the Desmonds and the Butlers. If he got a message to say that James Butler was wanted for murder then he would be only too pleased to start a war against his old enemy, Piers Rua Butler. And this would cause deaths – not James's death, but his father's also, perhaps. And, even at the very least, it would put an end to the ambition to remain in possession of the earldom of Ormond.

'I'd hate to see that nice young fellow dangle at the end of a rope,' said Master Beasley. He cast a quick glance around. Most of the kitchen staff had gone for their dinner. There were only a few pot boys left, industriously and noisily scrubbing at the pans and pots over one of the still red-hot fires. There was a cloud of steam and smell of strong lye around their heads and they were shouting merrily at each other. He pushed a small whole cheese over towards me and I concealed it under my cloak.

I had a sudden flash of inspiration. It might be easier to get a boat to Calais, than to do the obvious thing and make for Bristol. I could visit Richard Gresham in the city of London, draw out some money from him and then we could get a boat to Calais. The cardinal would, I was sure, give me an introduction to Sir Edward Guildford, Marshal of Calais. I might be able to get hospitality in his household while waiting for a ship to Ireland or even a position, perhaps, for the two of them. James, despite his lame leg, was an expert bowman and Padraig could turn his hand to anything. I would not mention James at any stage to the cardinal, I decided. The cardinal could not afford to go against the king's justice. But there was no reason whatsoever why I should not visit Calais before I went back to Ireland, and armed with the cardinal's blessing, I would be welcome as a guest in any household there. Calais still remembered the cardinal and the magnificence of the 'Field of the Cloth of Gold', where he set up a splendid tented village where the King of England and the King of France could meet and talk and have fun and games together. I had seen some of the sketches and paintings of the event and guessed that Calais would never forget the event nor the name of the man who had masterminded everything. 'The cardinal's signature was on two thousand pieces of paper,' George Cavendish had boasted to me when telling me about the event.

It would be a good idea, but it was an idea that I would keep secret between myself and the cardinal. Let the chase go down the road to Bristol. James and I, once I had found him, would make our way south towards the port of Dover.

'Were you one of the cooks at the Field of the Cloth of Gold?' I needed some more information about Calais and information was always easy to get from Master Beasley.

'Of course I was. Most of this household have been with the cardinal for years and years. Wouldn't serve another master, none like him. Myself, the serjeant, the chamberlain, the steward, the treasurer, all of us have been with him even before he built Hampton Court. You should have seen that sight in Calais – well outside Calais – nearly two years ago, it would be. It was June. I do remember that size of that bread oven, they built. Like a small house …'

'And the cardinal shipped everything over by ships, did he?' It was always easy to get this man to talk. I had noted his words about the king's serjeant's opinion of me. The cardinal liked me, but I was a stranger, a foreigner. He had given me until Monday, but after that he would trust to that man who had been in king's service for more than ten years, to solve this murder and to hand the culprit over to the law. 'I suppose it would take a long time to go by boat to Calais,' I added in a careless fashion.

'Not a bit of it! We were over in twenty-four hours, if my memory is right. Though the weather was kind to us – I'll have to admit that. But it's never too bad a journey, they say. It's not like going to Ireland, you know. The Earl of Surrey's cook tells me that his master is always complaining about that journey when the king, God bless him, sends him to Ireland to sort things out over there. No, Calais was pleasant. I enjoyed the trip. Had a good rest, too, on the way back. Tired out, we all were. It was no joke cooking for that lot over field fires with a tent for a kitchen.' Master Beasley looked around the neat order of his kitchen with the fires burning steadily, the tripods and the spits clean and ready for work, the charcoal ovens glowing gently and the tables scrubbed and ready for chopping and mixing.

'Well, some day, perhaps. I'd like to see it before I go back to Ireland.' I took a manchet from the basket.

'Try some of this cheese. We get it all the way from Gloucester. His Grace is very fond of it. If you like it, I'll send a ball of it over to your lodgings. Just the thing if you were to go on a long ride.'

'Thanks.' I got to my feet. I had no intention of confiding my plans to the cook. A nice man, but a great gossip, and information is currency to a gossip. I didn't want rumours flying around the courts and lodgings that I was going on a journey. This escape had to be done quickly and slickly and not divulged to any except to Padraig and Colm. The cardinal would not want to know. I half-smiled to myself as I went back towards the great hall. I could just imagine how he would hold up his hands and widen his eyes with horror when the story of my departure was brought to him.

The great hall was in almost darkness. There were a few candles burning on side tables but their glow was lost in the immense space. My own head and shoulders etched a black shadow on the wall. The hall was probably like this, empty, lit only by firelight on the night when Edmund Pace had been killed. It would have been about this time of the evening. I remembered the serjeant's words – stiff as a board, dead for at least twelve hours. Not while the pageant was on, of course, but later on. The use of the knife had made that certain.

But why had the man not cried out? Surely there would have been a moment between the producing of the knife and the fatal blow.

Unless, of course, Edmund Pace, a middle-aged man, had tired of the antics of the young and had slipped away from the sugar banquet, away from the music and the dancing afterwards, had come back into the hall, found that all had been cleared away and cleaned up, that the barrow of wood had been delivered to keep the fire going during the night watches. And Susannah? When exactly had she left the hall? By then, I hoped, but I could not be certain as I turned my thoughts back to the dead man.

And so he came in here, into this warm, dimly lit hall and he would have perhaps settled himself in a comfortable chair by the fire and had fallen asleep.

His murderer, a victim, perhaps, but still a murderer, had come in, seen his enemy there, asleep, had taken out a knife and thrust it through the man's heart.

There was a big chair beside the fire, shielded by a wooden-framed screen from draughts coming from the doors at the back of the hall. This chair would be the first choice of a solitary man in that large room. I crossed the floor and stood beside it. It was upholstered in leather, a dark brown leather. I picked up a candle from a side table and held it in my hand, moving it up and down and then feeling with my fingers. There was nothing: no stickiness, no change of colour as far as I could see. I replaced the candle and crossed to the end of the room, beside a screen. The cardinal had made provision for everything, including accidental fires. Behind the screen were a couple of iron buckets, each filled to the brim with water.

If blood had spurted from the wound, then the chair and floor could easily have been cleaned after the body had dragged away to its hiding place behind the tapestries. I moved the screen a little, just enough so that I could see the length of the hall, seated myself on the chair and stretched out my legs like a man who felt drowsy, closed my eyes experimentally. It would be easy for a man who had eaten a large supper and had swallowed numerous cups of wine to drop into a profound sleep quite quickly. There would be music and the sound of merry voices from the cardinal's chamber, but that would just form a backdrop.

And when I heard music and laughing voices, for a moment I almost thought that it was my imagination, but it wasn't; there were clear sounds from just outside the door. Gilbert, Thomas Arundel – I could hear them and Francis Bryan's high-pitched laugh, Harry Percy, stammering slightly over the word 'Anne' and then the voice of Tom Wyatt, a rich, smooth voice rising high above them all. I was no musician, but I liked the spare sharpness of Wyatt's verse and listened now, waiting for the punchline, the inevitable unhappy ending to all of his tales.

> Why sighs thou, heart, and wilt not break?
> To waste in sighs were piteous death.

There were a few uncertain giggles and a silence for a moment and then door opened. Tom Wyatt went on singing his verses but I was sharply aware only of the slight, graceful figure of Anne Boleyn. The light from the corridor glowed on the rich silk of her crimson gown and on the small heart-shaped cushion that she bore triumphantly aloft.

And then the door was gently pulled shut from outside. The song continued from behind the closed door, the lute forming a plaintive accompaniment. The girl had not seen me and I watched her as she prowled around the room, the heart still held in her hand. She seemed to be searching for something and she paused for a moment in the centre of the room and stood looking around its walls. It would, I guessed, take a minute or two for her eyes to adjust to the light. She moved uncertainly and then picked up a candle and stood holding it. The pinpricks of light glittered in the pupils of her eyes for a second and then she held the candle at arm's length and moving it backwards and forwards, examining the wall opposite to her.

And then she seemed to come to a decision. Wyatt had begun to sing his song again and the sound came sweet and low through the closed door.

Comfort thyself, my woeful heart,

He sang as Anne moved forward resolutely and placed the small heart-shaped object into a large silver chalice that stood on the wooden buffet between the windows. She replaced the candle on the table, but still she lingered, a shadowy figure now.

To waste in sighs were piteous death.

There was a torch outside one of the windows, placed to give light to the passageway leading to the chapel. I had noticed earlier how it had cast a precise outline of the window frame onto the floor and now the leaden bars were etched across the girl's figure with one black bar across her throat. She stood very still for a moment and then moved quickly to the door and flung it open.

Alas, I find thee faint and weak.

Wyatt led the way, still strumming the lute and then others followed, each carrying a candlestick, hands showing pale in its light, eagerly dashing from one corner to the other, raising the candles high up and casting dark shadows on the polished boards beneath their feet. Harry Percy was last and I saw Mistress Boleyn turn towards him, deliberately lifting her hand in the gesture of one drinking and then when he stared at her, she moved her head slightly, indicating the buffet. He smiled, a flash of white teeth from behind the candle flame and went straight over and plunged his hand into the silver chalice, holding up the crimson heart with a cry of triumph.

'Is this the latest game at court?' I rose to my feet as suddenly as I could and looked for a reaction.

The trouble was that I got too much of a reaction. One of the Howard girls almost fainted. Margaret Dymoke screamed. Lucy Brown spilt a long, lacy curtain of wax from her candle all down her green satin gown, Bessie Blount gave a moan of terror and Wyatt plucked a discord from his lute.

But I had to admit that neither Anne Boleyn nor Harry Percy showed as much emotion as any of the others. In fact, they hardly noticed me. The boy was bemused, holding up the crimson silk heart and she, well, she hardly took her eyes from his flushed face.

A man rising from a sleep on the chair by the fire seemed to evoke no bad memories in them.

I got to my feet and made my way towards the door. It was time to have a good night's sleep and let a fresh mind deal with the problem.

11

There was no one around when I made my way towards my lodgings. Apart from a few giddy youngsters, the rest of the inmates of Hampton Court were probably in their beds and fast asleep. A rush of damp cold air hit my face when I opened the door and I guessed that a heavy fall of snow was on its way. It was a very dark night, with not a glimmer of light from the moon or stars. I felt my way carefully through the gateway and into the clock court. The path beneath my feet was still icy in some places and I decided against crossing it, but stayed close to the wall, taking care to stay within the light of the wall torches as I tentatively slid one foot in front of the other until I reached the clock tower archway. There was something abnormal about that, something strangely and unusually dark, and it took me a moment to realise that the torch on the far side had been extinguished. I moved forward and then stopped at the far side.

The whole of the Base Court was in complete darkness.

Cardinal Wolsey, a hospitable man, had not only built quarters for the king and for the queen, and for their courtiers and waiting staff, in his palace of Hampton Court, but had also built, just inside the great gatehouse, the Base

Court which had forty-four lodgings for ambassadors, their staff and other guests. At this time I was one of the few occupying one of those lodgings, nevertheless, on every other night the torches had burned at regular intervals around the court until they were extinguished at dawn.

One torch might have blown out by accident, but not ten.

There was something about the deep darkness and utter stillness that made me feel uneasy. It would be possible to feel my way to number fifteen, but an instinct stopped me and made me stand, hesitant, sheltered beneath the clock tower.

'Coward,' I said to myself, grimly amused, but I did not have to give the matter much thought. I had seen how St Leger glared at me, had seen the appraising look of the king's serjeant, a look that he gave to his opponent on the tennis court. And then there were the indiscreet, drunken ravings from the Spanish doctor, Ramirez, which could have been overheard by anyone. I just did not want to cross the midnight blackness of that court without a light in my hand.

The cardinal's serjeant, John Rushe, like his sister Alice, lodged in the clock tower. I would beg a light from him, I decided and went back in through the doorway. A yeoman, just inside the doorway, was dozing peacefully on a chair in the hallway. I did not disturb him. There was something odd about every torch on the Base Court, where I lodged, being extinguished and I wanted John to see it for himself.

I knocked on his door and he opened it immediately. He showed no surprise at seeing me and I noted that he was fully dressed.

'Did you take the bow and the box of arrows belonging to young James Butler?' His abruptness took me aback.

'No, of course not, why should I?' I had not thought to look for James's bow. I supposed he had left it beside butts when he had heard the arrival of the barge. It must have been brought to the guardroom after he had made his escape

'I thought that you might have wanted to return it to him.'

'Don't be stupid, John,' I said irritably. 'If I wanted to reclaim James's property I would have asked you for it. So how was it taken? Stolen, I presume.' I glanced down at the lock to his door. It looked untouched.

'I ordered it to be placed in the guard room,' he said after a pause.

'I see,' I said.

The guard room was next door to John Rushe's lodgings. It was used as a place to confine a belligerent drunken man overnight, or an unruly offender before he could be sent under guard to one of the London prisons. Normally the room was locked. Now it stood open with what looked like John's keys in the lock.

'I found it was unlocked; I was checking doors,' he said. I bit back a smile. Alice and I often joked about John and his obsessive checking. I was a bit annoyed about that valuable bow and the arrows being stolen, but John would probably get it back. He would scour every square yard of Hampton Court in his search. I walked across and looked in. The room was bare, with nothing but a straw pallet and a bucket and I reckoned that would be the way

it was always kept. It seemed an odd place for a thief to
come looking for booty. I wondered whether there was
any possibility that John had accidently left it unlocked.
Unlikely. He was a careful man. Still James would not be
needing his bow for a while.

'Only I and the king's serjeant have the key to this place,'
said John and there was a worried frown on his face.

I stiffened. Why should the king's serjeant steal James's
bow? More evidence to be piled up against him? What
devilry was being planned now?

'Lend me a torch, John, like a good fellow,' I said. 'Some
idiot has extinguished all the torches in the Base Court.'

He swore. It seemed like the last straw to him. He left
me standing there as he went down to berate the yeoman
and when he came back his face was bright red. Grimly
and without a word, he pulled out one of the wall torches
outside his room and preceded me down the stairs.

The chastened yeoman was already relighting the
torches up by the gatehouse when we came out. I was
struck again by how cold and damp the air felt. It held
that strange stillness that sometimes occurs just before
snow falls and my unease doubled. It was impossible, on
such a still night, that all the torches in the Base Court
had been extinguished by anything other than deliberate
intent. And why just the Base Court?

'You don't think young James came back for his bow?'
asked John.

'Unlikely,' I said. 'Why should he put himself at risk?
The bow is not that valuable.'

He did not reply to this, just continued on, crossing
the court with confident steps, holding the light aloft. I
was behind him, but I was the first to exclaim.

Looking back at it, I realised that, subconsciously, I had been expecting something like this. John's eyes were darting here and there, checking to see that yeoman was doing his task efficiently, checking to see whether any mischief-maker was lurking in the darkness, poised to make a quick escape under the clock tower.

But I had my eyes fixed on the front door of my lodgings and so I was the one who cried out: 'There's a man lying there, just a few feet from my doorway!'

John quickened his step, holding the torch high and then stopped. A little light came from the window of my lodgings and it shone on the dark figure slumped there. A man, a big man, wearing a dark cloak, a face turned up to the sky, a man of my own size.

And an arrow protruded from his chest.

John lowered the torch. 'It's Ramirez,' he said, but I had already known.

The Spanish doctor must have, in a drunken impulse, decided to visit me. We were much the same size and shape and in the darkness he had been taken for me. That was my immediate thought.

'He had a wife and a new baby,' I said and heard my voice crack. John gave me an uneasy look and then signalled urgently to the yeoman. I avoided the body, went forward and hammered on the door of my lodgings. It was immediately answered. Colm, my servant, I had expected would be in bed and asleep. I had my own key and would let myself in. But he was wide awake, dressed, but hastily, I thought, noting the wrinkled hose and unbuttoned doublet. He had a scared look on his face and oddly did not even glance at the corpse and the men that gathered around it.

'I don't know anything about this,' he said hastily. His voice rang out in the quiet darkness.

'Don't be a fool,' I said roughly. 'No one thinks that you do. Did you hear a knock, any sound or any voices? Did you see anyone hanging around?'

He shook his head, but the frightened look persisted. He was not very old and perhaps two murders were too much for him. I gave him a pat on the back and told him to bring out a lantern. I would get more out of him when he was on his own. Leaving the door open for the extra light, I returned to John.

'Do you think that he was taken for you?' John bent down and touched the arrow almost as though he expected that this, also, would fall away from the wound. Colm came over, held the lantern high in a shaking hand. Now we could all see the arrow, lodged deep within the man's chest, but showing, just next to the fletched end, the two black initials: JB.

I didn't answer John's words. I was busy looking around the Base Court, looking into the shadows. The man who had fired that arrow was a man who would stop at nothing. He was a man who would take a chance.

'He took a terrible chance, committing a crime here where people come and go,' said John echoing my thoughts.

'Maybe,' I said. And then, thinking back to my law training, 'There are three people who do a reckless deed,' I quoted aloud. 'There is the man without fear; the man without hope and there is the man who has powerful protection.' I looked at John carefully and saw him flinch. I wondered how much he guessed. He had been present at the supper, had probably heard the drunken words of

Ramirez, no doubt but that he knew the king's serjeant and St Leger were thick as thieves.

'Young Master Butler's arrow,' he remarked.

'But not fired by him,' I countered.

'No, no,' he said absently. 'No, that was one of the arrows that I had in my custody. It's the arrow that fell from the wound in Edmund Pace's chest. Look,' he took the candlestick from Colm's shaking hand, 'look, just there, on that feather, there's a tiny smudge of blood. I noticed that. You can see that it is black blood, old blood. That blood has been there since the murder of the instructor of wards. And the arrow has been safely locked in my guardroom ever since.'

He had been speaking almost to himself, but then he became aware of Colm.

'Go back inside, my lad, this is nothing to do with you, don't you worry,' he said with a rough attempt at kindness and then when the door had closed behind my servant, he stood, irresolute for a few seconds. Very unlike him. He was normally a man of quick action.

'John,' I said after a moment. 'What's worrying you?'

He gave himself a slight shake, almost as though to shrug off his troublesome thoughts. 'Nothing,' he said defensively. And then he raised his voice and called his yeomen. I noticed a few lights come on in the clock tower. One of them was Alice's and I determined to go there and to talk with her. This affair was getting very dangerous. I had to see Colm, first, though, so I went back into my lodgings.

Colm had made no attempt to get ready for bed. He was standing, gazing through the window. His eyes were troubled and, I noticed, there was a distinct tremor in his hand when he lifted his arm to close over the curtain.

'Colm,' I said and then I stopped myself. His room, the outer room of the lodgings, was very dim, lit only by the glow from the fire. A man standing at the window, about to close the curtains, perhaps, might not be spotted by the assassin who crouched in a dark doorway on the opposite side of the court, crouched there with an arrow slotted through the bow, ready to shoot once his victim was on the doorstep. That was the way it had been. St Leger, probably with the connivance of the king's sergeant, had unlocked the guard room, removed James's bow and arrow, blown out the lanterns and then when a tall figure with hood over his head crossed the Base Court towards my front door, St Leger shot him.

'You saw his hair, I suppose, when he stepped forward to take aim. That silver bush of hair would catch any little stray gleam of light. And the lights under the clock tower were still lit so it wouldn't have been complete darkness. You saw his hair, didn't you, Colm?'

Colm gulped noisily. 'I'd like to go home if I could, Master, if you are thinking of sending Master James back to Ireland,' he said and I remembered that he was barely sixteen years old.

'So you shall, Colm. Don't worry, I'll take care of you. Keep close to me and there will be no problem. But it was him, wasn't it, Colm? It was the man who tried to shoot James. Sir George St Leger, it was him, wasn't it, Colm?'

He stared ahead and I could see that his face was white. I took pity on him. He was in a strange country, a place where everyone spoke a strange language and where customs were strange and where the people who surrounded him were mostly strangers. I squeezed his arm. 'Good boy. Now go to bed. I'll be back in twenty minutes, don't worry. Serjeant Rushe has all his men out there looking for the assassin. You will be quite safe.' He went without a word, but as he stripped off his doublet, I heard his teeth chatter.

'You'll leave a man on duty here, tonight, John, won't you?' I asked when I came back out again.

'Of course I will,' he snapped. 'Don't try to teach me my job, Hugh. There's someone loose with a bow and a quiverful of arrows, and I mean to find the scoundrel.' There was an uncertain note in his voice, though, and he had a baffled expression on his face.

'My servant is worried,' I said mildly.

'You're the one who should be worried,' he said harshly. 'I'd say that you have escaped with your life.' He paused for a moment and then said, rather hesitantly, 'Come with me to the cardinal, will you, Hugh? The queen will have to be told and he is the man to do that.'

I stood aside as he barked out some orders and then I walked to the clock tower archway and waited for him there. I could not bear to wait around and watch the poor dead body of a man, poor Ramirez, who had been so full of life and fun, carried, like dead meat, to repose in that frozen cellar.

Lights were burning in the cardinal's rooms. We could see them when we came out into the Clock Court. According to George Cavendish, His Grace had often worked right through the night and I felt sorry that we were about to add to his burdens. Cardinal Wolsey looked his usual benign self, though, when we were ushered in by a sleepy yeoman. Glasses of wine were produced and warm seats by the fire organised before he turned an enquiring face, not to me, but to John.

'There's been another murder, Your Grace.'

The cardinal's eyes went from him to me and then back again to John.

'It's the Spanish doctor, the queen's doctor, Your Grace. He was killed in the middle of the Base Court, perhaps on his way towards Hugh's lodgings.'

'By mistake for Hugh.'

'Could be.'

'We're about the same height and shape,' I put in. 'And all of the lanterns in the Base Court had been extinguished, presumably to hide the assailants.'

'Assailants,' he repeated, slightly emphasising the final s.

'Or assailant,' I amended, though there were two figures in my mind.

'How was he killed?'

'Bow and arrow. The arrow was marked JB, just like the one that killed the instructor of the wards. The same one, I think.' John went into a laborious explanation about the bloodstain while the cardinal thought hard.

'Too late to speak to the queen tonight,' he said after a minute. 'I'll do it first thing tomorrow morning.' He pondered for a moment and then raised his head.

'Thank you, John,' he said with finality and John got to his feet.

'Thank you, Your Grace.' He hesitated by the door, but I had not moved so he went out, shutting the door very quietly behind him.

'And now he'll go straight to Alice's rooms and ask her what he should do.' The cardinal smiled gently to himself, and then looked across at me.

'You're in danger, Hugh,' he said. 'Until this matter is cleared up, you are in danger. And James is in even greater danger. You are just the pawn, a pawn to be rid of, James is the target; the king you might call him if we are talking about a chess match.'

'The target,' I repeated. And then aloud, 'Is an earldom worth risking death?'

The cardinal did not answer this. 'They will make a case against James if they can lay their hands on him. They will accuse him of the murder of Edmund Pace. And they will find a good reason for the murder. He was a blackmailer, my instructor of the wards, that was it, wasn't it? And he had something on James. No,' he lifted a white bejewelled hand, 'No, don't act the innocent with me, Hugh. I can see how anxious you are and, no, I don't want to know anything about it. I can't interfere, you can see that, can't you? I have to uphold the king's justice. There are enough people who would love to pounce on any minor sin of mine, any hint that I had bent the law to suit my own purposes, to favour a friend or a protégé – well, I just can't do it, Hugh. I've gone as far as I can go. The rest is up to you.'

I nodded. I appreciated his straight talking.

'No, no, of course, not,' I said soothingly. 'You've been so kind to me, so hospitable. I've enjoyed staying here and meeting the members of the court, seeing a different land. I'm a man,' I said, watching him carefully, 'who loves to travel, loves to see new places, see strange buildings, admire the art of far-flung places. You'll hardly believe this, Your Grace, you who have travelled so often to France, you will hardly believe that I have never been to Calais. Normandy, Brittany, Bordeaux, yes, but never Calais. The cook, Master Beasley was telling me all about the Field of the Cloth of Gold and how you got him to prepare meals in a tent and all about the two thousand sheep and everything else that they cooked on that field. He told me that it didn't take too long to get there, too. Twenty-seven ships embarked at Dover at dawn and you were all safely in Calais by midday, that's what he told me. And your signature on two thousand pieces of paper, according to George.' I smiled blandly at him.

'Well, we can only hope that it was of use in the end and that these two kings can live in peace with each other,' said the cardinal with a sigh. And then with a sudden change of voice, just as though an idea had this moment popped into his head, he said casually, 'You should see Calais, Hugh. You're right. It is interesting to see foreign places. A man should travel as much as he can while still young. When you get to my age, of course, you just want to stay at home, say your prayers and make peace with your maker. But you, you are still young. Go to Calais.' Cardinal Wolsey, according to George Cavendish was in his mid-fifties, younger than my own father, but he loved to speak of himself as an old, old man.

'Do you know, I'd love to do that? What an excellent idea!' I spoke as though the thought had just popped into my head also and I saw the twinkle in his eyes.

'Well, so you must. Now, you may not go for months yet, but while I think of it, let me give you a pass for Dover and also pen a note to Sir Edward Guildford in

Calais. I find these days that if I don't do something on the spot, it gets pushed to the back of the long list of matters. Hand me my tablets, Hugh, will you?'

'You're very kind,' I said when he scrawled his signature, *Thomas Cardinalis* and added his seal. This would guarantee me a good reception in Calais and there would be no questions asked about anyone in my company. James could be my secretary, my gentleman usher, my page, anything like that. I packed the cardinal's letter safely away in the purse at my waist and looked at him interrogatively.

'And I have your blessing, Your Grace, is that right? So as to speak,' I added hastily. I had already confessed to him that I was not particularly pious and his response was to tell me that he was too busy a man to worry about his guest's religious feelings as long as the guest kept them to himself.

'But not a follower of Luther, I hope,' he had asked hastily. 'My master, the king, does not like that man.'

'Wouldn't dream of it,' I assured him, but didn't mention that I was no follower of the pope either. I, and most of my family, tended to follow the easy-going rule of the old Celtic church, where priests could marry and where ancient festivals, gods and goddesses merged imperceptibly with their Christian equivalent.

'And you have money to fund your trip?'

His kindness gave me a good opening. 'I have a draft from Sir Piers Rua on a merchant banker in London, Sir Richard Gresham, so I might just go up to the city tomorrow morning,' I said in a casual manner.

'Borrow my barge, if you wish.' He had risen stiffly, stretched himself, looked out of the window at meagre snowflakes still drifting, feather-like, down onto his knot garden below the window, but then sat down again with a weary sigh, stamped another piece of paper for the barge, and rang the bell for his secretary.

'Wrap up warm and take care,' he said without lifting his head from his papers and I took my dismissal. He had done all that he could for me and I was more grateful than I could express, or that he would want expressed. *Mine Owne Goode Cardinal*, the king always addressed him as, and I could understand the affection that had inspired this phrase. I went to the door and raised my hand in a farewell. '*Go raibh tú í Neamh, leathúair os comhaira bhfuil a fhíos ag an diabhal atá tú bás.*' I said and added: 'That's an old Irish saying, Your Grace, and it means "May you be in Heaven half an hour before the devil knows that you are dead",' I said the words lightly and his rich laugh followed me down the corridor.

The cardinal was right: John was with Alice. He looked slightly disgruntled to see me, as if I had discovered a secret weakness of his, but I greeted him with warmth.

'John thinks that the arrow was meant for you.' Alice was the first to speak. 'Now all you have to do, John, is draw up a list of people who wanted Hugh out of the way.'

'And make sure that you top the list with someone who is not great friends with the king, otherwise you may be wasting your time,' I said lightly and John frowned.

'Why should St Leger want to kill you? We're agreed, aren't we, that he could not have done the first murder, the murder of the instructor of the wards. He was playing cards with the king all night. I saw him myself. Alice saw him.'

'He was still there when I went to bed,' confirmed Alice.

'Well, he might just want me out of the way. He wants James convicted of the murder of the instructor of wards, and he may think that I will use influence to prove that he was not. He knows that I am friendly with the cardinal,' I said, but at the back of my mind I remembered the cardinal's warning. The king was mercurial. The cardinal could not afford to risk his displeasure.

Aloud I said, 'I'll ask you the question that I asked the cardinal: Is an earldom worth risking death?'

'And what did he reply?' asked John, and I turned to Alice.

'What do you think he said?'

She lifted the silky ear of her little dog and whispered something into it and then showed me a smiling face.

'You're right,' I said. 'He didn't reply. The cardinal is a cautious man. But what would you think, you two, in the privacy of this room, with only little Lily as a witness, what would be your opinion. Is an earldom worth such a risk?'

John looked doubtfully at Alice.

'The answer to that is probably, yes,' she said instantly. 'Yes, of course, an earldom would be deemed to be worth a risk. You know, Hugh, risks are run all the time by people in power. Charles Brandon, the friend of Sir George St Leger, was sent to France to fetch home Queen Mary when her husband died. He was warned by the king that she was not for him, but he married her and she was pregnant when they arrived back. That was treason! Charles Brandon took a huge risk. The king could have had his head removed for that, but he didn't.

And Brandon was made Duke of Suffolk. Ask him now if it was worth the risk and he'll tell you that it was. Ask St Leger whether getting rid of you, an Irish lawyer, and being unhampered in arresting and executing James Butler is worth the risk when the prize will probably be an earldom, well, in his secret soul, I would say that, yes, he would think he would reckon it's worth a risk, especially as he has a powerful protector.'

'There are three people who do a reckless deed,' I quoted for the second time that evening. 'There is the man without fear, the man without hope and there is the man who has powerful protection – one of the triads in our laws, Alice,' I explained.

'That's good,' she said. 'I might embroider that onto a cushion cover as a present for the cardinal, but we are straying from the point. What is the most important thing for you to do, Hugh, to convict St Leger of murdering Dr Ramirez, or to find out who murdered Edmund Pace on Shrove Tuesday evening?'

I didn't have to think about that. 'The latter, of course. I must clear James before St Leger manages to have him arrested. Once I find out who did that first murder then there is no case for James to answer about that second murder, especially as it can probably be proved that he was many miles away.' I looked across at John. 'Was it Richard Gibson who took that bow and arrow from your guard room?'

'I couldn't say,' he said stiffly.

'You said that he had a key.'

He looked at me stubbornly. 'It's a matter of good manners,' he said obliquely. 'The king brings a large number of courtiers and their servants with him when he visits. My brother serjeant must have access to the lock-up facilities. The cardinal would want all courtesy shown to the king's men.'

Alice stirred. 'Hugh, you are going off the point again. We've agreed that the important matter to solve is the murder of the instructor of the wards where James has been openly accused by two eyewitnesses of firing a lethal arrow during a pageant and in the presence of the king. That is enough to have him hung and it's enough to discredit his house and rob his father of an earldom. That's the puzzle that needs solving. The queen may well ask for an investigation into the death of her physician and that will be a matter for John and perhaps for the king's serjeant, Master Gibson, is that not right, John?' She looked across at her brother and he got to his feet instantly.

'I should inform him now, I suppose,' he said looking worried. 'I was thinking that I would wait for the morning, but perhaps it would be better done now.'

'You're probably right,' said Alice and I saw Lily open one eye and look up at her mistress. I hid my face by bending down to fondle the little dog.

'You have great diplomatic skills, Alice,' I said when the door had closed behind her brother. 'The cardinal will find you very useful during the visit of his imperial majesty, Charles V, when he comes to England in July.'

She ignored this. 'What's the matter, Hugh? You're troubled. Won't you tell me? There's no one here but Lily and I have trained her to be discreet.'

I got up and walked across to put some more logs on the fire. 'It's this dreadful death penalty. I just can't abide the notion of condemning anyone to such barbarity. That's why I shy away from naming a suspect.' I said the words without looking at her. Perhaps she did not feel like that. Perhaps brought up under English law, brought up to believe the biblical harshness of a life for a life, then she would find it hard to understand how I quailed at the idea of being responsible for one of those dreadful hangings or savage beheadings.

'Put it out of your mind for the moment,' she commanded. 'There is always a way. So who do you suspect?'

I gave the fire a kick and went back to my seat, picking up Lily to give me an excuse not to meet her steady gaze.

'I think that the murder was committed when the hall was empty, either during the sugar banquet or after it. Someone came in, some victim who had been blackmailed, met the man, had received a demand for more money, an unreasonable demand, perhaps, found the man asleep on a chair by the fire …' I fondled the little dog and did not look up.

'Why asleep?' queried Alice.

'There was no sign of a struggle,' I explained. 'He wasn't a big man, but he would have been considerably bigger and stronger than anyone who might have killed him that night.'

'Go on,' she said.

'So a knife is pulled out, the man is killed, the fireplace and chair cleaned of blood by means of that fire bucket …'

Alice nodded. She knew all about the fire regulations at Hampton Court. A couple of those buckets, elegantly painted in mulberry and gold, stood by her own fireplace.

'And then the body was carried, or more likely dragged over and concealed by the tapestry. There was a clumsy attempt to involve James by sticking an arrow through the tapestry and then into the wound in the man's chest.'

'And who do you think might have done this? Who could have been blackmailed?'

'It could have been one of the wards,' I said. 'Gilbert is a possibility, but I don't think that he would have involved James. And then there is Harry Percy. The man was blackmailing him about his gambling debts and Harry risked losing his position as heir to the Earl of Northumberland. His father had already threatened him. And also Harry had fallen in love with Anne Boleyn so that would give him a reason to involve James. Even an accusation of murder might have been enough to make the Boleyns back away from the projected marriage.'

'But Gilbert had no reason to involve James, that's right, isn't it?'

'It's possible that he didn't know it was James's arrow,' I said, but even to myself that sounded weak. The initials were burned into the stem of the arrow and the letters stood out black and clear.

Alice made no comment, just gazed into the fire for a moment and then turned back to me.

'And …'

'What do you mean by 'and'?' Despite the seriousness of the matter, I couldn't help smiling. Alice was always so astute.

'There's someone else.'

I took a long breath. 'There's a Flemish girl, Susannah Horenbout. Her knife was found in the hall by young Tom Seymour. It's possible that Edmund Pace may have been blackmailing her, or else she might have hated him for some reason. He may even have raped or attempted to rape her. The cook was talking about advising his daughter to carry a knife with her as a defence against being attacked, and somehow I wondered from the way that he spoke whether he was dropping me a hint, a hint about another girl who walks dark passageways in Hampton Court. Susannah Horenbout is a big strong girl, and, of course, she has a brother, Lucas. We met him, myself and poor Ramirez, and he had just come back from the Wildernesse where he had been to gather willow twigs for turning into charcoal sticks. Well, James lost an arrow when he was shooting in that place, only a few days before Edmund Pace was killed. Lucas could have found it …'

'So it was possible that one or other of the Flemish brother and sister might have been involved, is that right?'

I nodded. It was all that I could manage.

'What are you going to do?' Alice watched my face.

'Nothing for the moment,' I said, gathering my courage. 'I'm going to go up to Westminster tomorrow and see whether I can find James and take him away. If I can't find him, well, you'll see me back here and I'll have to work out something.'

'But if James is arrested?'

'If James is arrested, Alice, then he comes first.' I said the words bravely, but thinking about Susannah and poor Gilbert, I quailed at the idea of handing them over to the hangman. And Harry Percy, a boy so deeply in love. An image of his fever-filled eyes and his flushed face came to me, and I knew that I couldn't do it.

'I must leave you now, Alice,' I said. 'I plan to rise early.'

12

I rose at dawn and made my preparations. Colm looked as though he had not slept at all. I asked him no more questions, but bullied him into swallowing some bread and ale. It would be cold on the river and the boy was growing fast. He still had a frightened and worried look about him. I was almost certain that, despite his denials, he had seen something last night. I'd have preferred to leave him behind if it had not been for that, but as it was he would be safer with me. The killing of a foreign servant was not something that dangerous men would baulk at. The queen was, according to John who popped in, most upset about the death of her physician and would spare no pains to use her influence with the king to bring the murderer to the chopping block once she was sure of his identity. Colm, if he had seen anything, was in great danger.

'Letter for you, Master Brehon,' called out the boatman, just as I was about to enquire whether I could go back to Westminster with them. I took the paper from him quickly, my heart thumping.

'News of your missing young friend?' The king's serjeant was by my side in an instant, peering inquisitively over my shoulder.

'Perhaps,' I said in a non-committal fashion. I didn't know the handwriting on the paper that enfolded the message. The seal, also, was unknown to me. I cursed the mischance that had brought the man to the ferry wharf just at the same moment as I had reached it. I could not ask for the cardinal's barge, either, in his presence. If I did, he would make some excuse to accompany me to Westminster.

'Not the Earl of Ormond's seal, is it? Or Master James Butler's, either.' Without apology he took the letter from my hand and scanned it, holding it close to his eyes.

'Oh, a swan among the flowers. That would be Master John Skelton, the king's poet. Strange fellow. Never know whether he is laughing at you or praising you. Told me he would put me into a poem, once. Said I'd surely know myself, if I did read it. I told him that I didn't have the time for reading.' The serjeant's tone had turned friendly but I was not deceived. I knew this man well. I didn't know whether he would tell a lie, or whether he would manufacture evidence, but he would be tireless in his pursuit of a man whom he thought to be guilty. And resolute in delivering him up to the hangman.

Still, it didn't appear as though he had any further interest in the letter. He handed it over to me and then looked me up and down.

'Going on the river?' he asked.

'No, just for a walk through the Wildernesse,' I said. I had not yet spoken to the boatman and that was lucky. I would have to postpone my departure. I turned away from him decisively, tucking the letter into my purse and striding out energetically.

The Wildernesse at Hampton had been planted on the north side of the court's buildings and, although the hedges gave shelter, it was bitterly cold on that March weather. Nevertheless, the grass at my feet was crisp and the earth below it was rock hard. There would be little or no mud on the roads to Dover and no floods to negotiate.

As soon as I had made my way into the heart of the hedged pathways, I stopped and took the letter from my pocket, carefully prising loose the wax seal and unfolding the paper.

I wasn't sure what to expect, though a wild hope had arisen that in some way this John Skelton had met up with James and was sending me a note on his behalf. But I was disappointed. Two pages of poetry, written in a scrawling hand with several blots marring the surface of the paper.

'Anything interesting?' The serjeant, on second thoughts, must have come to the same conclusion as myself. He would have wondered why the poet had written to me, followed me silently on the grassy paths that twisted and turned in a maze-like pattern. And now he had caught up with me. Colm gave a frightened, convulsive jump, but I greeted him calmly and waved the letter at him. He frowned, but did not take it, looking sharply into my face.

Well, I wished him joy. I was no great admirer of John Skelton and thought that the cardinal put up too patiently with his scurrilous jokes. I read aloud some of the lines:

With turrets and with towers,
With halls and with bowers,

'Must be Hampton Court, don't you think?' I enquired
in a casual voice, glancing back and up at the red brick
towers that framed the Base Court. And then felt my
heart miss a beat. My eye had moved further down the
page and had picked out a familiar word. Hurriedly,
before he noticed my hesitation, I moved on to another
section.

'This must be about the tapestries, I should imagine,' I
said in my most nonchalant manner:

> Hanging about the walls,
> Cloths of gold and palls,

He was getting bored and restless, but relentlessly I read
on:

> With Dame Diana naked;
> How lusty Venus quaked,
> And how Cupid shaked …

'Oh, dear,' I said lowering the paper. 'George won't like
that! And here's another bit,' I continued:

> With wanton wenches winking …

'Well, well, I think that I must study these tapestries more
carefully.' Did I dare pocket the letter or should I go on
reading out extracts, but he solved the dilemma by saying
sourly that he had work to do and couldn't spend his day
listening to rubbish.

After he had left I did not yield to the temptation to
read the rest of the letter, but put it away and set out

briskly to reach the centre of the maze. James had shown me the trick of it and I knew that once I reached there that I would have a broad, empty space all around me and there would be no possibility of someone stealing up quietly beside me.

There was a statue of Venus in the centre. There was no doubt that the cardinal, as a great patron of what they were calling the rebirth of classical Greece and Rome, seemed to have a fondness for naked women – something that might seem inappropriate to a churchman. John Skelton could mock him all he liked though. The cardinal was serenely sure of his position as the king's advisor and chief minister. And this Venus was a beautifully sculpted lady. I sat on her plinth, leaned against her shapely knees and searched eagerly for the line that had caught my eyes. There it was:

'Pantlers run; Butlers flee,'
Rivers flow to the sea.'

There the faintest of blue marks below the word, 'Butler'. James went down the river towards the sea. That was relevant.

And then my eye went back to the business about the cupids:

'And how Cupid shaked
His dart and bent his bow
And landed on Canon's Row.'

It didn't make sense. Not even sense for John Skelton's type of verse. And the blue line was definitely under the two words *Canon's Row*. A row of canons? And then inspiration dawned. A row of houses. A row of houses for the canons at Westminster, perhaps? Or one canon, perhaps. I extricated myself from the cardinal's maze and went in search of George Cavendish.

George was fretting over the provision of silver ewers for the lodgings being prepared for the party of Spanish ambassadors. He had young Francis Bigod in attendance on him and was painstakingly instructing him in the nice graduations of the *bouche de court* according to the rank of the guest.

'Large or small, Hugh?' he asked in anguished tones as soon as I had put my head around the door. He had an ornately decorated and brilliantly shining ewer in either hand.

'Small,' I said promptly. George agonised so much over all decisions that the best way to handle him was always to give a decisive answer.

'Really? Well I suppose you are right. It might encourage them to drink less. Make their allowance seem greater. So the small ones, Francis. Make sure that there is one in each front chamber and that it is placed directly in the centre of the table and that there is a mat underneath it. Or perhaps it should be to one side, what do you think, Hugh? Or to the front? Some of these boys are so careless when they pour the wine.'

'Put a red linen mat and then no one will notice a few drips,' I said and George looked at me with admiration.

'What a good idea. See to it, Francis.'

'I suppose that you know Westminster like the back of your hand, George,' I said as Francis hurried away before any more instructions could be heaped upon him.

'You spend so much time at York Place with the cardinal, don't you?'

'He never travels to Westminster without me,' said George preening himself. 'He has so much business there what with the Star Chamber and other such matters. Of course I …'

'Would you know a place called Canon's Row?' Hurriedly I took Skelton's poem from my pocket and waved it under his nose for a minute. 'He wants to have my opinion on his poetry and I'm not sure whether he shouldn't try a different rhyming sequence. You see,' I said earnestly, 'I wonder whether he's rather forcing a rhyme in places, like for instance where he rhymes the word 'crow' with 'Canon's Row' – it does seem as though he couldn't really think of what else rhymes with crow and bow, doesn't it? Or is it a real place?'

'Oh, it's a real place all right, it's just near to Bridge Street, not far from Westminster Abbey. It used to be for the canons of St Stephen's Church, but that's rather derelict now. Most of the old canons are dead and haven't been replaced.' George wrinkled his brow over John Skelton's poem. 'I see what you mean, but you know he's supposed to be a very clever man,' he said dubiously. 'He was tutor to our king and now he is his poet.' He scratched his head. 'Is he making fun of the cardinal?' He asked the question with a note of rising indignation in his voice and I hastily took the sheet away from him.

'I'll advise him to abandon this – bad poetry.' I shook my head sadly over the closely filled pages.

He regarded me with respect. 'Do you know about poetry, Hugh?'

'Of course! Every Brehon lawyer has to pass examinations in poetry as well as in law.' I made a pretence of scanning the rhymes and once again shaking my head sadly.

'Really!' He was looking at me with respect and I knew that a hundred questions trembled on his lips.

'Well, I think that I had better give him my opinion about this. I'll get the letter written and then when the barge is going to Westminster it can be taken to him.' I had to get away from George. Francis had returned with three red napkins, all of slightly different shades, for the gentleman usher's perusal and I could see that I might be kept here half the day helping him to come to decisions. I waved a casual salute and made my way back down the corridor, opening the door into the court and coming face to face with the king's serjeant. He had a companion, but she disappeared with a flip of a cloak and toss of a veiled head. I recognised her, of course. There was no mistaking the grace of that walk. They had indeed trained her up very well in the French court. I lifted an eyebrow at the serjeant just to assure him that I knew whom he had been listening to.

Master Gibson drummed his fingers on the windowsill of the corridor. The pale light from outside drew flecks of silver from his eyebrows and the lines around his mouth looked deeper and harsher than usual. 'See here, Master Brehon,' he said abruptly. 'My task is keep the king's law in his palaces and anywhere the king visits. Here at Hampton Court on Shrove Tuesday evening a man was killed in the presence of the king himself. It's all very well for the cardinal to tell his serjeant to delay, to tell him to allow Master Brehon a few days, but why should you have a few days? Why should that young man, seen to commit murder by two good witnesses, one a friend to him and the other almost betrothed to him, why should he be still at liberty, that's what I ask myself. And you, a judge, a friend of the cardinal, I suspect you of knowing the whereabouts of this young man and refusing to reveal them. What if he is a murderer, and there are men like that, who will not be content just with one death but who will kill and kill again, just like a fox in a poultry house? Where would I be then? What will Sir Thomas More say to me?'

He had a point and a serious grievance. I set myself to talk to him seriously.

'But, you know, Serjeant, it would be worse if you got the wrong person, wouldn't it? After all this is not just a matter of a thieving clerk. James Butler is an important pawn in the game. The king doesn't want any trouble about the Ormond succession and he needs the Butler support in Ireland. Kildare is greedy, Desmond is unreliable, and as for the west and the north of Ireland, well, that's a tinderbox. All those petty kings: Turlough O'Brien of Thomond, his vassals, and his allies, the O'Byrnes, the MacNamaras, the O'Connors, the O'Carrolls and the O'Kennedys – I could name a dozen more – if Butler was to cease to assist Kildare, well the king might have to say goodbye to his possessions in Ireland.'

My words impressed him. I could see that. I could visualise thoughts cross his mind and could see his struggle with himself. This was a difficult one. If the instructor of the wards was systematically blackmailing his young charges, then some of the greatest names in the kingdom were involved: Ormond, Northumberland, Arundel,

Seymour, Bigod, Derby ... I could see those thoughts cross the mind of the man responsible for finding out the truth of this murder. His face darkened.

'Ireland!' he said contemptuously and a snarl parted his lips as he spat the word out. 'What about the north?'

And, of course, he was right. Trouble in the north of England would be worse than trouble in Ireland. However bad it would be to have James Butler dangle from the hangman's noose or see his head roll from the chopping block, it would be very much worse to have the heir to the earl of Northumberland hauled off to execution in the Tower of London and perhaps have a rising in the north among the Percys, the Talbots, the Dacres and others.

'There's no easy way out of this,' he said sombrely, 'but I have to do my duty and if you obstruct me, then I will arrest you.'

With that he turned on his heel and strode off. All the camaraderie engendered by our tennis games seemed to have ebbed away. I gazed after him thoughtfully. This threat to me was another reason to leave Hampton Court. Cardinal Wolsey would be very soon heavily engaged in negotiations about the Italian war and would have no time to deal with this domestic issue.

I would have to be careful about my departure though. I had planned to go to my lodgings and to pack a couple of travelling bags but would that be wise, now? I gazed thoughtfully around the court. A movement at a window caught my eye, a dark shape and then just frost-patterned glass. A man had suddenly stood back. The serjeant probably had given his orders. I would be followed wherever I went, not arrested, nor detained, just shadowed. I bit my lip, undecided as to what to do.

And then deliberately I walked rapidly across the court, not going towards the clock tower, but towards the north cloister. As soon as I got there I fumbled in my pocket, took out a handful of coins, began to count them and deliberately allowed one to fall to the ground. I moved forward another few steps and then whirled around. One of the yeoman stopped abruptly. I hailed him in a friendly way and he pointed out the piece of silver half disguised by the slivers of ice. He looked slightly embarrassed, stamped his feet energetically, but he did not go away. There was no doubt that he had been ordered to shadow me.

Thoughtfully I threaded my way down the narrow passageway, stood aside to allow the wood yard boys with their long flat barrows go past me and I looked around for inspiration. A light in an upper window in the Carpenter's Court caught my eye. I stopped. My shadow stopped also. Like all the yeoman serving the cardinal he was a tall, heavy man, and he made a lot of noise with his footsteps and almost overbalanced when he came to a standstill. I grinned to myself. It might not be too hard to fool him. I got out my knife and took my handkerchief from my pocket and began to scrape a little dust from the brick in the wall, making sure to take only a shaving from each of the crimson bricks. When I had a nice little pile I knotted my handkerchief around it and walked briskly towards a door in the court and knocked energetically.

To my relief, it was Susannah who opened the door. 'Got that brick dust for your paint,' I said in ringing tones, which I was sure would reach to the yeoman lurking in the shadow of the archway.

'Come in,' she said. She looked bewildered, but that didn't matter. He wouldn't be able to see her face. I went through the door rapidly and closed it behind me instantly. She looked sharply at me, but said nothing until we had mounted the stairs and were in the big, light-filled room under the roof. 'It's very kind of you,' she said. She bit back a smile and produced a wooden bowl which was filled to almost its rim with the very same crimson brick dust.

'Oh, well,' I said and tipped in my contribution. I walked across to the table and carefully examined her knives, taking them out one by one, replacing each in its slot and then I took out the narrowest and smallest of them and brought it to the window facing to the south. The sky was grey and there was no sun, but there was enough light to be able to see it clearly, the shining steel of the blade and the well-scrubbed wooden handle.

'You keep your knives very clean.' It was a stupid comment. And a stupid action. I had already inspected this knife. What did I hope to find? This was a work-room where there was every kind of scrubbing soap and cleansers available. She would probably make her own – varying degrees of fat, ley and ashes, according to the strength required. And there were graters, stiff bristled brushes and scrubbers, too, on that table in the corner of the room.

'Like a good craftsperson.' She replied to my remark with a quick smile. I didn't think that it worried her. She took the knife from me and replaced it within its slot. 'Now, tell me, what is this brick powder for?'

'I just wanted an excuse to come and see the fish.' I walked across to the 'Fishermen on the Sea of Galilee' panels. I scanned the picture, at first absent-mindedly and then focussed intently upon it.

'Yes, I see what you meant,' I said after a long moment when I swept a glance from bottom to top of the picture and then back again. Just that little hint of gold and a slightly more substantial presence due to the skeleton beneath the paint, both of these drew my eye immediately. She was watching my face, a half smile came and went on her lips and her very blue eyes widened suddenly with a look of pleasure.

'You like?' she queried.

'Very much,' I said. It would have to be Calais. A murderer in the abstract was one thing; in the flesh was another.

'I need to get away from Hampton Court without being seen,' I said turning around to face her.

'James?' she queried. I could see how her colour paled and her eyes darkened for a moment. Still in love with him, I thought with a slight pang.

'How old are you?' I asked abruptly.

'The same age as Mistress Boleyn.' She faced me and there was an angry glint in her blue eyes.

'Mistress Boleyn.' I smiled to myself as I placed the two girls side by side in my mind's eye. The one tall, well-made, blonde, blue-eyed with a straightforward gaze, an artist and a craftswoman; the other slight, small-boned, dark, subtle, sly, mysterious and, I had to admit, alluring.

'Can you help me?' I brushed aside all other thoughts. Only James and his safety mattered now. The cardinal had shown the way and now it was up to me to follow the path. This brother and sister might have parcels delivered, large pieces of wood for panels, panes of glass for painting upon, clay for modelling … They would know all about boats, about ways of transporting goods.

'What do you want to do?'

I would have to trust to her. She, above all people could not wish any harm to James. I suddenly remembered my father in front of a class of scholars telling them that preservation of the self was the strongest emotion within the human soul but I brushed the thought aside.

'I want to go to London without being seen, or followed,' I said.

'The cardinal,' she began.

'He has given me a note for his barge,' I interrupted, 'but …'

'But you are afraid that you will be followed and will bring disaster with you. You know where James is hiding.'

There was no hint of a question in her voice and she left me instantly and went to stare out of the window. I joined her there, glancing sideways at the thoughtful face. We both looked down up the figure of the patient yeoman, stamping his feet and rubbing his hands.

'I have to trust you,' she said after a minute.

I smiled to myself. 'I'm trusting you,' I pointed out.

'The clerk of the greencloth, he and the serjeant, they want to check everything, charge big sums for everything, not allow people to make a little profit,' she was stumbling over her words. 'We need oil, you see, all sorts of oil, lamp oil, mainly. We use it for making our paints, for a mordant, for all sorts of uses, we use barrel loads of it, but the clerk, you, you saw him, everything, money, money and we have to pay money, extra money, big money to buy it and people us do not pay until at end of process and we …'

'So you have a private way sometimes of getting free supplies,' I put in. I had thought that when I saw her in the kitchen. She was, I noticed, just purchasing very small amounts, enough to last her a few days, only. Looking at the activity going on in this large workroom, the room so full of projects, I could see that they would need large amounts of supplies. The goods placed on barges for Hampton Court would not be as meticulously checked as they were when they arrived. Cardinal Wolsey's all-seeing eye had not yet reformed the activity at the docks. But once goods arrived at the Hampton Court jetty they were meticulously recorded on their journey from storehouse, to kitchen, to plates, even the leftovers from the last sitting, which were given to beggars, were checked by one of the many clerks.

She nodded. 'Master Beasley is very kind. He help us. He tell us. We have a place, a secret place, there is a skiff, a so small skiff, we … I will be ruined, we will be ruined if you tell …'

'I won't tell.' I hoped that my voice would quieten her. Her own had begun to rise. These windows filled with glass were elegant and useful, but they did not block sound in the way that a good wall, or even shutters would do.

''There's a stream that joins the river, just by the pond where they keep the fish for the kitchen. They have a boat there. Master Beasley told us.' She had lowered her voice and I nodded encouragingly – yes, the kitchen would have to have a supply of fish for times when bad weather would cut off supplies. And it made sense for the kitchen to keep a boat there, much easier to transport large quantities of fresh fish by boat and land it just next to the fish larder. And a boat could be used to meet the barge on its way with the supplies.

I could see what Susannah and her brother did now in order to get their supplies without the knowledge of the clerks, and I could see how this could work. The Thames wound its way with loops and twists between London and Hampton. I could just imagine that there might be a little concealed place where goods could be unloaded secretly. There might not the same strict system of checking the loads from the docks. Hampton Court was the size of a small town. And the consumption of oil for cooking and for lighting myriads of lamps and torches for corridors and courts would be enormous. One barrel here and there would not be missed.

'How do you get there?' I asked aloud.

'You go down the gallery, past the terracotta roundels of the Roman emperors. This is what I always do. I pretend to be checking that there is no injury to the clay.' She lowered her voice to a whisper. 'And then I slip out the far door. Go through the south-easterly garden, keep facing south until you reach a little patch of willow trees. If you go through these you will find the stream. The skiff is tied to one of the trees. Row towards the river and then wait for the barge.'

There was one more question that I needed to ask. If the attempt to get to Calais failed, then I needed to save James in some other way.

'Mistress Horenbout,' I said, 'would you be very unhappy if you had to go back to Flanders?'

She gave me a long and enquiring look and eventually she said, 'If I had to, well, I would go. There is still plenty of work for someone like me in Flanders. I would go

back to doing illustrating, I think. It would be a change
to work small again.' She gave a glance over towards the
fishermen picture and half-smiled to herself. She did not
look too concerned. Perhaps for an artist like her the
most important thing was the work.

I kissed her quickly, impulsively, on her soft lips, and
then went down the stairs, opened the door and stood
for a moment pretending to examine the sky. My shadow
was still hanging around, pretending not to look in my
direction and after my one quick glance, I did not look
at him again. I walked briskly through the gatehouse,
through the Base Court, under the clock tower and
heard him behind me, but then he stopped as I turned
in through a door. The gallery was quite empty and I
slammed the door loudly behind me. My watcher would
not dare to follow me in here; he would be too conspicu-
ous. He would, I guessed, lurk beside the clock tower,
waiting to see whether I returned to the jetty. There was
no one but me there in the empty gallery, but I took
care not to come out too quickly. I followed Susannah's
example and studied the eight roundels of the Roman
emperors, fashioned from baked clay, London clay, apparently, and each had cost the cardinal about three pounds
sterling. I could see how one could study them for a long
section of time as they had such intricate detail. I could
write a treatise on those roundels, I stayed so long gazing
at them.

Eventually I took a chance and stole out by the far
door. Some boys were pushing wood barrows towards
the cardinal's quarters and I ducked behind them and
slipped through the clock tower archway and stood in
its dark shadow. Colm had just finished putting away

the wood and was idly sweeping up some scraps of bark from in front of the door. He was on edge, uneasy, I could see that, and when I softly said the Gaelic words '*anseo, Colm!*' he started violently, but he was a quick-witted lad and he gave a cursory glance around before sauntering over towards me.

'Come with me when it is safe.' Once again I spoke Gaelic; saw him take a quick glance around and then join me in the shadowed archway.

I waited until the boys came back and then with a quick gesture to Colm moved along beside them on their journey back to the wood yard and then slipped through the gate to the south-east. Colm followed closely on my heels and neither of us spoke.

There was a pathway sheltered by a hedge on either side and I went rapidly along it, thankful that it was not gravelled, but was just grass underfoot. Quite soon it finished and then, looking in the direction of London I spotted the little woodland of bare-twigged willows. Now I broke into a run. I could not afford to miss the next barge and I didn't quite know how long it would take to row down the stream that joined the river.

I saw the pond first. It was constructed so that the stream flowed into it, through a metal grill and then out again through another grill so that the water would remain fresh and the fish were trapped inside. The skiff was there, as she had told me, at the far side of the pond, facing down stream, tied to a tree. Another huge and ancient willow had fallen into the stream at some time. Its crown – branches and all, had been removed, but a section of the trunk had been left in place and the rounded surface of this had been roughly planned into a makeshift jetty. The boat itself looked old, but well maintained, painted black both outside and in – something which I guessed must make it very difficult to see in the distance. I gathered my dark mantle around me, beckoned to Colm to follow me, took my seat, lifted the oars and then a figure appeared from behind the trees. For a moment I feared my watcher had managed to follow me despite my precautions, but the voice was gruff and cracked, a familiar voice.

'Not so fast, Master Brehon, if you please. I'm coming with you.'

13

My heart lurched unpleasantly and I tasted blood on my tongue as I bit through its tip. For a moment I had thought it to be the king's serjeant, but it was only this stupid boy.

'I thought that you were up to something,' said Tom Seymour breathlessly. 'Let me in or I'll tell the king's serjeant that you are off. He's been telling Harry Percy that he is keeping an eye on you.' He grabbed a branch and swung himself into the boat.

'Get out,' I said between my teeth. I clenched my fist around the oar. Colm looked at me for instructions.

'As you please. Should I give the serjeant a message to tell him when you will be back and why you are leaving in the kitchen boat, not going in the barge like a gentleman?'

He had me there. I held the oar as a threat, but he was too clever not to guess that I would not knock a boy of his age insensible. It was not in me. I couldn't do it to a child. I didn't want to take him with me, but how could I convince him to let me go without him?

'Look, Tom,' I said coaxingly. 'Just keep your mouth shut about this. You and I are friends, are we not? I did give you an hour's practice and teach you a lot of tricks on the tennis play, didn't I? And who knows, the next time I go there I might teach you some more.' I wished that I could bribe him, but I was going to be short of money for myself if I did.

He wasn't fooled. 'You're going to look for James, aren't you? Don't worry, I won't get in your way. I just want to make myself scarce for a couple of hours. The serjeant has threatened to have me beaten and I thought that if I could hide until my brother Edward comes to Hampton Court for supper this evening, then I might escape. Edward is in high favour with the cardinal. He'll intervene for me. But it would be best of all to go to Westminster and come back with Edward. That way, I can have plenty of time to explain everything to him. It was just a joke, anyway, making that slide in the courtyard. How did I know that he would come down with such a bump?'

'Well, come on, then, take that oar and make yourself useful,' I said roughly. I suppressed a smile. It was an ice slide, I supposed, probably cunningly disguised with a scattering of sawdust. Now that he had appeared he just might be useful. Tom had a knack of getting on well with everyone. Also, he had his bow and arrows with him and this would give an excuse for appearing at the riverside, half a mile away from the official Hampton Court jetty. I would tell the boatmen some tale about forgetting the time while we were hunting and this would account for our unscheduled arrival.

'How much money have you on you?' he asked casually as we came within sight of the river.

'What's that to you?' I strained my eyes towards the west. It was not dark enough for torches, but the light was fading fast.

'I was wondering how much you are going to give me to keep my mouth shut about something that I know.'

'Keep rowing,' I said roughly. 'By God, you'll never make a decent tennis player if your muscles are as puny as that.'

This annoyed him, as I knew it would. He made the water fly behind us as he scooped energetically with his oar.

'That's better,' I said after a minute. I was finding it quite hard to keep up with young Tom. He was certainly an asset to me in the boat. He was looking at me hopefully so I relented. 'Well, tell me now what you know,' I said.

'James, well James and the artist lady, what's her name, Mistress Horenbout, well they were ...'

'I know all about that,' I said glancing over my shoulder. 'Stale news, my boy, stale news.'

'Not just that.' He was stung by my assumption of lack of interest.

'So?' I made the boat leap with a vigorous sweep.

'So Master Pace caught them,' he said in my ear. 'They were in the archery house. We heard Master Pace shout, myself and Francis Bigod. We thought there was something wrong and we came running in.' He stopped for a moment to breathe, or perhaps to visualise the scene and I heard him chuckle to himself before he resumed with an energetic sweep of his oars. 'And then I could see her pulling her shift down over her head. She had nothing on. I could see her ... well, you know what. Francis went out – he's very religious – but I stayed hidden behind that big wooden press.'

I bet you did, I thought grimly, but I said nothing. The less interest I showed now, the cheaper the price later.

'Master Pace was in a wild temper. He was roaring and yelling at them, threatening all sorts of terrible things. He said that he would get the cardinal to send Mistress Horenbout back to Flanders, that she would be disgraced.'

I was busy prodding a floating branch away from the boat with my oar as the words came to my ears and said nothing. In a cursory glance over my shoulder at the floating piece of timber, I glimpsed his face. Like most boys of his age, he would have stared avidly at the half-naked woman, but that did not prevent a shrewd youngster from correctly estimating the value of his information once Master Edmund Pace was rumoured to have been killed by James Butler. As for James himself, no doubt that the man had made threats against him, also, but the cardinal was a broad-minded man, and the instructor of the wards would probably not have bothered him with such a matter. No, the most serious threat was to Susannah, and James was an earnest and conscientious young fellow. That would have filled him with fury, especially if he had any hint that Master Pace desired Susannah for himself. I remembered the hints dropped by Master Beasley, the cook and was fairly sure that he had been talking about the Flemish girl when we had the conversation about knives. Yes, there was no doubt about it. Master Seymour's information might be enough to hang James if Dr Augustine persisted in saying that the man had been killed by the arrow with the initials J.B. scratched into it.

'Five shillings,' I said after a minute. James and I would be on our way to Calais by this time tomorrow, I hoped, but Susannah was left behind and I owed it to her, for James's sake, to safeguard her position as much as I could.

'Make it ten,' he said.

'Twenty-four groats and six pennies. And that's my last word,' I said.

He considered that. In groats and pennies it probably sounded better to his young ears. The Seymours of Wolf Hall were not rich. There was a large family of them. His eldest sister was Mistress Jane Seymour, one of the queen's ladies-in-waiting, and there were, I seemed to remember, another six or seven of them scattered around in various posts at court or among noble families. Edward, the oldest brother, now at court in the household of Princess Mary, had been brought up by the cardinal, as was young Tom now.

'Done,' he said. 'I won't say a word to the cardinal.'

'You won't if you know what's good for you. And hold your tongue now. When we get on the barge, leave the talking to me. I don't suppose that you want to be found with a knife between your ribs, do you?' I purposefully made my voice aggressive. This boy was going to be a nuisance to me. He was sharp and inquisitive and I would have to lose him in London before I went anywhere near to James. And then on the still air I heard the rhythmic sound of oars.

We were now in sight of the wide expanse of the Thames and Tom put all his energy into his strokes. Like most boys of his age, he enjoyed an emergency and I found it difficult enough to keep up with him.

The interesting thing was that, even before I raised a beckoning hand, there was a shout from the man with the tiller and barge had slowed down and begun to steer its way towards us. I allowed Tom to do the work now, while I sorted a piece of silver from my pocket. In theory as a guest of the cardinal I need not pay. In practice, small coins grease the wheels that made life flow easily in this place without ties of clanship and community, such as I was used to back in my homeland.

'What's the best way to get from Westminster to Bradstrete in the city of London?' I put the question to the steersman and saw young Tom turn an interested face towards me. I could see how his lips silently repeated the word. Well, even if he were minded to play the traitor, that piece of information would not do him much good. I wished him luck in exploring the many streets in London City.

'Bradstrete, Master, well, that's a tidy way. That's near to Austin Friars, isn't it? You could have had a word with Master Cromwell if you had thought of it. He lives by there. He generally takes the ferry from Westminster Steps to the Temple Steps or else you could hire a horse, sir. Very good stables at Charing Cross, sir.'

'Thank you,' I said. If there were good stables at Charing Cross, I might be able to purchase a pair of horses there. Much as I regretted my own horse and James's horse, it would not at the moment be safe to send for them. No, I would have to draw on my master's credit with Sir Richard Gresham and then buy a couple of horses. In the meantime, I would follow Master Cromwell's example and get the ferry from Westminster.

I bade a brisk farewell to Tom after ladling out his bribe which he pocketed instantly. And then I and the silent Colm went straight down towards the Westminster steps in order to find a ferry. I did not dare even have a cursory look around to locate 'Canon's Row'. Master Seymour was a bright young man and would be alert for any such move on my part. I doubted he would follow me to the city, though. He would have to make contact with his brother or else he would be in double trouble when he returned to Hampton Court.

Nevertheless, I made sure that I was the last one in the queue to board the ferry and that there was no sign of the boy anywhere. And while I was making conversation with Sir Richard Gresham, while I drank a glass of his excellent wine, greeted his wife and admired his three-year-old son Thomas – '*Sharp as a needle, I do assure you, Master Mac Egan*' – I still made opportunities to go from time to time to the window of his splendid house and look down on the busy street, just to make sure that I had not been followed.

Westminster was even more crowded when we came back. I had thought to suggest to Colm to have a look around the abbey and other sights, but the boy looked terrified of the crowds so in the end I suggested that he waited at the steps until I came back. He could pass the time looking at the boats and barges and I could easily pick him up from there as soon as I made contact with James. I did not want to bother the lad with any extra information in case matters went wrong so told him only that I had an errand for the cardinal. He seemed happy to do this and promised that he would not stir until I returned and so I left him and went in search of James.

I had reckoned that if I could find St Stephen's Church, then I would be well on my way to finding Canon's Row. But it wasn't as easy as that. I seemed to be wandering in circles, always ending up by St Margaret's Church, every time I followed the sound of chiming bells. Eventually I stopped a priest.

'Reverend Father.' I removed my cap at the sight of priest clothed in a floor length surplice.

'My son!' His hand automatically rose to bless me, though I caught a sharp look of curiosity from his eyes as he noticed the different accent. I hoped that he would have no contact with the Seymour brothers.

'I'm looking for the king's poet.' That was better than saying the name, but I wasted my time.

'Master Skelton,' he said loudly and with a note of commiseration in his voice. 'I do hope, my son, that you have not come a long distance to see this man.' He waited for me to explain my business, but I waited also and my silence lasted longer than his. 'He is very ill,' he said eventually. 'By now, indeed, he may well be dead. God bless his soul.'

'Ill?' I repeated.

'A case of the sweating sickness,' he explained, dropping his voice and he looked around furtively.

'The sweating sickness,' I blurted out. 'But I had a letter from him this very morning.'

'Ah,' he said sadly. 'You are a stranger here, my son, or you would know that they say of the sweat: "Merry at dinner; dead at supper".'

I had heard of the expression and the tips of my fingers, even inside my warm gloves, grew icy cold. What if James was also ill? I had to see him.

'I should wish to do honour to his remains,' I said stiffly. 'Would you be kind enough to direct me to his house?'

He stared at me as though I were mad, but lifted his hand and pointed to a narrow laneway. 'Go down there and you will find Bridge Street,' he said. 'The unfortunate man lives, or lived in Canon's Row. You will find another laneway that will bring me you to it.' He gave a quick glance at me. His face looked as though he had seen enough of me, that he was beginning to be suspicious that I, too, might be bearing an infection and he sketched a cross in the air a few safe cubits away from me and then hurried off. I was glad to see him go. He had a loud, carrying voice and I wished that he had not mentioned Canon's Row.

It took me some long fifteen minutes or so wandering up and down small laneways until I found the name, 'Canon's Row' etched into the side of the first house on one of them. The houses here were a better quality and from one a trim man servant issued forth on an errand. I was wondering whether to chance using John Skelton's name again when I saw another of the doors open and a young man thrust an anxious-looking face out from it and look up and down as though waiting for someone.

'James!' I exclaimed. In a second I was beside him. 'Quick!' I said. 'Let's get inside. I may have been followed.'

He did not move, but stayed standing squarely in the doorway. 'Don't come in,' he said. 'We have sickness in the house.' Once more he looked down the road. 'Where the devil has that man gone? The blackguard, the cowardly hound. I bet he has absconded. I sent him for a cooling draught. John Skelton is very sick.'

'I know. The sweat. I heard it from a priest.'

He snorted. 'He didn't offer to hear a dying man's confession, though, did he? Bet he's the one I sent the serving girl for. She hasn't come back either. Hugh, could you go to the apothecary? Down there on Bridge Street. You'll find it easily. You'll see bunches of dried herbs in the window.'

'And then we'll talk?'

'Never yet managed to shut you up, have I?' Suddenly he seemed more like himself. He certainly did not appear ill in any way, though I tried to avert my mind from that fatal phrase of the priest's. *Merry at dinner; dead at supper.*

I rushed down the road as quickly as I could. The bell at Westminster Abbey chimed the noon hour and I grimaced with anxiety, blaming myself for agreeing to run this errand. Still I had a good sense of direction and Bridge Street was not large. I could be there, make my purchase, tell James the position, buy a couple of good horses at Charing Cross and then we could be off before, if we were lucky, one o'clock of the afternoon.

'The sweat, is it? Man or child?' The apothecary was wearing a strange mask and he sniffed continuously at an orange stuffed with herbs and spices. 'Drop a groat into that bowl of vinegar,' he ordered and only when I had done that did he produce a flask from his shelf. 'Pour two spoonfuls of this down his throat three times a day. If his jaw is clenched, break a tooth or two and open it with a chisel. He'll thank you if he recovers.'

'Will he recover?' I asked, dropping the groat into the pungent liquid and then adding another. 'Give me two of these,' I ordered. James, I remembered, had been with this man, Skelton, and might succumb to the illness while we were on our journey. I would take the remedy with me so that I was prepared. I had heard a lot about the sweating sickness in London. It started with a shivering and then sweating. The cardinal had told me how he had had the disease several times but always recovered. James was young and healthy, surely healthier than an overweight, middle-aged man, but I would take no chances. I would insist that he did not go too near the sick man, just leave the medicine within reach.

James was waiting anxiously on the doorstep for me when I came back into Canon's Row.

'God's bones, I've never seen anything like that before in my life,' he said. 'He was fine. He was having fun slipping lines into that poem of his, and then he walked down to the wharf to send you the note. I needed some money, otherwise I wouldn't have bothered you, Hugh. But when he came back he was shaking from head to toe and his teeth were crashing against each other.'

'James,' I said urgently. 'You have to get out of England before Monday. The cardinal can do no more for you. This affair will be left to his serjeant and Master Rushe is determined to believe that you murdered that man, the instructor of the wards. I'm off to buy a couple of horses at Charing Cross. I'll be back in less than a quarter of an hour. Be ready for me by then.'

He grimaced. 'I can't do that, Hugh. I can't go off and leave this man here. I need to look after him.'

'Oh, fiddlesticks,' I said roughly. 'Let a servant do that.'

'None left,' he said. 'All gone.'

'Well, even so …' I looked at him tentatively. I was familiar with that expression.

'I'd be a poor sort of fellow, wouldn't I, if I walked off and left that unfortunate fellow – a man who sheltered me from the law? He needs someone to look after him,' he said evenly.

'Well you're not an apothecary or a physician,' I said roughly. I clenched my fingers with frustration. 'James, you … you must come,' I burst out. I made my voice sound pleading. With James it was never any good to order him or to try to bully him. He always had to be made to see reason. 'James, the man will live or die as God commands. No one knows much about this sweating sickness. The cardinal himself says that he only recovered because it was the will of God, because God had work for him to do in the realm of England. Take the medicine and leave it next to John Skelton and then you will have done all that you can possibly be expected to do. No one will blame you.'

'I'll blame myself,' said James and there was a steely note to his voice. 'The man needs nursing. Now give me some money if you can spare me some.'

Dumbly I handed him two pounds; it should buy plenty of medicine and food. The rest I would keep to myself. I still had enough to buy two horses and to pay for our journey through southern England and across into Ireland. Could I find lodgings nearby? It was not a long illness, this sweating sickness. Either John Skelton would be cured or dead before a week was out. I shrugged my shoulders and began to turn away, but then turned back.

'What on earth possessed you to tell Gilbert Tailboys your secret?'

'What! He didn't say anything!' James also had turned away, but now he had whirled back to face me.

'Yes he did.' I took pity on his air of stunned disillusionment and added, 'But luckily only enough to let Mistress Boleyn and Harry Percy know that you have a secret.'

'I can't believe it.'

'Well, he was very drunk.' And then, when he didn't comment on that I said, 'And did the secret involve your birth?'

He nodded slowly and looked rather shame-faced.

'Your mother told you,' I said resignedly.

'No, it was my father, actually. He told me that they had changed my birthday; that I was really four months older than I thought I was. My mother had been promised to another man, but when she told her parents that she was pregnant, they allowed her to marry my father.' James smiled a little. 'Piers Rua said that it was all nonsense; that under Irish law there would be no problem.'

'But not under English law,' I said grimly. 'Under English law you are illegitimate and would have no right to the earldom, or even to inherit lands from your father. I wonder why he told you.'

'He was afraid that someone might tell me; in fact, he thought I might know already. He was anxious to tell me that it made no difference at all, that I was his eldest son and would always be that no matter who might say nay,' finished James.

'You do realise how it would change your position under English law. It would ruin everything. Why on earth tell Gilbert Tailboys?'

'It was stupid. I was drunk. I was trying to prove something, I suppose. Trying to prove that it didn't matter.'

I looked at him closely. 'Did Edmund Pace know about this? And don't tell me any stories about gambling or getting drunk.'

He shook his head. 'No, I swear to you. But he held over my head that I had a fight with St Leger while the king himself was in residence. Pace ordered that I should have a hand chopped off, but Master Cavendish talked him out of it. But Pace never let it rest; he kept telling me that he could still get an order to have my hand chopped off. And he and the king's serjeant were as close as a pair of thieves. I was afraid that he would do it and so I paid what he asked.'

'Well, keep your mouth shut from now on; you won't just lose an earldom. You'll lose your head,' I said brutally.

'I know. Makes a good reason to kill a man, doesn't it, a secret like that.'

'But you didn't do it.' I made it a statement, not a question and he nodded his head.

'No, I didn't do it.'

'I still think I should get you out of here.'

'No,' he said and there was a warning note in his voice.

'Have it your own way.' I was about to make a joke that I didn't know where he got his stubbornness from, but something about that white face stopped me. This was no obstinate boy. This was a young man with firm principles and I was proud of him. I raised a hand, almost a salute rather than a farewell, and turned to go.

'Hugh,' he said then.

'What?' I turned back.

'I didn't do this murder, Hugh. I had nothing whatsoever to do with it. I swear by all that I hold holy. I swear on my mother's life. Are you listening to me, Hugh?' He looked up and down the empty street, but nevertheless, lowered his voice a little and moved somewhat closer to me.

I nodded. James was not a liar; I had known him all his life and knew that even as a child he was always too proud to lie. And swearing on his mother's life. James adored his mother and would never have used that phrase lightly.

'I believe you,' I said. 'But others may not.'

'Well, then you find out who did do the murder,' he retorted quickly. 'I'm not going to run away, to run back to Ireland and to upset all the plans that my father has made, undo all the years of diplomacy. We want this title Earl of Ormond and we are going to keep it. The old earl trusted my father to look after his Irish interests. The Boleyn and the St Leger female heirs can divide the English property between them, Ormond is a place in Ireland, it's an Irish title and we deserve it. So, listen to me, Hugh, listen carefully. I'm not going to run away. I'm going to stay and face my trial if necessary.'

I stared at him dumbly, suddenly visualising the aftermath of that trial. He read my face and grinned with a sudden flash of white teeth.

'Go on, Hugh, you can do it. You can clear my name. My father always said that out of all the clever Mac Egans you were the most brilliant of them all. Go on, go and do it. I bet you have a notion. It's just a matter of working out the proofs. Thanks for the two flasks. And for the money. Just go now, Hugh. I'll send you a message, another poem, when it's safe for you to come back.'

I left him then. There was nothing more that I could do. And if I were to return to Hampton Court in time for supper, then I would have to go quickly. The cardinal's barge was due to bring his guests in good time for supper, plenty of time to rest, relax, and to get ready for one of the splendid suppers. It would leave Westminster Steps with great punctuality and already the first strokes of the abbey bell sounded on the air.

'Don't leave me to guess,' I said urgently. 'Find some more of Skelton's doggerel or make up some. By God's wounds it can't be too difficult. I've never read such rubbish. But keep me in touch. And remember, remember, day or night, you must be ready to leave.' Skelton, I reckoned, would be dead or recovered within a few days. From all that I had heard of the sweating sickness those who recovered did so quickly.

If a warrant was issued for the boy's arrest, then it might be too late, was my thought as I made my way back to Westminster steps to be greeted by Colm with great relief. It had been a boring day for him, but at least he was safe.

The cardinal's barge with his distinctive badge and men dressed in the livery of mulberry and gold was moored in its usual place. I was not the first to arrive. Already Tom Seymour was ensconced under the cardinal's awning with his brother Edward beside him. I took a seat opposite them. And then realised that Sir George St Leger was already beside him.

'You know Master Mac Egan or Master Brehon as the cardinal calls him,' said Edward politely to him. Edward, unlike young Tom, was a very smooth and diplomatic young man. He paid me several compliments about attaining the rank of judge at such a young age and then switched to St Leger, enquiring about his lands in Devon.

'I'm sorry to hear about my young relative,' said Sir George to me and Edward seized the opportunity to enquire about the state of Ireland. Edward Seymour was probably not much older than James, Harry Percy, Gilbert Tailboys and Thomas Arundel, but they were boys in comparison to this smooth and assured young man. He would do well in the service of the Princess Mary. And so I sat and watched Edward listening respectfully to Sir George about the recent happenings in the House of Commons and what an excellent Speaker that Sir Thomas Neville was reckoned and how much power he, as a member of the House of Commons, held. And all the time while St Leger chattered, Edward, with an adroit question or an exclamation of interest, encouraging the man into a state of happy contentment. By the time Princess Mary was old enough to assume the role of Princess of Wales, Edward would be an accomplished diplomat and probably head of her household, in the same way as the Earl of Ormond had risen to be Lord Chamberlain of her mother's household. Even his normally irrepressible young brother was very subdued by his presence and his flow of talk and looked at him anxiously from time to time.

Was Tom Seymour really in that much trouble? I began to ponder this. Why should the king's serjeant-at-arms, a man whose ambition it was to be a judge, concern himself with a scrubby little schoolboy. After all he had no responsibility for these boys. There was a clergyman from Oxford, a protégé of the cardinal's coming next week to superintend their studies. In the meantime the normal tutors came and went, giving them lessons in archery, tilting, music, dancing as well as Latin and composition. Why was the serjeant concerning himself with Tom? I wished now that I had cross-questioned the boy, but I had been too anxious about James to worry about other matters. Certainly now he was his usual bumptious self. Whatever worries he had, he was relying on Edward to sort them out.

'And how was your day in London City?' Edward said to me, and I saw Thomas's eyes light up at that question. One long leg moved slightly and his knee nudged his brother's leg. There had been speculation between the brothers about the real purpose of my errand to London and I had a feeling that Edward had been waiting for the opportunity to ask that question.

'Excellent!' I said enthusiastically and turning to Sir George I explained about my need for funds, so much more important in England than in Ireland, and how my patron, Sir Piers Rua, *your Butler relation, Sir George*, I could not help adding, had given me a draft on Sir Richard Gresham, a merchant banker. Tom shifted his position impatiently a few times as I related in boring detail all the stories told by Sir Richard about how he had been Cardinal Wolsey's agent in the purchasing of various tapestries and how he had selected eight chairs upholstered in black, 'each of them,' I said solemnly, 'having a high back fringed with green silk, and having my lord's arms and letters embroidered on them. And I think,' I said, drawing out the description, as I could see Thomas fidgeting restlessly and glancing under his black eyelashes at his brother every few seconds. 'Yes, I do think that he said there was, also, four gilt apples on each of them. Can you remember where those chairs are kept, Tom?'

'No,' he muttered, and once again his knee nudged against his brother's spotless hose and he gave an impatient sigh.

This time Edward responded. 'So you are leaving us and going back to Ireland, then, are you, Master Mac Egan?'

I gave what I hoped sounded like a hearty laugh. 'I rather doubt that. I think that I am enjoying the cardinal's hospitality too much,' I said. 'Hampton Court is such a beautiful place. Italy is wonderful, but Hampton Court would rival some of the palaces in Venice or Rome. Such pictures, such statues, such tapestries.' I went on with giving them a short summary of all that I knew about the new learning, about the new ways with art and architecture based on Greek and Roman ideas, and bored them for while about my praise of the symmetrical plan for Hampton Court. 'I must say that I envy you, young Thomas,' I said with a heavy-handed imitation of the late instructor of the wards, 'it's an education in itself to live amongst such beauty.' The more restless he got, the more I warmed to my subject. 'When you think that even the smallest rooms … just think of that closet in the cardinal's lodgings with the gold and blue ceiling above you and the priceless carpet from Turkey beneath your feet …' I drew in a deep breath and shook my head with the wonder of it all. Tom was flushed with impatience and that amused me, but I had to admire the grace with which Edward managed, simultaneously, to greet other guests getting on the barge and at the same time appear to give me his undivided attention.

'And, of course,' I put in a light laugh at this stage, 'the cardinal's wine is superlative. Why, Master Seymour,' I enquired, 'did you think that I was going back to Ireland?' He had been, I remembered, present on that Shrove Tuesday evening.

Gently, almost unobtrusively, his hand pressed down on his young brother's knee. *Leave this to me.* I could almost hear the words so silently conveyed in that gesture. Tom heard them also. His mouth; that red-lipped mouth now mirrored in Susannah's painting of the fisherman in the Sea of Galilee had opened impetuously, but then it was shut firmly. Tom sat back and left me to his brother's superior tactics.

'Oh, servants' gossip,' he said nonchalantly. 'Tom gathered from James Butler's man that you were all on your way back to Ireland.'

'Really, goodness!' I shook my head sadly. I didn't believe a word of it; Padraig wouldn't have said such a thing. Why was Master Edward Seymour trying so hard to probe? I thought back to what James had said. Even when Skelton either recovered or died, I doubted whether I could force James to go back to Ireland. He was a very thoughtful boy and his father's position meant a lot to him. Ormond was an Irish title – came from the two Gaelic words *oir Mumhain* meaning east Munster, one of the four provinces of Ireland. The original member of the family had come to Ireland with King John, over 300 years ago and though he had been an Anglo-Norman named Theobald Walter, soon to be rechristened Butler after his office to the king, the family had steadily become more identified with Ireland down through the centuries. Piers Rua was determined to keep the title of Ormond in his family and not allow it to go to England, through a female inheritance, something forbidden under Irish law. And James was determined to do his father's bidding and act as his advocate in the court of King Henry. No, it was no good thinking about fast horses and ships. James would stay and would need his innocence established. One way or another the affair of the murder of Edmund Pace had to be solved and James cleared of all suspicion.

As soon as we arrived back at Hampton Court, I left the others to make their obeisances to the cardinal and made my way towards my lodgings. Colm had gone ahead of me and the king's serjeant was there, chatting to him as he supervised the unloading of the firewood.

'Ah, the wanderer has returned.' He was falsely genial, like a man ordered to play a part. We got on fairly well, on the whole, but it was in a sharp, competitive sort of way where each was anxious to convince the other of the superiority of his native legal system.

'You must be cold; not a great day to be on the river. What about a game of tennis before supper? Will warm you up.'

'Do you know, I'd enjoy that,' I said in an easy manner. 'Give me an appetite for my supper.'

I didn't quite trust him, but I might be able to influence him. Present him with another and more plausible candidate, or perhaps, I amended, thinking of the rope and the axe, with a signed confession and he might be willing to abandon his case against James.

He was scrutinising me carefully, and then unexpectedly he smiled.

'Well, I'm looking forward to it,' he said lightly. 'Meet you at the tennis play in a few minutes. Did you have a good day?' he asked over his shoulder, but did not wait for a reply.

14

I collected my racquet and soft shoes, leaving Colm occupied with receiving our stores for the evening. It was one of the busiest times of the day when the second instalment of firewood, candles, wine and bread was being delivered to those lucky enough to have the cardinal's generous *bouche de court*, and he would have plenty of company at this work for an hour or so. I could leave him without any worries.

'Do you want me to bring around your stuff in an hour, would that be about right?' asked Colm.

'No, don't trouble yourself. I'll take a change with me,' I said. The king's serjeant never bothered with a servant and when I played him I followed his lead in this matter. We had had many interesting discussions while we washed and changed after a match on the differences between the law that I had been taught at Brehon law school and that he had learned in the Inn of the Courts. It would be interesting to hear what he had to say today. The game of tennis was fast and furious with little opportunity for talk. At the most, a few shouts could be exchanged as the dozens of distinct serves with different trajectories and spins sent the ball sliding over the net, or bouncing from a penthouse roof or slamming against a netted window.

No, the best time for talking would come afterwards, afterwards while we stood together in the small lodging attached to the court, enjoyed the heat of the fire that was always kept burning there, mopped our perspiration with damp sponges, rubbed dry our hair and changed our sweat-soaked shirts for clean linen. The king's serjeant carried what he needed in a neat leather satchel. I would do the same thing. We would both be wearied after the exercise, and no matter who won we would both be pleased with ourselves.

I seized a spare shirt and a soft linen towel and crammed them into a bag. Richard Gibson had been, when I met him earlier, very uncurious, most uncharacteristically so, about my visit to London. He knew, I could bet on it, that I had been missing all day and undoubtedly saw me descend from the cardinal's barge in the company of other guests from London but he had only asked a perfunctory and conventional question about my day and had not followed it up with any further questions. Perhaps he hoped that I would unbend when we matched our racquets.

When I emerged from my lodging, after telling Colm that I would back in an hour, I could see that it had eventually begun to snow at last, real snow, falling thickly and heavily, covering over the Base Court as I went through it and making the wood yard boys shout with excitement. The narrow passageway was filling with snow and some child from the kitchen, armed with a broom, was sweeping it up as soon as it fell, stopping occasionally to throw a snowball at the wood yard boys scurrying past

with their flat-stopped barrows. The boy's heart was more
in those skirmishes than in his task and he was leaving a
thin skim of snow on the paving stones – more dangerous than soft piles would have been and I resolved to
be careful on my way back. But the real danger would
only come if the stuff froze overnight. Still there was little
chance of that. I looked at the sky. The soft heavy pale
grey clouds were full of snow and snow held little threat
for the cardinal's magnificent dwelling with its wood
yard piled six foot high with well-seasoned oak and large
bundles of faggots and its larders, pantries and storerooms
bursting with food. Even if the snow lasted a week or
longer, it would not be a threat to supplies. By morning the roads might be impassable, but Hampton Court
would still have its waterway open to London and to the
fields and farms to the west of it. Nevertheless, it probably meant that the guests would not be in any mind to
rush away. Apart from the king and his privy servants, all
of whom had been playing cards all night, everyone who
had been present in Hampton Court when the instructor of the wards was murdered was still there. I would do
as James told me. Turn my mind to finding the killer and
stop worrying about him. I reached the tennis play with
my face stinging from the cold, but with an odd feeling
of exhilaration.

The king's serjeant was waiting for me when I arrived
and was armed with a coin which he tossed as soon as I
came in the door and while my eyes were still adjusting
from the bright glare outside to the candlelit shadow-
filled interior. 'Heads, me, tails you,' he said before I could
speak and then snatched up the coin as soon as it fell.
'Tails! The hazard end for me,' he said with a grimace.

I did not argue. He had the worst of the throw. The service end gave a player a great advantage and to get it at the beginning of the game when one was still fresh was a piece of luck. And yet, somehow, just before he clapped his hand over the coin I had thought that I could see on the coin the sombre head of the old king, the present king's father, seated on his throne. My lips twitched as I went to my place. Serjeant Gibson was trying very hard to get me in an expansive mood. I swung my racquet. I might win this first game, I planned, but allow him to win the match in the long run. I chipped the ball viciously with the edge of my racquet, causing it to rise up and strike the penthouse roof. It rolled there for a moment and then fell down with an odd bounce. He hit it, but half-heartedly and it went into the net. I gave a shout of triumph.

'James well, was he?' he called suddenly as I let the racquet smack the ball down towards the winning galley. The bell rang. Another point to me.

'What did you say?' I yelled the words just as the ball hit his side of the court. I had placed it badly and he managed to slam it into the grill. I saw him smirk.

'Just wondered how he was. There's supposed to be sweating sickness in that part of the city.' The king's serjeant must have made time to talk with young Tom. I smashed the ball back to him. His return shot landed close to the wall under the gallery and my racquet stroked the wall instead of the ball, making me swear aloud. Well, let him think that his verbal shot caused me to lose my poise. He could spend a month of Sundays searching the city for James. Perhaps, after all, it was a piece of luck for me that young Seymour insisted on coming to London.

The king's serjeant was a man who had lived in the city of London during his student days, knew it as well as the back of his hand, he had told me once. Let him send a man to search Bradstrete and Austin Friars if he wished. It must be a good hour or so away from Westminster. I smiled to myself as I served again. The score was deuce. In wits as well in tennis we were well-matched.

This time he hit the ball well and skilfully. It went into the chase and I had lost my superior position in the serving end. First game to him. As I waited at the net post for him to pass me, I had a good look at his face. He didn't look triumphant, or as one who was scanning my face for information. No, he seemed, oddly, as though he were listening intently and his eyes went towards the door to the outside. But when I turned to look over my shoulder, he nudged me, held out his hand and I handed him, as tradition ruled, two balls.

And then he was in the serving place and my back was to the door. He served with great vigour, bouncing the ball up and down three or four times, and continually driving it overhead so that it clanged against the tin penthouse roof at the side and from time to time aiming directly at the tambour.

There was a sharp, cold wind in the back of my neck for a second and then a click as if a door had been cautiously closed. I turned around and then back again. Richard Gibson was hopping his ball vigorously and had served before I had completely straightened myself. Another point for him. I was younger, just over thirty, while he must have been edging towards his middle forties, and in general I was a slightly better tennis player. However, today everything seemed to be going his way

and I allowed it to do so. I played carefully, with great
subtlety and skill, diving for balls and just reaching them
a minute late, but then missing. The score was adding
up for him and I was happily allowing myself to slide
into defeat when I had the oddest impression that I was
being watched.

And then I exerted myself, using every trick that I
had learned over the years, driving the ball towards the
net at a deliberately low angle so that he relaxed and
then, when the ball barely trickled over, raised his racquet just too late. My game! Now it was I that passed
him at the net post, I who accepted the two balls with a
gracious salute.

Before I served, I looked up towards the 'dedans',
the long, netted window behind which spectators
could watch the match in safety. There did not seem to
be anyone there, but I did not look at it for too long.
I concentrated on playing well, for now. Even if I won
this game, I could easily arrange that he would win the
match. But, with such an astute character, I didn't want
to awake any suspicions that I was deliberately trying to
lose. Once he had begun to despair, I could ease back.

And so I pulled out all the tricks that I knew, swerving
the ball cross-court, spinning the ball with an underhand
flick of the wrist, holding the racquet ankle-high one
moment and above my head in the next. And then, deliberately and swiftly, I changed a stroke at the last minute
and aimed my ball towards the 'dedans'. I hit as hard as I
could. The net was strong, but it vibrated with the force
of the ball.

And I saw the movement beyond the net, deep in the
darkness behind it.

It would have taken nerves of steel to have continued to crouch unmoving in the darkness there while a ball came pelting towards his face at twice the speed of a galloping horse. For a second I saw the movement of a pale face, and then a flash. The person in the gallery had a weapon, sword or knife, steel, anyway. There was no mistaking that flash. I cast a hasty glance across at the king's serjeant. Like myself, he had stripped to his shirt and I could see no sign of a weapon on him. That was not to say, though, that he had not left a dagger with his clothing. I had not watched him with any care while I had undressed.

Now I deliberately began to lose. I wanted to bring this game to an end. It was pointless, anyway. If a friend had come to watch, well, he would depart instantly, wrapped in his warm cloak. We would have no time together to chat and there would be no opportunity for me to put firmly into his head the possibility that James was not the only possible suspect. I needed to convince him that the arrow was not the cause of death. If he could accept the conclusion of the queen's physician, Dr Ramirez, that a knife had killed Edmund Pace, then at least the field was opened up.

I was worried about that silent watcher in the gallery. Should I shout a question? I decided that it would be more sensible to wait until the game was over. It was probably, I tried to tell myself, one of the young men in the household, at a loss for some outdoor pursuit in this bad weather who had been attracted to the sound of balls and racquets and who had come in to watch the match.

The king's serjeant sent the ball spinning across the net, a short bouncing stroke that came too near for comfort.

I made a clumsy effort to leap back and then a spectacu-
lar stumble, which gave a good excuse for missing the
ball. A point for him. The king's serjeant had a spurt of
new energy, as anxious as I to get this game over and
done with, perhaps.

Why?

The question filled my mind. I missed the next ball
and heard the bell ring as it entered the winning galley.
The sound reverberated around the long, narrow court,
echoing from the concrete floors and walls.

'Game, set and match to you,' I said. And walked forward to shake his hand.

He pretended not to see. We gathered up the balls in
silence, well, not full silence because he whistled loudly
as he did so. He tossed the balls into the box and rapidly
changed his soft slippers for his boots, slinging his fur-
lined cloak around his shoulders and making rapidly for
the door.

'See you at supper,' I called after him and he raised a
hand in reply.

At least I think that he did, but I was not sure as a
moment later a sudden sharp blow on the side of the
head knocked me sideways and that was really all that I
remember happening after my tennis match.

Until I woke up, or came back to consciousness.

★★★

For a moment I thought that I was in bed. It was dark
and very quiet. But the beds provided by the cardinal
for his guests were soft featherbeds on top of the straw-
filled mattresses. I was lying on hard boards. I slightly

raised my head and bumped it. Wood beneath me, wood above me. I moved a hand, didn't need to extend it too far. It touched wood. Moved the other hand. Wood again. Stretched as far as I could. My feet, still in the tennis slippers, touched wood. Wriggled up a little. My head bumped against something. More wood. I was in a wooden box. My foot felt something, I wriggled my toes and lifted the foot. Something hard and round. I guessed instantly what it was. I had often rolled my foot over one of those cork-filled, seamed tennis balls and the feel was familiar. I was in the long wooden box where the tennis balls were stored. Someone had emptied the box, leaving a ball behind by accident, probably, and I was shoved into the empty space.

I was not tied up. My legs and arms were quite free, my mouth, though dry, was unencumbered by a gag. I lifted my arm and pushed against the top of the box but it did not yield. I tried again, using both hands and feet, pushing against the lid as hard as I could, but it didn't work. I tried to lift my head and add its pressure, but it ached so badly that I let it slip back down again. I had been hit on the side of the head and I could feel a swelling there. I tried to picture one of those boxes: rather like a coffin, I seemed to remember. Yes, I thought, the lock, as one would imagine, was on the side of the box: just a padlock and hasp, if I remembered rightly. No great security. It was unlikely that anyone would seriously want to steal tennis balls, but some of the boys that worked in the kitchen or the wood yard might purloin a ball for their games around the narrow passageways of the service buildings. Surely I could rip the hasp from the wood if pushed hard enough.

But it was no use. The blow on the head had weakened me and extra exertion made me feel slightly sick. My legs trembled. What time was it? I had no means of knowing how long I had been here. It would have been about half an hour before supper time when I had been stunned. I was not feeling particularly cold; my doublet, jerkin, and cloak – even my linen towel had been spread on top of me, as though some kindly person had tucked me into my bed. Even so, I reckoned that I had not been lying in this wooden prison for too long. The chances were that everyone would be busy now with the evening supper, serving, eating, cooking, the wood yard boys busily delivering more wood as the fires died down, and the pot boys starting on the everlasting washing of dishes and pots. If I were right about the time, then it would be of little use to try shouting for help. The tennis play was situated at a distance from kitchen, hall, great chambers and lodgings. There would be little chance that anyone could find me.

My best chance would still be to tear the hasp from the lid, and so I would be better off lying quietly for a while in order to regain my strength before trying again. A faint light came through, now that my eyes were accustomed to the darkness. It was not airless in there and I remembered that the lid of the tennis balls' coffer had a few holes bored it in so that the balls would not become mildewed. I did my best to calm myself with that thought.

Looming in the background of my mind was a feeling of panic. I hated to be shut up anywhere, always liked to have a window open, hated even to go into small store cupboard. I focused my eyes on those small round spots of pale grey light. Plenty of air, I said to myself. I tried to force myself to sleep, but knew that I would not be able to do that. Think of something. Use this time for thinking. No action is required, no talking, just thought. I should be able to do this.

Firmly I shut my eyes and thought of the garden at Hampton Court, admired the tapestry-like patterns of the knot garden, the jewelled colours of summer flowers enclosed with tiny walls of purple and silver lavender. And then, more calmly, I moved my thoughts back to the affair of the murder of the instructor of the wards. Surely I could solve this case. James had confidence in me, so I should have confidence in myself. I went through the last ten years in my mind and thought of cases where I had worked out the truth.

I set myself to forget that there was barely two inches of space between my mouth and the lid of the coffer that imprisoned me and began to ponder this strange case. Someone, I reckoned, came into the hall that night, no doubt while the king was partaking of the sugar banquet in the cardinal's room, or perhaps even later when the king himself and the young gentlemen and pages from his privy chamber were dancing with the queen's ladies in waiting. Most of the household, except those that were on night-time duty would have gone to their beds by then. Master Beasley, the cook, had told me that he made a habit of retiring at eight o'clock on winter evenings and made sure that all the kitchen scullions did likewise. After the pageant castle had been removed, the torches on the artificial branches quenched and packed away, the floor swept and the fires refurbished, the great hall would have been empty for the rest of the evening.

And then I considered one that had remained and shifted uneasily in my narrow prison. The picture of Susannah came to my mind. Nevertheless, when it came down to it, James had to come first. Who, I asked myself, was likely to kill that unpleasant man? There would have been a motive – the motive for all the people that I had suspected from time to time had been the same. Blackmail. An ugly word and an ugly concept. Not so important in Gaelic society where everyone seemed to know everyone else's business, but here amongst the king and his nobles there was always an edge of fear. The threat of disembowelment, of an axe, a frequently blunt axe, descending on one's neck, the fear of hanging, hanging from a rope, even worse, hanging from chains and dying an agonisingly slow death … there was a miasma of fear among all of those bejewelled and bedecked gentlemen and ladies, and among those who served them.

And fear would have been the root of blackmail.

Holding firmly to my thought and endeavouring to breathe slowly and calmly. Edmund Pace had been blackmailing someone. This person found him in the great hall. With a knife such as Dr Ramirez had described, a thin, very sharp knife, then the murder could have been committed very easily. There in the dim light, with most of the candles blown out and just a glow from the fire, it would have been easy to pull out that sharp knife and plunge it into the man's heart. But the arrow. Where did the arrow come from? Had the murderer brought it? Unlikely. Everything seemed to point to the murder of the instructor of the wards being an opportunist crime. I tossed impatiently, hitting my shoulder against the solid wood at the side of the box and bringing my mouth dangerously near to the lid. Drops of moisture fell from it now and I had to suppress my panic-stricken feelings that the air might be getting used up.

Did someone deliberately try to inculpate James? I asked myself. Desperately I fastened my mind on visualising the great hall in the dim light on that March Shrove Tuesday. Something had come into my mind in that elusive way that things sometimes pop in and then hang at the back of the memory like a skeleton leaf on the forest floor in autumn. It was something to do with that red glow from the fire. Why the fire?

And then suddenly I got it!

Fire! That was the key. I remembered my conversation with poor Ramirez. The body. Stiff as a poker.

And the arrow.

James had said that he had lost the arrow firing after a duck near the moat. But the wood yard was there, on the other side of the moat, just near to the water. And I had often seen, during the day, the hard-working boys piling up the wood, talshide after talshide of it, and also bundles of faggots, onto those flat, four-wheeled barrows, leaving them all ready to be pushed out to replenish the fires at regular times during the day, and last thing in the evening so that fires could be quickly revived with dry wood first thing in the morning. There must be about one hundred of those barrows lined up under the shelter of a penthouse roof. As soon as wood was chopped and graded it was quicker and most efficient to pile it onto a barrow, rather than stack it on the wet ground of the wood yard, open to the rain. What if James's arrow, flying across the moat, and then dropping down, had fallen into a space between some of those rounded logs? No one would notice it.

But my murderer, having killed his victim, might seek to divert attention, might spot the arrow there on a barrow beside the fire – I visualised a sudden flame spurting up and the light catching the steel tip, a sudden flash and a sudden inspiration. The scratched initials may not even have been visible.

And so the whole pantomime began. The arrow was used to pierce a hole in the tapestry, right through the hub of the cart – that was a mistake; yes, that was a mistake. Unlikely that an assailant would take that much care as to aim at the stitched hub of the cart. A picture of the murderer began to form in my mind. Naïve, perhaps? And then the body was dragged over, placed lying down behind the tapestry, the arrow was stuck into the wound and *voilà*, as the cardinal would say, the scene was set. The murderer could retire and await the discovery. In my mind's eye, I began to write a list. *Name, Motive, Opportunity* were my headings, scribed in my best Italian hand.

But the list was too long. Almost anyone could have slipped surreptitiously into the hall at a time when corridors and passageways were lit dimly and ladies and gentlemen went to and fro between their lodgings and the cardinal's rooms. And pages, secretaries, gentlemen and ladies in waiting were sent on errands by their masters and mistresses. Hampton Court was guarded like a fortress with moat, and barred and locked doors; but on the inside, once a face was known, people came and went as they pleased. In the end, my list, hanging there in front of mind's eye began to mesmerise me and I slept.

And woke to a feeling of terrible panic. I was stone cold, my legs and arms seemed frozen to my side; the box seemed to have shrunken overnight. I screamed. It escaped me before I could control it, but once it erupted, I lost all control. I might be here for days. I and the two serjeants were the ones who played the most tennis these days. Others preferred the sport of hunting or jousting.

'Help! Help me!' I screamed and wished that I believed in prayer. I tore with my nails at those tiny dots of light which were the only thing that rested between me and suffocation. Slightly brighter light. No good, though. No good unless someone decided to play tennis. I screamed for help again and then stopped. My voice had torn through my throat and the sound had come out, ragged and hoarse. I struggled violently for control. I would have to preserve my voice until I heard a door open. I had to lie very quietly and wait until I heard the welcome click of the key in the lock. Surely someone would come? If not to play tennis, then perhaps to clean the place. My throat was sore with shouting and now I realised that I was also desperately thirsty. There was no way that I could get a drink so I tried to thrust that realisation away. Once more I went back to visualising my list but this time it brought no measure of calmness with it. I was consumed with regrets. Why had I agreed to play tennis with a man whom I suspected? Why had I not secured a couple of horses at the very first word of 'murder' and taken James back to Ireland, back behind the stoutly barred doors of Kilkenny Castle? I could just as well conduct marriage negotiations from there. I moved my legs fretfully and tried not to imagine a long drink of red wine from the barrel in the corner of the kitchen. I began to recite in my mind all the heptads that I had learned in law school: *seven ways in which a church building can be destroyed without legal claim, seven bloodsheds that do not incur fines, seven women who …*

And then I heard a click. I heard it and I was dumb. For a long moment I could say nothing. When my scream came out eventually, it was rusty and seemed to die half way out of my throat. I tried again. There was a silence, a croak from a dry mouth. Violently I kicked at the lid of the wooden box.

And then a frightened voice, a young voice, half-broken said: 'God's wounds. Who's there?'

'Tom!' That came out better. The flood of relief was oiling the cords in my throat. Whoever was responsible for hitting me over the head and locking me into the tennis balls' box, I certainly did not suspect a boy of doing that. What would be the point?

'It's Hugh, James's friend,' I managed to say.

'The key is in the padlock. Wait, I'll turn it.'

It seemed too easy. I told myself not to hope, not to expect that the key would work, but it clicked with the precise sound of a well-oiled lock. Tom raised the lid instantly, staring at me, open-mouthed. For a moment he looked like what he really was, just a child. He had left the door open and a blast of cold air rushed in on me. There was light too, very bright light coming from the doorway. I tried to raise my head and felt as though I would vomit so lowered it again. I turned my head away from the door and swallowed hard. My head was thumping.

'What happened?' His voice, for once, sounded frightened.

I did not answer. I tried to sit up, but the wave of sickness came over me again. I had seen enough, though, to realise that the light came from the snow piled up outside the still open door. I began to shiver and I couldn't control it.

'Shall I fetch someone?' Tom came a little nearer. He had a tennis ball in his hand. He looked frightened.

'Why did you come?' The words came out in a croak.

Tom held up the tennis ball. 'I was borrowing this, I wanted a tennis ball.'

So it was sheer luck. Another wave of sickness overwhelmed me.

'What happened to you? What were you doing in that box?'

The words echoed in my head but I could make no sense of them. I concentrated on not vomiting, swallowed hard. I closed my eyes tightly against the glare from outside and tried to breathe in slowly and deeply.

'Do you want any help?' Now he was kneeling beside the coffin, as I now thought of it.

'No.' I pressed my hands over my eyes. 'No, go and get Colm, my servant, in my lodgings, but take that key with you! Don't leave that key. I don't want anyone to lock me in again.' My voice had risen with the last command and with shame I heard it crack.

He sounded embarrassed. 'I'll be very quick. Don't worry.' He was gone before I could repeat my command about the key, but when I reached out, and felt the lock, there was no key in it.

It seemed a long time, though. I kept my eyes shut. The deadly waves of nausea were less troublesome like this. Tentatively I moved my legs and my arms trying to work the stiffness out of them. It was wonderful to have that lid removed from on top of my face, but I was beginning to think that I was suffering from concussion. That had happened to me before in Kilkenny when I had slammed my head against the concrete floor of the tennis court. Only time would cure it, I knew, but time was not what I had at the moment. I needed clear wits. Once again I tried to concentrate on those lists of names. From outside I heard the noise of a shovel and then the swish of a broom. They were clearing the snow outside my prison and the sound was comforting. There were plenty of people outside there, ordinary people doing an ordinary job. The murderer, whoever he was, could not come in and finish his deadly task.

And then Tom came back, the door swinging open bringing light and the sharp fresh smell of snow.

'He's not there. Colm is not there. Not in your lodgings. There is no sign of him,' he said breathlessly.

15

I sat up carefully and slowly feeling the wave of nausea come back. 'Fetch a doctor,' I said. I changed my mind. Useless to have Dr Augustine. He would just bleed me and make me feel worse.

'Find Master Cavendish. Find him and send him here instantly.' I was beginning to feel less sick. I would manage. The important thing was to make contact with the cardinal and talk to him about what to do. My head ached, but my mind was very clear. Now I knew the truth.

But this imprisonment of me for a period of less than a day just did not make sense to me.

'See if you can stand. Lean on me.' Tom stretched out a hand. There was a slight spurt of warmth within me and I felt my muscles respond as I thought of James, with shame for my shortcomings and my past stupidity but with a surge of determination to get the boy out of this affair in safety.

'Here.' He held out my fur-lined cloak and then without waiting for me to take it, draped it around my shoulders and fastened the ties under my chin.

'Shall I go now?'

I nodded. My legs were still stiff and the muscles trembled. I would soon be back to myself, though and when he had left, I sat on the bench and rubbed my legs. My boots were there in the corner of the room. It was a strange affair. Why not throw me in the river once I had been knocked unconscious. This violence towards me and the imprisonment in such a public place which could not have lasted too long made no sense with what I had been painfully working out last night.

It was almost as though someone just wanted me out of the way for a number of hours.

Had my release been planned?

And where was Colm? Had something happened to James?

Master Cavendish crashed through the door a few minutes later.

'Hugh! What a terrible thing! What happened? Are you all right? This is a terrible business? Nothing seems to be going right these days! And His Grace is so upset! I've never seen him like this!'

I fastened on what was for George the most important matter.

'Why is His Grace so upset?' I asked mildly, wishing that he would help to pull my boots on. What with the stiffness of my joints and my aching head, I was having quite a struggle.

'And wait until he hears about this, now!' George confirmed my view that my small mishap would not be of huge importance to the man who was not only legate, but also Lord Chancellor of England.

'So what did upset him?'

George looked evasive.

'I think I had better allow His Grace to tell you about that himself.' He turned his attention to the lesser matter, looking down into the opened tennis ball container.

'Don't tell me that you spent the night in that little space,' he said with horrified pity. 'Poor Hugh, you must be cold and cramped. Was it one of the boys, do you think? Young Tom Seymour, perhaps? Not Francis. He's a very pious boy, but perhaps George Vernon …'

'Tom released me,' I said. I didn't think it was a boyish prank, but I decided I wanted no more talk about it. 'So, let's go and see His Grace, George. Do I look respectable?'

'A little creased.' He eyed me as narrowly as though I were a linen tablecloth for His Grace's high table. 'Still, your cloak will hide most things.' To my relief, he seemed no longer interested in my overnight incarceration, but fussed around me, brushing some chalk from my cloak and offering me a comb, even reaching up himself to put a finishing touch to my hair.

'Well, considering everything, you don't look too bad,' he said with his head on one side. That would be the last of his speculations about my imprisonment, I guessed. He went ahead of me into the cardinal's room and, I suppose, told his story rapidly, because he was out again within minutes, beckoning me to come inside.

The cardinal had an angry look. His eyes, usually so good-humoured, had the bleak colour of chipped flint stones. He was wrapped in his splendid scarlet cloak and he huddled into it as though, despite the blazing fire, he felt a mortal chill.

'Sit down, Hugh,' he said gravely. 'You will take a glass of wine?'

Almost before the words were out of his mouth, and without waiting for any reply from me, George had poured some wine into two silver goblets and now carried them across, placing each carefully on its silver tray on top of the priceless carpet from Turkey. I drank thirstily. Not the best thing for a man with a thumping headache, perhaps, but it put new heart into me.

'You were not at dinner, Hugh,' said the cardinal. I noticed that he stated the fact, but did not ask a question. He had doubtless been told the whole story by his gentleman usher and would have drawn his conclusions. I saw a glance pass between them and the cardinal nodded gently, pleased that I had said nothing. I guessed that I was about to be enlightened.

'George, have we something to offer our guest? Perhaps you might fetch something? You feared that there would be more fish, doubtless, that's why we did not see you at table. But, since today is not a fast day, the kitchen might have something to tempt our guest's appetite, what do you think, George?'

And thus, neatly, George was got rid of and in the silence after his departure, the cardinal eyed me across the table for a long moment.

'I made you a promise, Hugh, and the promise is broken.' His voice was bleak with, if it were possible, an undernote of fear in it. I looked across at him in a puzzled way.

'I promised you that you would have until Monday to solve this matter, but it appears that I had no right to make such an assurance. There is a proclamation on the very gate of Hampton Court, and in all public places in the city of London, that a man is sought for the murder of

Edmund Pace.' The cardinal took a longer draught than usual from his wine goblet and took from a drawer in his table a large piece of paper. It was printed in the usual rough style of public proclamation, the words etched carelessly into a block of wood and then stamped on the page. But, blotted and blurred as it was, the message was quite clear:

'Wanted for the MURDER of Master Edmund Pace,
Instructor to the Wards at Hampton Court,
JAMES BUTLER
Aged about 20 years. Very tall. Red hair, red beard, walks
with a limp.'

'I see.' I handed the poster back to him. No doubt that there would also be men crying the name of James Butler in the streets of London and brandishing pamphlets. My blood seemed to have turned to ice and I imagined James as I had seen him last, standing on the doorstep of that house in Canon's Row, red hair and red beard both blazing forth his identity. And the limp, that would be the final touch.

'It wasn't I, Hugh. I've had nothing whatsoever to do with this. The king overrode me in this matter.' He compressed his lips and sat for a moment, his eyes fixed on the ornate pattern of the table covering. I waited quietly. There was nothing that I could say and nothing now that my friend and patron, Cardinal Wolsey, could do for me. But why? The king, I knew, was capricious, impulsive, easily led. But who had brought this matter up? Who had persuaded the king to take this matter into his own hands? There had been no talk of relatives –

Edmund Pace was a man who had come to London in his youth, from somewhere in Cornwall.

I had a notion.

'I travelled back on the barge with Edward Seymour. Sir George St Leger was there, also. He would be a first cousin of Sir Thomas Boleyn, would he not?' I allowed the words to hang in the air and saw him nod.

So it was St Leger who had procured the 'wanted'.

'The Ormond inheritance,' I said slowly.

He smiled but there was still a worried look in his eyes. I understood that. The king had overridden him, had taken the matter out of his cardinal's hands, for the sake of a low-ranking courtier. That was a grave rebuff to a man who normally held such power. Who was behind it, who had persuaded the king to do this? I raised my eyebrows at him.

'You must understand, Hugh, that Sir George St Leger is a boon companion of the Duke of Suffolk,' said the cardinal.

So that was it. The Duke of Suffolk was married to the king's younger sister, but that was not all. He was also a prime companion at arms to the king, and had been brought up with him in the court of his father. The king and the Duke of Suffolk were as close as brothers. If St Leger was sponsored by Suffolk, then there was little that my friend, the Cardinal of York, could do for James. But what was the reason for my imprisonment?

'I see,' I said. That would be about all that I was going to get from the cardinal. The king had taken the matter from out of his hands. A slight insult to a proud man such as the cardinal, but a disaster, perhaps, for James Butler.

'Sir George St Leger has a lot of influence at court,' said the cardinal. There was a glint of a warning in his eyes and I bowed my head.

'So James had been judged and found guilty,' I said.

'You really should attend some law lectures at the Inns of Court, Hugh; the law in this country is different to your rather strange, rather utopian laws in Ireland. The man has now been accused and so he is guilty until he manages to prove his innocence.'

'Whereas it should be innocent until proved guilty, if we kept to Roman law, as well as Irish law. *Ei incumbit probatio qui dicit, non qui nega.* You know that quotation, I'm sure, Your Grace.'

'I shall miss you, Hugh,' he said affectionately. 'No one else in my household argues with me.'

I understood what he was saying. He wondered, probably, why I had turned up again, why I was not, even at this very hour, boarding a ship at Dover.

'Well, I'm sure that Your Grace is familiar with the reverend gentleman, Thomas à Kempis, and his saying: *Homo proponit, sed Deus disponit.* And, of course, we have often agreed, have we not,' I went on carefully, watching his face as I spoke, 'that youth is God these days.'

His eyes sharpened. He got up, went to the door, looked up and down the corridor, then came back in, turning the key in the lock. A careful man. He then went over to the space in front of the oriel window, twenty feet above the ground, and beckoned to me to join him.

'The horse won't run,' he murmured. He had guessed instantly that James had refused.

'No, Your Grace. He has refused.'

He raised one white, bushy eyebrow while still staring ahead at the snow-clad brick walls.

'Motives can be mixed.' I, too, fixed my eyes ahead, and kept my voice low. 'A mixture of pride, family feeling, foresight for the future.'

'Both wise and discreet,' he murmured and I remembered his words to the king about James. I wondered now whether he was speaking ironically, but he gave a decisive nod after a minute.

'Well, then this matter has to be cleared up, no matter how powerful the interests,' he said and I guessed that he was speaking of Sir George St Leger.

'I should, as you have often remarked, Your Grace, study some English law, but perhaps you will enlighten me as time is of the essence in this matter. Would a signed confession be acceptable in an English court of law?'

He frowned slightly. 'It depends on the credibility of the person who presented the confession. Who would witness this confession?'

'Who would Your Grace consider to be an excellent and impartial witness?'

'A lawyer, of course,' he said decisively. 'And, of course, a judge would be even better, would he not? I presume that the signature at the end of the confession could be verified?'

Despite the seriousness of the matter, I smiled. 'Your Grace, in your drive for efficiency and accountability, has ensured that we are all signing pieces of paper all day long. Yes, this signature can be verified.'

And then there was a sharp rap on the door. The cardinal went across, turned the key noiselessly in its well-oiled lock, returned to his desk and took his seat behind it, tucking his long white hands into the flowing sleeves of his scarlet cloak. I returned to my position opposite to him, feeling as I often felt in the presence of the cardinal, as though I were taking part in some pageant.

'Come in,' called the cardinal. He dipped pen into inkpot and held it while the jet-black ink fell drop by drop back down again.

'Yes, George,' he said tranquilly. And then, 'What, no food for my guest!'

'I beg your pardon, Your Grace, and yours, Hugh. I felt that you might want to know immediately what has happened. I was told about it when I was on my way to the kitchen. It's very bad news, I'm afraid, Hugh.'

'What?' Had James been taken, been placed in prison? I stared at him, numb with terror. All the terrible events that would follow this arrest flashed through my mind.

'It's your servant, Hugh,' said George. 'I'm very, very sorry to have to tell you this. He's been found. His body was in the water, by the edge of the pier. The boatmen were clearing the ice away with long poles and one of them prodded something. They've taken him out now.'

I got to my feet without a word, pushing past George and running down the stairs and was out of the door well ahead of him.

I had seen many dead bodies during the years when I had worked as a lawyer, first for my father and then on my account. And during my life time there had numerous battles and skirmishes. Ireland was never at peace and cousin fought cousin in bloody battles. And yet, somehow, this sight of the body of my poor Colm was almost unbearable. Barely sixteen years old. I remembered how he had sung on the ride down to Wexford, how excited he had been on his first sea voyage, how awestruck by the magnificence of Hampton Court, ten times the size of Kilkenny Castle, how cheerful a companion. I thought of the pride he had in speaking English and tears stung my eyes.

And then I blinked them away. The body was naked. His clothing had been stripped from him. There were marks on the body, dark stripes across the torso and the legs. A livid streak across the face, deep marks on his wrists. Colm had been tortured. He had been hung by the wrists, interrogated, no doubt, not believed when he said he knew nothing. For a moment, I almost wished that he had known something. James could have defended himself better. Poor Colm was always so deferential to the gentlemen, so impressed by their fine clothes, by their authoritative manners. My anger surged.

I turned to one of the yeomen standing looking down at the body. 'Go to the lodgings of Master James Butler in the Clock Court,' I ordered. 'See whether his servant is there. Send him to me. If he is not there, bring me word immediately.'

Sir George St Leger had joined the crowd now. Very pale, he looked, this morning. I tried to keep an eye on him unobtrusively. He had two servants with him. I had seen them on the barge from Westminster. Big, strong-looking fellows, speaking Cornish in low tones to each other. I remembered thinking idly that the cardinal, who was always on the lookout for fine yeoman, might offer a sum to Sir George to secure these Cornishmen for his palatial residence.

They had not looked at poor Colm. And that was strange. Every eye of those gathered around, men from the wood yard, clerks from the green court, bakers, even kitchen boys sent out to get fresh air and exercise by a vigorous sweeping of the narrow passageways, all of those eyes went immediately to naked body and only withdrew when the sight became unbearable. But not the two Cornishmen. Each of these men had their attention fixed on their master: Sir George. And so had I.

But why not me? If anyone knew the truth of James's whereabouts I did. Why just lock me into the tennis balls' chest and leave me there while they tried to flog from poor Colm a knowledge that he did not have? I clenched my teeth. Why had they not interrogated me, but I knew the answer to that. I was a favourite of the cardinal's, a man who had conversed with the queen. And I was a tough man, powerfully built, as good with my fists as with a sword. They might have been able to kill me, but they were unlikely to get me to betray James.

Poor Colm was gentle, peaceful, easily impressed. And his disappearance would have caused little disturbance. If it were not for the accident of the overnight frost, his body would have been swept away on the tide and it might have been assumed that he had gone back to Ireland, or perhaps gone to join James, or just run away as servants often did. Even I would not have been sure.

'Does the cardinal know about this?' I asked the question, not to George who would have been flustered and unsure but of the serjeant himself.

'I'll make a report of His Grace as soon as I get the facts. I've sent for Dr Augustine.'

'To certify that the man is dead, I suppose,' I said curtly. 'I don't suppose that he will be of much more use than that, and I can save you that trouble. He's dead. He's been hung by the wrists, tortured and then a knife was stuck in him so that he could not identify the man who tried to get the information from him.'

I saw his eyes look away from me and go in the direction of Sir George.

'Did you see anyone in the yard when you came out of the tennis play yesterday?' I asked abruptly.

'Just Tom Seymour and Francis Bigod collecting snow.' He did not enquire why I had asked and he left me abruptly, going towards the distant figure of Dr Augustine.

And then the men I had sent on the errand were back, bringing Padraig with them. I saw them come through under the arch of the gatehouse and I went hastily to meet him. He was older than Colm, older and wiser. I didn't see him allowing some strange men into the lodgings in the absence of his master. And, of course, if my suspicions of Sir George were correct, then the existence of Padraig, still faithfully waiting for his master might not have been known.

'Give me half an hour with the fellas that did that,' he said.

And then when I looked at him hopelessly, he nodded. 'There'll be no justice for him, I suppose. Well, I'll move in with you; should have done that before. Perhaps the poor lad would still be alive if I had done that,' he added.

I made up my mind. Everything was beginning to come clear to me. I would get Padraig out of the way.

'We're going to bring poor Colm back to Ireland. His mother would want him to be buried in Ireland in the grave with his father before him.' I said the words loudly and clearly. Sir George St Leger was approaching me, no doubt with condolences about the death of my servant. 'We'll bring him back to Ireland, the pair of us, Padraig,' I said even more loudly, just in case Sir George had not heard my first remark. I turned around and beckoned to the king's serjeant. He took a leisurely few minutes to make his way over.

'When the doctor has examined the body then I want it put into a good box, placed on a cart and tomorrow Padraig and I will take it back to Ireland. I'll have a word with the cardinal. He won't mind me borrowing a cart and some men to get to Bristol. They can return once we reach the boat.'

He looked at me through narrowed eyes. 'But what about the investigation into the murder?'

'Which murder?' I asked the question with an air of innocence and he looked annoyed.

'I have only one in hand at the moment.' He gesticulated towards the boathouse. One of the posters with James's name and description had been hammered to the door with four nails. I pretended not to see and kept my eyes fixed on the body of my poor Colm.

'Well, I'm sure you will solve it without this body once Dr Augustine has given you the benefit of his excellent advice. You don't need me here. I must take my servant's remains back to Ireland. It's a sacred matter with us,' I said solemnly.

'And so you are leaving us?' There was a hint of relief in his eyes.

'Yes. I must make my farewells. Come, Padraig, we'll go to the carpenter's yard together. Master Cavendish,' I called, 'will you come with us?' Just as well to get his authority to commission the carpenter and, of course, one could always count on George to spread the news through the whole of Hampton Court.

'I would like to see the poor lad safely under his native soil,' I explained as we walked across towards the carpenter's yard with the bitter wind blowing in our faces. I pulled my hood up over my head. It would be a hard ride to Bristol, but that wind was coming from the east now and a journey to the west would not be too difficult if the cart set off first thing in the morning. I looked quickly at George. His face was an easy one to read and it wore a puzzled expression.

'I've decided that I should get James's father, Piers Rua, over to London,' I confided in a low voice, placing my mouth quite close to his ear. 'The earl, well, he is always known as 'the earl' over in our part of the world, the earl is a very forceful man. He knows the king distrusts Kildare and Desmond, so there's just him and his people to fall back on him. I think his arguments might be more forceful than mine, what do you think, George? But, of course, don't tell anyone about that, will you?'

The air of puzzlement vanished from George's face. 'Yes, of course,' he said enthusiastically. 'You're quite right, Hugh. That will be the best thing to do. His Grace will be so pleased. No, I won't tell anyone, just say that you are determined to bring the body of your servant back to his family. I won't say anything about the other matter.' George knew very little about political affairs but he was eager to learn, and so I fed him a lot of facts about the dangerous political situation in Ireland, bewildering him with a multiplicity of unpronounceable Gaelic names. And he was helpful and authoritative in the carpenter's yard, deciding immediately that the coffin should be made from elm, picking out a large trunk already hollowed to serve as a water conduit and getting a promise from the clerk of the carpenters' yard that the work would be started instantly and finished before nightfall.

'It won't be a perfect job by any means.' The chief carpenter had a worried look about him.

'A few rough edges and splinters won't hurt,' I said reassuringly. 'Just make the lid thick. We have a four-day journey ahead of us.'

'Master Carpenter will do his very best for you,' said George and the man looked pleased.

'Just a plain coffin.'

'That's right. Nothing fancy,' I said. 'No hinges, no brass plates, nothing. When it's made, send a lad for me.'

'We'll load it onto a cart and then it will be ready for the body.'

'Good,' I said, resolving to get the body onto that cart as soon as possible. It would be important that the little procession would move off early in the morning before many people were astir.

'Thank you, George,' I said as we walked away. 'You're a great man to manage people. Now perhaps you might go and tell the cardinal all about it. I'll stay here. I don't think that I should desert the poor man at this stage.' I sent him off, beaming happily, to spread the news that I was leaving Hampton Court and to hint at secret reasons for my decision. I waited until he vanished and then went across to the group around the body beside the ferry pier. The king's serjeant had taken himself off and so had most of the other bystanders, including Sir George. Tom Seymour and Francis Bigod were hanging around near to the boathouse and I walked across to meet them.

'I've never thanked you properly for rescuing me, Tom,' I remarked. I placed a coin in his hand and looked at him speculatively. 'What made you come in this morning? You were by yourself, you weren't going to play tennis, were you?'

'Just wanted a ball,' said Tom in his insouciant manner. 'Edward gave me the idea. I thought it would give someone a bit of surprise if they were hit by a snowball and there was one of those hard tennis balls inside it.'

'I wouldn't do that if I were you,' I said. 'I've heard of a tennis ball killing someone. You're already in the serjeant's bad books. You don't want to be accused of murder, do you?' Boys of his age could be hanged under English law, I knew, and the thought of a hanging made an icy shudder run down my back. I hoped that I could convince the cardinal. I was taking a huge responsibility on my shoulders. Nevertheless, it had to be done. If only I could have convinced James, I would have mounted my horse and disappeared back to Ireland. But I knew that James had made his decision. 'Stick to snow,' I advised Tom. 'I don't want to see your head roll, or your ankles dance on the end of a rope. Now, you two better be off and get yourself ready for dinner.' Francis was glad to go. It had probably been Tom's idea to watch what might be happening to the dead body, now lying on a large loading slab with the elderly doctor bending over it.

There was a question that I needed to put to Dr Augustine. I wished that poor Ramirez were still here. Still, it was not a very difficult question. I probably knew the answer to it already. I stood silently behind him for a moment as he gazed down at the body, with its gaping knife-hole. He did not do any of the things that

Dr Ramirez did, but said in a self-important fashion, 'Yes, death would have been instant after that knife wound.'

'Could it be self-inflicted?' The serjeant cast an uneasy look at me.

'Possibly.' The doctor didn't sound too interested.

'And so he killed himself and then walked over to the river and threw himself in,' I said in a sarcastic manner. 'You know very well that he was murdered. I would say that you know why.' And probably know who, I added silently, but aloud said: 'Why has the body not stiffened, could you tell me that, doctor?'

Dr Augustine drew himself up and looked pleased. 'Ah, well that is one of the secrets of our trade,' he said pompously, 'but perhaps I can enlighten you. For some reason, intense cold stops decay, just as when we put food in cold storage. The river water froze last night. Once the body is taken into the warmth then *rigor mortis* will set in.'

'And the opposite,' I asked carelessly.

This puzzled him for a moment, but then he understood.

'Certainly,' he said. 'A body left in intense heat will stiffen fast.'

I turned to Padraig. 'You'll stay around, won't you? They won't take long in the carpenter's yard. See that the coffin is nailed down and left on the cart. And then pack your belongings and mine. We'll both be off first thing in the morning. But I have to see the cardinal, now.'

16

The first trumpet giving everyone half an hour to get ready for supper was blown at the time that I left Susannah. I decided I had to visit the cardinal, but would leave it until just before the meal. The cardinal, who suffered from a bad stomach, would rush through last-minute urgent correspondence before appearing exquisitely groomed and dressed to sit in calm and solemn meditation for ten minutes before the meal, as his physician had advised. In the meantime, I had things to do. I sorted out my belongings, put some useful things in a bag, and then went through the money that I had got from Sir Richard Gresham, dividing it up into neat piles. This would be the sixth time for this journey from Wexford to Bristol and I had a fair idea of how much the journey would cost for two men. And then, of course, there was the cost of transporting the coffin. Extra had to be allowed for that. No need now for elaborate preparations of hardened bread, no need to sneak out surreptitiously. The kitchen, would, as always provide provisions and use could be made of wayside inns. Padraig had made the journey even more times than I, and he would know every inn on the route. And as I dressed in my best and beautifully embroidered shirt and doublet, and covered it with a sleeveless jerkin in glossy black marten fur, I was turning over in my mind what to say to the cardinal. One matter, at least, I could try to put in train on this very night. I owed it to poor Colm, my faithful servant, now lying cold and dead on a cart.

But first of all I went through, once again, my instructions to Padraig. I did not want to burden him with any knowledge that could endanger him but it was essential that he understood the importance of carrying out all of my instructions with absolute accuracy.

'And for tonight, once I leave for supper, bar the door behind me, and the window. Open for no one and under no pretence, until you hear my voice,' I warned him. 'If necessary move that table in front of the door also, and keep your knife handy. Make a lot of noise, too. Hampton Court is a law-abiding household. The cardinal would not countenance any violence. So if you are attacked, shout for help, immediately. There are enough carpenters and woodcutters only a hundred yards away. Shout the place down!'

I left him with that advice. I wasn't unduly worried, though; he was a careful, experienced man.

I tapped on the cardinal's door five minutes before the second gong sounded and entered without waiting for a summons. He was completely ready, and the pile of letters that his secretary was placing in a bag had all been signed and sealed.

'Ah, Hugh,' he said with a nod. 'I thought that I might be seeing you.' He had a quick glance at the clock.

'Brian,' he said. 'Would you please tell George Cavendish to place Hugh beside me and Her Grace at table, tonight: we may not have time to finish our conversation, is that right, Hugh?'

'I'll be brief,' I said, the anger still bubbling within me, but waiting until the door closed behind Brian before saying, 'Your Grace, my servant has been tortured and murdered, and I want the man responsible for it to be publicly named and restitution to be given.'

'And the name of the man?' The cardinal raised his thin eyebrows at me.

I hesitated for a second, but only to gather my thoughts. 'My servant, Colm, now lying dead, Your Grace, saw and would have been able to bear witness to the man who murdered Dr Ramirez, in mistake, I do believe, for me. Young Colm saw Sir George St Leger raise the bow and fire an arrow towards the front door of my lodgings; I'm sure of that. Unfortunately for poor Ramirez, he had decided to pay me a late-night call and in the darkness was mistaken for me.'

The cardinal absorbed this calmly. 'And the king's serjeant, did he have any connection with this affair?'

Once again I was surprised by the detailed knowledge that the cardinal had of what was going on in this huge place.

'Only one man was seen by my servant,' I said and noted the slight sigh of relief, no more, perhaps, than the releasing of a breath.

'Nevertheless, this is a very difficult matter, Hugh,' he said, speaking in a very low tone of voice. 'You must understand that I can't go against the king. St Leger is high in his favour. In fact,' he continued, raising a white hand, as I impetuously opened my mouth to protest, 'in fact, I think that there is only one person now who can handle this matter, and that is the queen.'

I could see that he was thinking hard so I did not interrupt him. He was a man who always visualised a situation with great exactitude and never left his subordinates in any doubt as to the desired outcome.

'I think,' he said after a few moments, 'that this would be best if it came, not from me, not from you, but from the queen herself. You're a man who is good with words, Hugh, you tell the queen, but keep it obscure, vague, you'll know how to do this. Let the queen to be the one to ask questions and to take any measure that she wishes, yes, I think that is the way to handle it.' He rose to his feet to take the prescribed three turns around the room before descending majestically to the hall, while I pondered what he had said.

'Let us go, Hugh. You would not wish to be late when Her Grace, Queen Katherine, does us the honour of dining with us.'

I took the hint and went rapidly ahead of him, running down the corridor and taking the stairs two at time so that I reached the hall well ahead of the cardinal and was already in my place when he entered the room and waited by the door to escort Her Grace to her seat.

★★★

'So, you've had bad news, Hugh.' Once he had pronounced grace, the cardinal made that announcement loudly in a voice trained to reach to the back of any church or cathedral. Most people at the table, even those who were helping themselves to pottage, stopped what they were doing and looked at me.

'Yes, Your Grace.' There was a large mirror of burnished steel hung on the wall halfway down the hall. If I were giving judgement on the hill of Kyle back in my native Ossory then I would have aimed my voice at a bare patch of rock across the field, but the mirror would do just as well to throw the sound through this enclosed space.

'My poor servant,' I said and waited for the words to sound in all ears. The noise of spoons and knives paused, I took in a breath and let out on the next word. 'Murdered,' I said and heard the long *uuur* sound reverberate around the room. There was a stunned silence. Startled eyes flickered in the candlelight just as though a hundred flames had suddenly flashed. I looked down at my plate.

'Another murder! Jesu!' exclaimed the queen. She turned her head and looked at me past the cardinal's paunch. 'When did that happen?'

'Just this afternoon,' I said, still in a carrying tone. 'His poor body was fished out of the river not long before suppertime. He had been murdered with a knife stuck into his heart.'

'What is happening, here? My Lord Cardinal!! This is terrible!'

I paused for a moment, but she said no more. Her face was thoughtful, but this was a very discreet woman, a woman who had learned diplomacy in a hard school. I could understand why the cardinal did not want to approach her directly.

And so I bowed to the queen, said nothing, just waited respectfully while she carefully selected a small venison pasty, shaped and ornamented like a needlework pouch with elaborate 'v's appearing to be stitched around its four sides. Only when the pasty was half demolished did

I turn back to the cardinal. It was time, I thought, to disseminate another piece of news.

'Your Grace,' I said, not lowering my tone. 'I feel that I must take my servant's body back to Ireland, back to his poor mother who had entrusted him to my care.'

'May God have mercy on his soul!' The cardinal made the sign of the cross and everyone bowed heads and held spoons aloft for forty seconds. I noticed Anne Boleyn, who had managed to upset George's seating plan again, had turned a questioning face to Harry Percy, listening eagerly. Gilbert was on her other side and his face was very grave. Both of the boys were enlightening her and I could see a look of shock on that smooth face. I warmed to her. She was self-centred and ruthless, but she was young. If I could get James out of this mess, and I hoped that I might, well, perhaps the marriage would take place after all. It would be nice to see her busy around Kilkenny Castle and the small town that was growing up around it, arranging for stonemasons to be taught the latest style of Italianate building, setting up a school of artists, rearing a brood of seven sons as the Irish proverb for newly wedded women would have it. But then she touched Harry's hand, quite gently with her own and smiled tenderly at him. I shrugged my shoulders. I had more important matters to think about. Now was the moment for the second act of the play.

'May I tell you a story,' I said to the cardinal. We had finished our pottage and we, too, had begun to help ourselves to the small, pouch-like venison pasties. I cut one open, mopped up some of the gravy with a piece of bread, took a piece between finger and thumb, chewing appreciatively on the deliciously tender meat. There was an amused twinkle in the cardinal's eye, and he inclined his head graciously, exchanging a smile with the queen. Sometimes, with the cardinal, I felt that my role was like an amalgam between learned judge and Patch the fool. I adopted a clear, storytelling voice, but kept my eyes fixed on the cardinal and resisted the temptation to look at the queen.

'Well, Your Grace, as in all the best tales, there is in my story a man with a great longing, not for a princess, but for a kingdom. Or at least,' I added, thinking of Ossory as seen by him, 'at least a portion fit for a knight.

'Your tale interests me.' The cardinal blandly chewed on his venison and then joined in the chorus of delight as a peacock, dressed in all its feathers, was carried up to the top table.

'The man with the great longing, I fear, is the villain in my story. You see, he hoped to snatch that kingdom from the true heir,' I kept a smile on my face and the cardinal's face showed a polite interest. I chanced a quick glance at the queen. She was listening intently, not smiling and I mentally paid tribute to her sharp mind.

'The only villain?' The cardinal conveyed a crumb of pastry to his mouth.

I bowed. It needed some such tribute to his quickness of mind.

'Not the only villain,' I said, 'because we have also the unjust steward.'

'Bribed by the villain, with gold, of course, though not, we hope, *fairy gold.*'

'With high honours, Your Grace.' That, I thought, was true. Every sergeant-at-arms had ambitions to be a judge.

'I see,' said the cardinal thoughtfully. He helped himself to a generous portion of ginger sauce and ladled it

on top of some chicken mortis. I followed his example.
It was delicious. The ginger brought out the delicate
flavour of the almonds and cream in that chicken pâté.
The queen was still listening intently and I noticed the
cardinal had leaned back in his chair to allow my words
to flow past him and to her ear. His gaze was fixed on
the Mess which held the two serjeants, together with
St Leger and George Villiers. His eyes had a hard look
and his mouth was tight.

'And the true heir,' he queried after a minute.

'The plan was to throw him into the deepest, darkest
dungeon,' I said. The peacock, now in neat bite-sized portions, was placed before us. The cardinal helped himself,
but I took a beef aloe. Trussed, stuffed and spit roasted,
the sirloin went very well with the smooth richness of
the wine from Burgundy.

'And has your story got an ending?' queried the queen,
leaning across the cardinal and looking at me intently.

'No, not yet, Your Grace. The ending requires, I think, a
master-hand.' I watched her face, but now it was inscrutable as she chewed thoughtfully.

'Yes, I suppose so,' said the cardinal with a sidelong
glance. 'One always felt with the unjust steward that there
was a certain lack of supervision.' He sighed heavily. It
was his constant wail that he did not have enough time,
and having seen his workload I could well understand it.

'Still,' said the queen unexpectedly, 'better an unjust
steward than an unjust judge.' And I knew that she was
thinking of the ambitions of her husband's sergeant. She
would, I hoped, put a spoke in the wheel of his progress.
'But your villain. He must be punished. We cannot have
murder, you know.'

'I agree, Your Grace,' I said. 'Murder destabilises the whole community.' I left a silence after that. Food, I decided, made very useful pauses. I chewed another beef aloe to point my words. 'No kingdom, to go back to my little story,' I said lightly, 'no kingdom, is worth a human life, certainly not worth two human lives.' I left it at that. She was meditatively eating some spinach tart, but her eyes were not on her plate, or turned towards the cardinal, but were gazing past us to where St Leger sat, uneasily picking at some shrimps. She would manage the matter carefully, I decided. She would take no action herself; that might anger the king. She would be more likely to catch the king in a good humour and then tell the story to him. In the meantime, St Leger would know that her eye was upon him.

'A very good maxim,' said the cardinal with a note of finality in his voice.

'Indeed,' I said and decided to leave the matter. The queen would take care of St Leger and I would see that justice was done to poor Colm in my own manner and in accordance with that law wherein I was trained. The cardinal also seemed to think that the subject was closed. Queen Katherine had turned to her neighbour on the other side.

'So, Hugh, you leave tomorrow on your journey to Ireland.' He rubbed his shaven upper lip with his forefinger and contemplated the dish of beef olives. 'How do you stay so slim, Hugh? I suppose it is all that tennis.' He looked at me benignly. 'You should start your journey early,' he said. 'If I were you I would go at dawn, go while everyone is at Sunday morning Mass. Best to go when no one is around. Farewells,' exclaimed the cardinal with an energetic wave of his hand, 'well, they are always well meant, but they do delay one so much.'

''Your Grace is always so perceptive,' I said with a smile.

'I will give you a dispensation to excuse you, and your man from going to Mass. You are on a merciful errand, are you not? It was St Paul, I think, who enjoined the faithful to bury their dead.'

He, normally the most hospitable of men, didn't ask whether I would pay a return visit, something that made me feel that he had a suspicion about my sudden resolve to go back to Ireland. I need say nothing and he would say nothing.

When the meal was over, he pronounced a Latin grace, reminded everyone that he would see them at the dawn Mass and then gave his blessing and retired. I thought with compunction about the number of papers that he would need to attend to on this very evening in between and after seeing the ambassador from Scotland and felt slightly sorry that I had placed another problem on his overworked shoulders. Still, I thought, the queen may just deal with it herself and leave the cardinal out of the matter.

St Leger was still with his friend, the king's serjeant-at-arms, when we all made our way to the bottom of the hall to partake of the sweet course. And then I saw the queen's gentleman usher, Senor De Montoya, touch him on the shoulder and whisper something in his ear. St Leger started, moved away, began a whispered conversation with De Montoya and the king's sergeant was left alone, at the end of the table, prodding some wet suckets with a fork. I went over the facts against him in my mind. Neither murder could have been accomplished without his help; I was certain of that. He had fetched out James's bow and arrow and had stood by while the Spanish doctor was killed and I was certain, looking back at the end of that tennis match, that he had helped to shut me in that box while he and St Leger tried to flog information about James out of my poor Colm. Whether he would be convicted in an English court was something that I did not know, but I was sure in my own mind of his guilt and was determined to get justice for the boy who had been my servant. I went up and stood beside him, very near to him, so that I could say the words into his ear.

'The fine for killing is twenty-one milch cows and this is doubled because it was a secret killing not acknowledged within twenty-four hours,' I said, repressing my anger under a show of judicial firmness, and I saw him look at me with a suddenly blanched face. 'And one milch cow, I would say, for the honour price of the victim.' I helped myself to a cinnamon wafer and bit it in halves. 'Still,' I added, 'since the laws of this country would have discouraged you from making a speedy and full confession, I will limit the fine to twenty-two milch cows.' I crumbled some white gingerbread and looked around for the man who had a finger in every pie.

'George,' I called heartily across the room. 'You know everything. You have a country estate, don't you? How much would you have to pay for a good milking cow, here in England?'

George looked slightly flabbergasted, but did not fail me. 'About forty shillings, about two sovereigns, I would say.'

'Hmm,' I said. 'They are more valuable in Ireland. We rate our cows more highly there. Still, I suppose, *when in Rome, do as the Romans do.* Was it St Augustine who said that?' I blandly asked the company and added, 'What a pity that His Grace is not here to answer that little question.'

I did the sum quickly in my head and so, judging by his sour expression, did the serjeant. That was forty-four sovereigns, a very large sum, but I was determined to prise out of him as much as he could lay his hands on. I wasn't sure how much he was paid, but he had the reputation of being a careful man. I would get, I thought, as much as possible from him. It was the least that I could do for poor Colm's mother and his six young sisters.

'Are you betting on it? Betting about cows?' asked young Wyatt. He had been circulating a piece of paper, folded to look like a butterfly, but with lines of poetry written inside each fold. Girls were snatching it from each other and giggling over it. But now, as was typical of him, he had grown bored with that and was interested in this game of mine.

'I never bet,' I said reprovingly, 'and neither should you.' He was probably only about nineteen and he was getting thoroughly spoilt here at court. His father, the keeper of the jewel house, and, according to the cardinal, a brilliant accountant who had found many new and creative ways of raising money for the king's father, was now employing young Wyatt as some sort of clerk in the jewel house. He should, I thought, think to send the gifted lad to university, to Oxford or Cambridge. He could write good poetry and an education wouldn't do him any harm. Still, I was grateful for the boy's intervention. It meant that the king's serjeant was suddenly aware that he could be overheard. I saw Alice look at me with a half-smile on her face and place a restraining hand on her brother's arm.

'I was talking about the mother of my poor servant who was killed,' I said loudly and clearly. 'It would be good to be able to buy her a cow,' I continued. 'She is a widow with lots of small children and she lived on the money that poor Colm sent her from his wages.' There was a flash of interest and comprehension from Tom Wyatt and he turned and called across to his friends:

'Listen everyone. We're getting up a collection for the poor lad's family, the one who was fished out of the river this morning.' Tom Wyatt said the words quite loudly and I saw Sir George St Leger, now at the doorway, swing around to look at me, standing beside his accomplice. He left the room hurriedly and the candle above the doorway showed the whiteness of his face as he glanced back at us over his shoulder. The king's serjeant, however, stayed very solemn, very straight-faced and looked along the lines of the supper guests. Finding many pairs of eyes on him, slowly and deliberately he fished in his pocket and took out from his purse, one by one, six sovereigns and counted them into my hand. I bowed and thanked him profusely and resolved to get more out of him in some way or other.

They were a generous crowd, I had to grant them that. Most would be playing cards later in evening and so were well equipped with silver for the betting on results. Mistress Anne Boleyn took out from her the bosom of her gown the padded heart that they had been playing with yesterday. It turned out to be a little pouch with a hollow centre and she went from guest to guest, giving her graceful curtsy, her demure sweet expressive smile and a flash of her dark eyes to the ladies and the gentlemen. When she handed the pouch to me, it was stuffed with silver.

I bowed my thanks, took the serjeant by the arm and escorted him firmly to the back of the room. He dared not make a protest. By now he was, thanks to his own quick-wittedness, thoroughly linked into this charitable enterprise. 'Two sovereigns per cow, well I make that forty-two sovereigns,' I said, 'and so you owe me a lot more. This,' I continued in a low conversational tone, 'will be sent back with the body to Ireland to the young man's sorrowing mother and sisters. I'm sure you can give me a draft for the remaining cash. One way or other, I shall see that the poor woman gets that money.' I put as much menace as I could manage into my low voice and ushered him out of the room and into the small chamber next door. I had been there on the night of the pageant, drawing up the marriage contract between James Butler and Anne Boleyn, and I knew that there were pens and paper there. It all seemed a long time ago, I thought as I watched him pen a draft for twenty sovereigns, his entire savings, according to him.

When I left the building with the money carefully concealed inside my cloak I made my way back to the lodgings. The lights were still on in the kitchen as the last dishes and wines cups were washed and dried. Soon they would all be in bed, ready for an early rising. I stood back for the wood yard boys wheeling in a barrow filled high with wood, twigs, faggots and talshides. Already the fires would have been banked down, but this wood would spend the night in the warm kitchen and would be ready to catch fire from the smouldering embers in the morning when the first person up would resurrect the fires.

And, of course, one barrow would be wheeled into the hall so that the dry, warm wood was ready to kindle a fire in good time before the morning dinner.

The sky was clear of clouds when I came out into the Base Court, but it was not cold and there was a light south easterly wind blowing which would prevent a frost next morning. Ideal riding conditions! I tapped quietly on the door of my lodging and went in to give Padraig some last-minute instructions and then to send him off to bed.

I would not sleep tonight. I had things to do, plans to make and three documents to write. The first was a letter to Piers Rua, Earl of Ormond. The second one would be quite short, a page in length with plenty of room for the signature and for the name of the witness. The last, meant for the perusal of the sharpest brain in Europe, needed to be carefully thought out. Not long, this man had little time at his disposal, but every word had to count, every piece of evidence had to be listed. It would be important. He would be the first to judge the case on the evidence provided and I would work on it as if it were my first law case.

17

The sun had not yet risen when I slipped quietly out of the lodgings by its back door. It was a bitterly cold morning with a sharp easterly wind, but no sign of frost and my double layer of cloaks saved me from shivering. The moon was setting in the western half of the cloud-free sky. The River Thames was a pale grey and a couple of white swans rocked on its surface. There was no sign of anyone there. The cardinal's barge was moored to the pier and a few small skiffs were tied up beside them. I looked up at the '*towers and bowers*', as poor John Skelton expressed it. There were no lights other than the usual night lights burning. It did not look as though any of the guests had yet risen. I breathed a prayer to the gods that all would remain undisturbed for the next hour or so and then crossed the carpenters' court and made my way out.

I went first of all to the stables. The cart, with its quiet burden of poor Colm's corpse, stood in one corner, its shafts facing the door. Everything seemed to be ready for a quick exit. One lad only was there, rapidly tacking up one of our horses. I had promised a large bribe to him last night and now gave a nod of approval at his punctuality and tucked a sovereign into his hand, carefully pulling the hood of cloak over my head before going near to him.

'We'll soon be out. Remember, not a word to be spoken,' I whispered before I left. I did not go back to the lodgings, but passed down the narrow lane to the paved passageway.

I had never been in the kitchen as early as this. The first thing that struck me was how tall it was. The walls stretched to a good twenty feet above my head, and the oak branched ceiling, normally shrouded in a mist of steam and smoke, showed every detail of intricate carpentry with its rounded arches and its carved bunches of corn. The whole place seemed incredibly large and I realised that on any other occasion when I came in that there were innumerable cooks and boys everywhere, turning spits, chopping vegetables, beating eggs, stirring sauces. This morning there was just one man in this immense space.

'I've never seen you alone in here before,' I said to Master Beasley.

'You're early. I was just getting some food ready for your journey.' He had greeted me in his usual friendly fashion and now added that everyone would miss me. I saw that he had a couple of pairs of leather paniers, easy to tie onto the horses, already stuffed with some bread and he was now wrapping a chunk of cold pie in a napkin. A basket of hard-boiled eggs was steaming gently on the table.

'I remembered that you said you were always the first up.'

'Been up for a good hour.' He was still friendly and unconcerned. 'I like this place first thing in the morning.

It reminds me of my young days, in my father's alehouse. It was just me, then. Just me, moving around, cooking, tasting, not too many orders to give, a couple of boys to turn the spit …'

'Rather different here.' I had more important things to talk about, but nevertheless, welcomed his reminiscences. 'Big numbers to cater for here,' I said, walking across the kitchen and going to stand beside the chopping block. He had a knife in his hand, but it was an ordinary table knife. The really sharp one, the knives that could cut through raw flesh, were all present, stuck into the leather holster on the wall above the chopping block, ranged in size order, graded according to width rather than length.

'You're right,' he said emphatically. 'Nothing but numbers, these days. One hundred, two hundred messes to cater for. A man begins to lose his interest in trying new recipes, devising new subtleties. And all these clerks, driving you out of your mind, accounting for this and for that. If they could do it, they would make you account for every drop of oil that you used.' He sounded bitter and angry, but he handled the eggs carefully, rolling them into the folds of another napkin and inserting them into one of the satchels.

'Whereas in the past, I suppose that it was always a part of the cook's perks to be able to dispose of excess stores.' I had been amazed to find that the cook, who managed such a huge staff and produced such tons of well-cooked food, was paid less than fourteen sovereigns a year, when Francis Bryan had received twice that amount as a present from the king after a particularly splendid jousting display. No doubt it had been understood in the past that they made some money on the side.

I had made the remark about perks as lightly as I could, but I saw him look at me sharply. I had to go ahead. The crackle of the piece of folded paper in my pocket reminded me of what I had to do.

'I think you were in the habit of disposing of anything that you had not used up,' I said. 'You probably had a buyer on the docks and a full barrel could easily be sent back with the empty barrels of wine, oil, butter, anchovies, anything that you had not used up. It became a little more difficult in the past few years when the new system was set up by the cardinal, but you still managed it,' I said. 'The skiff by the fish pond helped, didn't it and I suppose you had some sort of agreement with the ferrymen, didn't you?'

It would not have been anything unusual at one stage. I knew that James's father, Piers Rua, always swore that the sailors took a ten per cent by way of a levy on all of the goods that were imported into New Ross harbour in Wexford and that the carriers took another ten per cent. And judging by the poor food that we were served, probably the cook took his share of the good wine, of the tasty cuts of beef and left the poor stuff for us.

Nevertheless, the cardinal, with his genius for organisation, was trialling a scheme to stop all of this waste at Hampton Court. If it was a success, and it looked as though it might be saving quite a lot of money, then he was going to persuade the king to work the same system in his ten palaces. Then any such thefts would be punished with the utmost severity, perhaps with the loss of a hand.

'Edmund Pace, the instructor of the wards, loved to ferret out secrets and to blackmail anyone who had a secret. He discovered yours, didn't he?' I said and saw his florid face turn white. He said nothing, but closed up the last of the four satchels, buckling it with care. I watched him intently, almost as though he were a wild animal who would spring, but he didn't make a move towards the knives. He glanced once at the door, but it was safely closed. It would be some time yet before the boys who tended the fires would arrive to heap on them the warmed wood from the barrows and to wheel one of the barrows into the great hall to resurrect its fire before dinner at half past ten. 'That was why he died,' I added.

'I don't know what you are talking about; the man was killed during the pageant on Shrove Tuesday. I was in my bed and snoring then; you can ask anyone. Ask the pastry cook; he sleeps in the compartment next to mine. He's always complaining about the noise I make. Says it keeps waking him up. He'll tell you that I was there all night. He says he gets his sleep when I get up an hour before dawn.' He spoke bravely in quite an assured manner, but there was a sheen of sweat on his forehead. We stared into each other's eyes but he was the first to look away.

'I think you killed him in the morning, not the night time,' I said gently. 'I think that he came here on the morning of Ash Wednesday, quite early, before anyone was up. Just as I have done this morning. Everyone knows that you are the first up in the morning. I think that was when he was killed. Yes, the body was stiff by eleven o'clock, but that was the heat of the tremendous fire that you have here. You didn't know what to do with him. Everything would still have been very quiet indoors. I think that you put the body on one of the empty barrows, and then piled the logs all around it and bundles of faggots on top, covering it completely. You rule your kitchen. If anyone suggested using the wood from that barrow, you would have told them to leave it alone. And then when you had sent the boys away to have some breakfast, at about eight o'clock, then you moved the barrow to the great hall. Not something that you would have done in the normal way of things, but no one would question you. If they did, you could just have said that one of the boys forgot to do it. And, of course, because of the intense heat of the fire, the body was now rigid. You placed it behind the tapestry.'

Then he did take a cautious step nearer to the knives. I held up a hand.

'Wait,' I said. 'I have a solution. I won't turn you over to the hangman. I think that was a spur of the moment crime, something that you will never do again and I don't want you to lose your life for it. You and I are the same height. Take this cloak of mine, the Irish mantle, everyone in Hampton Court knows the look of my Irish mantle. Wear it and everyone will think it is me. You can go straight to the stables. Carry the paniers with you; no one will question you. I've arranged for you to go to Ireland. The Earl and Countess of Ormond will welcome you for my sake and once they taste your food, once they sample your cooking, they will keep you for your sake. You will have a small kitchen compared to this one, nevertheless I think you will be happy with it. But James must be cleared of this accusation.'

I took from my pocket the folded piece of paper and handed it to him. He held it in his hand and looked at me hesitantly.

'And I am not the only one who knows this,' I said. 'I have told my man Padraig. He will see you safely back to

Ireland and bring you to Kilkenny Castle. He is sworn to secrecy, and carries a letter from me to the earl, but,' I said warningly, 'if you don't join him in the stables fairly soon then he will come here to look for me. And he is armed with a good sword.' I waited a moment to allow him to digest this. 'You'll like Kilkenny,' I added. 'They have a wonderful garden of herbs, the river runs past your kitchen window and it's filled with fish. There's a big poultry yard. The earl will love your cooking and the countess will be happy to see him content. And the place is full of wild duck and deer and there is a mill down the road.' I seemed to be always trying to persuade people to go to Kilkenny. Perhaps I should make another effort to persuade Mistress Boleyn.

'Sounds good,' he said decisively. He took the paper over towards the small desk in the corner of the room, picked up a pair of glasses, held them in front of his eyes, read the words carefully and scrawled his signature; the bold, almost square loops on the B would definitely identify it as his. I took it from him and held it to the heat of the fire for a second then folded and replaced it in my pocket.

'Don't expect too good a supper today,' he said. 'The dinner is already worked out, but the supper may be new territory.'

I slipped off my Irish mantle and handed it to him. 'Wear this. Pull the hood right up. No one will challenge you. The cardinal has given orders for the gate to be opened for us. They will be expecting two men on horseback and a cart. Tell me one thing more,' I said as he put the cloak around him and pulled the hood forward over his head and half-covering his face, 'why did you try to implicate James?'

'I never meant to,' he began.

'You found the arrow in amongst the wood, was that it?'

'Stuck right through the bundle of faggots.'

'I thought that was it. I remembered James saying that he shot at a wild duck from across the moat. I worked out that his arrow might have fallen into a bundle of faggots. I just wondered why …' And then I stopped. 'And, of course, you couldn't see the initials, could you? Not without your eye glasses.'

'That's right, blind as a bat without them. I was very sorry about that.'

'Go in peace,' I said gently. It was what was always said after judgement day back home on the hill of Kyle. I had issued no fine, but perhaps banishment from his native land might be punishment enough. Our Irish law always took into account the provocation for the deed. And the crime of ridding the world of a man who blackmailed young boys did not seem to me to be too heinous.

'Give my love to the countess,' I said lightly as he left the kitchen. I gave him a few minutes and then slipped out of the back door. Susannah would hide me for a few hours and then I would go to see the cardinal. I had thought of trying to get to London, but decided against that. It would be important that James was publicly cleared of this murder before he came back to Hampton Court. I would tell her the whole story; she was fond of the cook and would be sorry, so I would conceal the fact that Master Beasley had tried to throw suspicion on to her when he had purposely visited her rooms with an unexpected gift of fish soup for her glue, had taken her knife and left it in the great hall. He had tried to throw suspicion onto Gilbert Tailboys, also, of course, reporting that he had seen him hand money to the instructor of the wards. Fear will make a man do evil things and perhaps we should just remember his good deeds, his affable company and his superlative cooking, I would tell her.

And so I dallied there in that quiet workroom, talking with Susannah, mixing her paints for her and waited until the first warning trumpets sounded for morning dinnertime before making an appearance. By now Padraig and Master Beasley would probably have gone past the town of Reading. Even in the unlikely event of the cardinal deciding to send men after them, the pursuit would take some time to organise and by then they would be well on their way towards Bristol. I slipped back into my own lodgings without causing any comment and then made my way to the cardinal's rooms.

18

Despite the early hour the whole of Hampton Court seemed to be in uproar. Messengers, page boys, stewards, sewers, footmen, yeomen, riding clerks, writing clerks, chamberlains, gentlemen ushers, all were hurrying up and down. Outside, there was just as much bustle. Men riding forth the stables. The cardinal's own barge disappearing around the corner of the river. George pacing up and down on the pier, his face white with anxiety. I wondered whether to question him, but thought it might all be a bit long-winded. He gave me a startled glance, but when I nodded towards the cardinal's window where His Grace stood, looking down at the scene, George looked up, also, and, like me, saw a hand raise, and then lifted his own hand signalling his acquiescence.

'Well, what's all the excitement about?' I said, as I opened the door into the cardinal's room.

Hugh.' He acknowledged my presence but gave no sign of surprise. He had guessed, of course, that I was not going to be the one on the second horse leaving Hampton Court during the dawn Mass, though I ventured to think that he was probably mistaken about the identity of that rider.

'James?' he queried. And I knew that I was right. I smiled a little, thinking of what I was about to reveal. It was not often that I surprised the cardinal. But I would postpone explanations for the moment.

'Safe, I hope.' I kept my voice non-committal and he nodded.

'What's happening here? What's the excitement about?'

'You may well ask. In fact, as the legal representative of the prospective bridegroom, you have indeed, a right to ask.'

This was slightly puzzling. I raised an eyebrow at him and he leaned back in his chair, his long white fingers just touching at the tips, forming a perfect steeple beneath his chin. He gave me a moment to enjoy the picture of a calm man before saying coolly, 'Mistress Boleyn and Master Harry Percy have disappeared. The birds have flown.'

'Indeed.' I took a seat opposite to him. 'And Master Thomas Boleyn?' I queried.

'I've sent a boat to Westminster for him.' The cardinal's tone was slightly grim, but personally I did not blame the father. The lady would probably have hatched the whole plan herself.

'And where have they gone?'

'Well, according Mistress Dymoke, who got the information from Mistress Dorothy Bouchier, who got it from either Elizabeth Bryan or Elizabeth Darrell, who got it from Mistress Jane Parker, they are on their way to Hever Castle where there is an obliging clergyman, enslaved by Mistress Anne Boleyn's black eyes – please don't ask me who said that, but it was one of the young ladies. Anyway,' finished the cardinal, 'a proper marriage ceremony is, one

of these young ladies confided in George, planned by
Mistress Boleyn and no doubt it will be followed by a
rapid consummation.'

'When did they leave?'

'This morning, early, I believe. Apparently neither
was at Mass. I've sent men to the north for the Earl of
Northumberland. He will not be pleased. But there you
are, I could not have been expected to have locked up
the boy.' The cardinal shrugged his shoulders but his eyes
were angry.

'Goodness! Busy morning at the stables.'

His eyes came back to me. 'Indeed,' he said. 'Now tell
me all your news.'

'You've lost your chief cook,' I said baldly.

That surprised him. His bushy white eyebrows shot up.

'I didn't want to see him hanged, and I don't suppose
you did either.' The cardinal was such a busy man that he
tended to lose interest in long-winded stories and return
to his never-ending pile of letters. I could see a half-
written letter to Dr Knight, Ambassador to France, on his
writing pad before him. My tactics worked. He replaced
the pen and stared at me.

I waited for a second. His eyes were completely blank,
staring straight ahead, always a sign that his mind was
working fast.

'Blackmail,' he said finally and I bowed my head. *You
should have paid him what he was worth*, I thought, but I said
nothing.

'Tell me what happened,' he said, closing down the lid
of his writing bureau.

'Edmund Pace, as well as blackmailing your wards,
his pupils, was also blackmailing the cook for selling off

various kitchen stores. He came to the kitchen early on Ash Wednesday morning.'

'His ghost presumably. Wasn't I informed that he was murdered on Shrove Tuesday night?'

'That was a mistake,' I said. 'That's the trouble with science, I find. It can mislead you. The medical men misled us. The corpse, they said, was stiff as a board and so he was murdered during or quite soon after the pageant. Not by an arrow, that was a clumsy effort to mislead; the queen's physician, Dr Ramirez, proved that to my satisfaction. He believed the man to be murdered by means of a small sharp knife plunged into his heart. But he, too, believed it had to be as early on Shrove Tuesday evening as was feasible because of the stiffness of the corpse.'

The cardinal shook his head impatiently.

'You're confusing me, Hugh.'

'If Your Grace would just listen to me patiently …'

'And ask no questions.'

'Your Grace has taken the words from my mouth.' I pulled up a chair and sat opposite to him sinking my elbows into the soft carpet on the table. I gazed for a moment at the gold engraving of his little portable writing bureau as I tried to put a complex story of fear, hatred and human ingenuity into order within my mind.

'Edmund Pace came into the kitchen, probably to catch the cook out secretly selling off goods; he challenged him, demanded yet more money, from a man who was only paid fourteen sovereigns a year. Your cook, Master Beasley, snatched up a knife from his array by the chopping board and plunged it into the man's chest. It was, I would think, a crime totally without premeditation, a flash of anger, of desperation and it resulted in a dead body. He didn't know what to do. In a few moments the boys would be coming into the kitchen to collect the brooms for sweeping the yards, the first task of the day. Hurriedly he put the dead man onto an empty wood barrow, piled up wood on either side of him and placed bundles of faggots on top of the body. And then, and this is significant, Your Grace, he pushed the wood barrow into an alcove very close to the fire. No one would touch this wood without his permission. It was kept hot so that the heat of a fire could be suddenly boosted.'

'And the body stiffened fast in the heat, is that what you are trying to tell me, Hugh?'

'It's a pleasure to talk to Your Grace.' I meant it sincerely, though he cocked a sceptical eye at me.

'I remember the bodies at the Battle of Thérouanne in France, in the heat. It was in the month of June. They stiffened fast.' The cardinal glanced at his letter to the ambassador to France and sighed a little at the recollection of this battle of almost nine years ago. 'And then I suppose he wheeled it into the hall.'

'When he had sent others off on various errands,' I confirmed. 'The boys always have breakfast in the pantry and the other cooks could have been sent to collect the stores.'

'And the arrow that caused such trouble?'

'He found it inside a bundle of faggots. He had some desperate idea of pretending that this was an accident. He didn't realise that it belonged to James. He's very short-sighted; he needs eye glasses to read,' I explained. I took from my pocket the summary of the evidence that I had written out last evening. He read it, twice, and put it carefully in the drawer.

I had expected him to demand an explanation as to why I had not come to him to or the serjeant about this matter, but I underestimated him. The Cardinal of York always got his facts straight before passing judgement. He got up from behind his desk, walked across to the fire, and pulled out a chair for me before taking his usual comfortable place between the burning coals and the thick draught-screen.

'Tell me how you worked out all of this, Hugh,' he invited.

I thought about that for a while as I stretched my hands out to the heat. 'I didn't think it was a very clever crime,' I said slowly after a minute. 'Not the sort of murder that I would expect from a man with a trained mind, or a woman with sharp wits. There was something very naïve about this business of pretending that an arrow, a whole arrow, had gone through a small hole in the tapestry and then pierced the man's heart. That could only have been the thought of a man, or woman, who knew nothing about archery. The feathers at the back of the arrow would surely have been wedged into the tapestry and the tapestry itself would have been soaked in blood and probably been pulled down when the body fell. I don't suppose anyone would have believed it for a second if it hadn't suited the king's serjeant, Master Gibson, to throw the blame onto James. He was already hand-in-glove with Sir George St Leger, as you know. And there was something else: when the cook lent his knives to Dr Ramirez, the small one was missing – so that it wouldn't be identified, I suppose. Well the idea did enter my mind when I remembered that. And when I realised that there was a way of secretly conveying goods from the kitchen back to London, well I began to be pretty sure that the cook had something to conceal, something that laid him open to blackmail. I didn't want to believe it, but eventually I knew it had to be him.'

The cardinal's eyes were still fixed on the fire and I could read nothing from his face. A silence is always difficult to interpret and I began to realise that I might be putting my own life in danger. I could be accused of conspiracy, aiding and abetting a murderer to escape justice. Still there was nothing to be done now, but to trust to him.

I took the confession from my pocket and handed it to him. 'I think that the signature will be well known in the kitchen clerks' offices.'

He read it through carefully and then thought for a moment. Carefully, he folded it and held it in his hand for a moment and then walked back to his desk, held a stick of wax to a candle for a moment and then dropped a blob on the fold of the letter. I had seen him do this on innumerable occasions, but now he did not press his own seal down on the hot wax, but left it as it was. Then he rang his bell twice as was his usual summons for his gentleman usher.

When George appeared the cardinal was once more busy with his correspondence.

'Oh, George, good news. Hugh decided that it was not necessary for him to go to Ireland after all. And so we will have the benefit of his company for some time longer.'

George turned a beaming face on me and said how pleased everyone would be, and then reverted to his worried expression.

'No news of them yet, Your Grace. I've sent off the best riders and with the best horses. With luck we will catch them before they reach Hever.'

'With the help of God.' The cardinal crossed himself solemnly. 'Oh, and George, Hugh was given this letter. I want the clerk of the kitchens to see it. Send for him, will you?'

'The great thing about George is that he never asks questions.' The cardinal made the remark as soon as the door was closed. 'Well, I'm glad to see you back, Hugh. We've lost another guest. Sir George St Leger has returned to London, bearing a message for the king from Her Grace, Queen Katherine.' The cardinal did not look at me when he said this, but returned to his work on his letter to the ambassador, filling the page with his small, spikey handwriting. I sat opposite to him and neither of us spoke until the clerk arrived back with George, both of them panting.

'Apparently a message from our cook, Master Beasley.' The cardinal smiled benignly at the clerk and George looked bewildered. I handed over the sealed sheet of paper.

Nervously the clerk broke the seal and scanned the few short lines.

'Read it aloud,' commanded the cardinal.

The clerk read the confession tonelessly. George gasped and the cardinal sighed gently. I preserved a solemn legal countenance.

'And the signature?'

'Master Beasley's certainly, Your Grace.' He did not, interestingly, look too astounded and I wondered how much he might have suspected. He did not comment either on my signature, just below the cook's, verifying that this confession had been signed in my presence.

'Perhaps, Master Lynsey won't mind signing to that effect, Your Grace,' I said and received a gracious nod from the cardinal. George brought me an inkstand and I penned a few words, thinking that if I were to stay in England I should follow the queen's advice and study English law at the Inns.

'I attest that the above signature is known to me and that it is the signature of Master Beasley, chief cook to His Grace, Thomas Cardinalis,' I wrote and then read the words aloud. Master Lynsey signed it with the rapidity of a man who normally signs forty pieces of paper before he has his morning dinner.

'Thank you, Master Lynsey, we won't keep you any longer. Master Cavendish, you are busy, I know, but perhaps you could send the king's serjeant, Master Gibson, to me.' With that the cardinal dismissed them and then turned to me.

'You may leave this other matter in my hands, Hugh,' he said. 'I won't delay you now. I know that you will want to fetch James back to Hampton Court in time for supper.'

Author's Note

James Butler and Anne Boleyn, did not, as everyone knows, marry. Ironically, James, who married a cousin, Lady Joan Fitzgerald, had seven sons who all lived to adulthood.

The match between them would have been good for both sides of the family because there was a disputed inheritance. Both James's father, Piers Rua, and Anne's father, Thomas Boleyn, laid claim to the title of Earl of Ormond and to the Ormond lands in Ireland.

When Thomas Butler, Earl of Ormond, died, he left only two daughters (both quite elderly women), one of whom was the mother of Thomas Boleyn and the other the mother of Sir George St Leger. Under English law the inheritance was to be divided between the two daughters, but his nephew, Piers Rua, claimed the earldom in Ireland under Brehon (Irish) law which states that women were only allowed to inherit 'land sufficient to graze seven cows', and also because he was the choice of the Butlers in Ireland. Piers Rua's mother (Saibh Cavanagh) was from a Gaelic clan and he had been fostered by a Gaelic family. As an adult Piers Rua lived by Brehon laws and employed members of the Mac Egans, the largest legal family in Ireland, as his Brehons or lawyers. Cardinal Wolsey sorted out the matter by getting Thomas Boleyn to agree that the earldom would go to James Butler on condition that he married Thomas's daughter, Anne Boleyn. James was described by Wolsey's biographer, George Cavendish, as 'my lord's favourite page' and Wolsey spoke highly of him as: '*right active, discreet and wise.*'

Harry Percy & Anne Boleyn:

It may look as though I am tampering with history by describing a possible elopement, but I do think that Anne Boleyn's possible prolonged stay at Hever and absence from the court, two years according to some (and with no marriage contract for a girl who was definitely 'getting on'), must have resulted from something a little more serious than just a boy/girl flirtation. In any case, there is a strange gap in the history of Anne Boleyn from 1522 to the mid 1520s. Professor Eric Ives, in his definitive biography, *The Life and Death of Anne Boleyn*, has an interesting few pages about this puzzle and confesses himself baffled. He says that it would have been unlikely that her parents would have missed two years or so of opportunity to find her a husband. After all if she were born in 1501, and that seems to be the consensus of opinion now, time was getting on for her in an era when marriage contracts were normally made for girls under twenty. I even wonder whether Anne had a baby. Henry VIII seems to have been notoriously bad at discerning virgins!

And, of course, no one, not even Professor Ives, has ever found a sensible explanation for why the marriage with James Butler, so good for both families, did not take place after all. Nor for why Anne Boleyn, at the age of twenty-four or twenty-five, was still unmarried.

True & Not True:

Untrue: I've taken some liberties with the historical record by transferring the Shrove Tuesday pageant of *Château Vert* from York Place (which no longer exists) to Hampton Court, where the reader can make a good effort at imagining the scene. Most people seem to think that it was the young choristers who played the parts of the unpleasant women (*Malbouche, Disdain, Jealousy* etc.), but I have used the cardinal's wards and this may be untrue – though plausible, I think.

I found the titles of officials in the cardinal's household from the gentleman usher George Cavendish's *Life and Death of Cardinal Wolsey* written after the death of Henry VIII, but, apart from George, I have invented their names. There is no record of an Irish lawyer coming over to the cardinal to draft a marriage treaty and Hugh Mac Egan is my creation, though it is **true** that Piers Rua Butler employed the Mac Egan family as legal advisors and judges.

True: George Cavendish in his *Life and Death of Cardinal Wolsey* (George joined the cardinal's household in 1522) talks about the cardinal's wards – eight of them. The only three he mentions by name are James Butler, Harry Percy and the 'little earl', fourteen-year-old Edward Stanley, 3rd Earl of Derby, but I have, I think, with a lot of effort, discovered the others. Very often one name led to another. For example, I saw mention that Francis Bigod was a friend of Edward Stanley, Earl of Derby, when they were adults, and when I looked him up I found that they were the same age and that he, too, had been a ward of the cardinal. A letter from Queen Katherine of Aragon to Cardinal Wolsey about a match for one of her ladies-in-waiting to his ward led me to Thomas Arundel. The only one that I am not quite sure of is Thomas Seymour, who would later marry Catherine Parr and would be involved in a scandal concerning the young Princess Elizabeth, but his older brother Edward had been in the care of the cardinal so I thought it was feasible. Gilbert Tailboys' father was a lunatic in the care of Cardinal Wolsey, and Bessie Blount, mother of King Henry's illegitimate son, was married off to him.

True: The details about Anne Boleyn's upbringing in France.

True: Leather mâché, mixed with glue, was used for a lot of the medallions that decorated the great hall at Hampton Court. Apparently they were always thought to be made from wood – such was their appearance – until taken down for repainting etc. It's my own idea to use it for mock arrows, but I think it is feasible.

Controversial: It is often said that Henry VIII built the 'real' tennis court, or 'play' at Hampton Court when he took possession of it in 1529, but when I was looking through the workmen's accounts I saw that not only was it referred to as the 'new' tennis play, but also that new 'lodgings' for the tennis play (changing rooms?) had been built prior to building the new tennis court itself. It seems to me very likely that the cardinal, knowing how much Henry liked the sport, had one built at around the same time as the royal rooms for the king and his court.

Controversial: It has been generally thought, that Henry VIII designed and had built the 50ft-high oriel window in the great hall at Hampton Court, but recently archaeologists, on closer inspection of the window, realised that is untrue and now believe that it was part of Wolsey's Hampton Court. The accounts bear this out as they only list, in the royal expenditure on the great hall, a sum for new stained glass.

True: Wolsey owned two of the four *Petrarch's Triumphs* tapestries in 1522. He acquired the set of four around 1523.

Helpful Books

I have a couple of shelves filled with books about this era, but the ones below have been the most useful and most often consulted.

Brears, Peter, *All the King's Cooks: The Tudor Kitchens of King Henry VIII at Hampton Court Palace*

Cavendish, George, *The life & Death of Cardinal Wolsey*

Cennini, Cennino d'Andrea, translated by D. Thompson, *The Craftsman's Handbook*

Ives, Eric, *The Life & Death of Anne Boleyn*

Krznaric, Roman, *The First Beautiful Game: Stories of Obsession in Real Tennis*

Law, Ernest, *The History of Hampton Court in Tudor Times*

Matusiak, John, *Wolsey: The Life of King Henry VIII's Cardinal*

Weir, Alison, *Henry VIII: King & Court*

Worsley, Lucy, *Hampton Court Palace*

Acknowledgements

Many, many thanks to my erudite and indefatigable agent, Peter Buckman, who is always able to sprinkle whole-some criticism with the sugar of his wit. Thanks also to the workers at the History Press: Mark Beynon, who has been encouraging and enthusiastic, and Lauren Newby for her meticulous and knowledgeable editing. My husband Frank shared pleasurable hours in the second-hand bookshops at Hay-on-Wye, uncomplainingly carrying large bags of long-forgotten books to the car, and my medical engineering son, William, was very useful in solving computer problems and matters to do with dead bodies. I am, as always, so very grateful to both.